I was going to be young
looking for...

all in return for a few minor drawbacks, like not being able to take sunlight – who does, these days? I secretly thought I'd got the best deal of all…until half an hour ago.

That's when the hunger came over me for the first time.

So here I am, standing in the dark on the bell tower of St Jude's Episcopalian church. Just one step and the ones I love will be safe from me. But maybe it's fitting that Jude is the patron saint of lost causes, because I don't think I can take that last step.

And oh, God…

I can feel the hunger coming on again.

On their twenty-first birthday, the sexy and stylish
Crosse triplets discover their mother was a vampire
slayer – and that each of them is destined to carry on
their family's legacy with the dark side.

A new mini-series from author

Harper Allen

Darkheart & Crosse

Follow each triplet's story:

Dressed to Slay – February 2010
Unveiled family secrets lead sophisticated
Megan Crosse into the world of shapeshifters
and slayers.

Vampaholic – March 2010
Sexy Kat Crosse fears her dark future as a vampire
until a special encounter reveals her true fate.

Dead Is the New Black – April 2010
Cursed by her own blood, wild child Tash Crosse
leaves her family, only to learn her death
might save them all.

DEAD IS THE NEW BLACK

BY
HARPER ALLEN

MILLS & BOON

First published in Great Britain 2010
Harlequin Mills & Boon Limited,
Eton House, 18-24 Paradise Road, Richmond, Surrey TW9 1SR

© Sandra Hill 2007

ISBN: 978 0 263 88289 6

89-0410

Harlequin Mills & Boon policy is to use papers that are natural, renewable and recyclable products and made from wood grown in sustainable forests. The logging and manufacturing processes conform to the legal environmental regulations of the country of origin.

Printed and bound in Spain
by Litografia Rosés S.A., Barcelona

Harper Allen, her husband and their menagerie of cats and dogs divide their time between a home in the country and a house in town. She grew up reading Stephen King, John D MacDonald and John Steinbeck, among others, and has them to blame for her lifelong passion for reading and writing.

For Tara

Prologue

One step, and everything's finished—the pain and the guilt and the cold, sickening fear washing over me, making my grip slick with sweat and turning my legs to rubber. With one step this nightmarish hunger ends, too. But I don't know if I have the nerve to take that step off this ledge into the darkness. Apparently I'm also a coward, among other things.

Or maybe I'm still in denial. I can't help thinking that this isn't the way my life was supposed to turn out, even though I finally understand that whining about fair and unfair is useless. But still. I mean, I should have been Mrs. Dr. Todd by now, right? I should have had the triplet wedding thing with my sisters, Megan and Katherine: summer brides, the three of us, ready to say the vows that would have ensured us the same uneventful life Grammie Crosse has. We would have been on the Maplesburg Hospital committee. We'd have played tennis at the Maplesburg country club. Megan would have hosted parties with her investment-banker hubbie, Dean, Kat would have done the same for Lance as he climbed the ladder at his corporate law firm and I would have played the part of a cosmetic surgeon's wife to perfection. And if once in a while we lay awake in the middle of the night and asked ourselves if this was all there was to life…well, remembering the nightmares we had when we were kids would answer that question for us.

But instead of getting married a few months ago we ended up having to stake our fiancés the night before Megan's wedding.

It's a long story, and in my current position I'm not sure I'll have time to finish it. I'll just say that our fiancés were turned into vamps by a bitch called Zena, the Queen *Vampyr* who killed our father, David Crosse, and Angelica Dzarchertzyn, our mother—for those of you who don't know, our mother was a Daughter of Lilith, a hereditary vampire killer—when we were babies. Carrying out his vow to his dying daughter, Angelica's father, Anton, made sure his triplet granddaughters had a normal American childhood by placing us with Grammie and Popsie Crosse.

So for the next twenty years Megan and Kat and I were adored, shop-till-we-dropped princesses in a small upstate New York town. Our closest encounter with a vamp was on a box of Count Chocula cereal and in barely remembered nightmares from our childhood. But then we turned twenty-one and Zena tracked us down to Maplesburg.

Which is when our perfect world was torn apart, never to be put back together again.

As I say, I don't want to dwell on the dreary details, mainly because I hate thinking about how dumb I was back then. When Anton Dzarchertzyn—Grandfather Darkheart, as he said we should call him—showed up on our doorstep the night we staked Lance and Todd and Dean, and told us the truth about how our mother had lived and died, I was convinced I would turn out to be the Crosse triplet who'd inherited Angelica's Daughter of Lilith destiny. I was equally convinced that Megan would fulfill Darkheart's other prediction.

Our mother had died trying to save her babies from Zena. She'd failed. One of us bore the mark of the Queen *Vampyr* and would turn vamp herself during her twenty-first year.

My theory about Megan being the vamp and me being the Daughter was blown out of the water during our final battle with Zena, when Megan proved herself to be the true inheritor of Mom's title. So I fell back on theory number two: that Kat, the languidly sexy middle Crosse sister—born half an hour before me and twenty minutes after Kat— was the one Zena had marked when we were babies.

Wrong again. When we went up against Master Vamp Cyrus Kane, Kat learned that her legacy didn't come from Mom or Zena, it came from our father, a Healer who'd been able to restore the souls of vamps and turn them back into the humans they'd once been. And after that revelation, it didn't take a rocket scientist to figure out who among us was left to turn fang-girl.

Me. Little Tashie Crosse. The shallow sister, the bratty sister, the sister who hadn't grown up, according to Megan and Kat. The sister who now never would.

I was going to be young and hot-looking forever. I'd never need Botox or have to trade in my Manolos for double-width Naturalizers, all in return for a few minor drawbacks like not being able to take sunlight—who does, these days?—and cringing if some insensitive clod shoved a crucifix in my face. All in all, I secretly thought I'd gotten the best deal of all…until half an hour ago.

That's when the hunger came over me for the first time and I understood what being undead was really all about.

It's about killing. Killing for the love of killing, killing for the sheer, unholy joy of it, killing because killing's better than sex, better than breathing, better than falling in love. I knew instinctively that making the kill last by torturing the victim would notch the thrill up even higher, and choosing a victim close to me would be a rush of dark nirvana.

I wanted to kill Kat. When I'd had my fill of her blood and her body had been torn beyond recognition, I wanted to take on Megan. Daughter of Lilith or no, I didn't think she'd be able to stake me before I overpowered her. Grandfather Darkheart would have been next, and then I would have contented myself with acquaintances and strangers, biding my time until the two people I loved most returned from the months-long cruise they were on.

Welcome home, Grammie. Your darling Tashya's missed you, Popsie.

Just for a moment the vision of killing them had been so clear in my mind that it had seemed like I'd already done it, and the horror that rushed through me had beaten back the hunger, breaking its hold on me. But it'll be back, and when it comes a second time I don't know if I'll be strong enough to fight it off again.

So here I am, standing in the dark on the highest point in Maplesburg, which happens to be the bell tower of St. Jude's, the Episcopalian church where

I was baptized. There was no problem sneaking in—Maplesburg churches still remain unlocked after-hours for the benefit of any sinners looking for redemption, and I didn't have to go through the church proper to get to the tower staircase. I won't have any problem getting out, either, as long as I can bring myself to do what I have to do.

Just one step into thin air and it'll all be over. Just one step and the ones I love will be safe from me. But maybe it's fitting that Jude is the patron saint of lost causes, because I don't think I can take that last step.

And oh, God…

I can feel the hunger coming on again.

Chapter 1

When I bumped into the muttering derelict with the shopping cart glaring at me through his tangle of matted hair I knew I'd hit rock bottom. Worse yet, I didn't care. Well, okay, I cared. I was so worried that someone I knew might see me that I was in disguise, which explained the short brunette wig bulging out like the Elephant Man's cranium where I'd crammed in my own hair. I'd pulled a trenchcoat over the mint-green Beth Bowley summer-weight cashmere sweater and short, tiered silk skirt I had on. I also wore dark sunglasses, although maybe they weren't the smartest idea, since it was eleven at night and I was in a dim alleyway. In the five blocks from where I'd parked my noticeable white Mini I'd walked into two fire hydrants, almost stumbled off the curb into the gutter and now I'd nearly knocked an old street loony off his feet.

But rock bottom or not, I was so churned up with anticipation and nerves that I was shaking. When the weird cat lady who lives in the apartment above mine had told me about old man Schneider and his after-hours service, she'd warned me he sometimes ran out of product. Actually, as I learned during that same conversation, her name was Kathy Lehman, but I couldn't shake the habit of calling her Weird Cat Lady in my mind, mainly because she was weird and had about twenty cats. In fact, I'd met one of her feline buddies before I met her.

How it happened was this way: I was just passing the Dumpster behind my building earlier in the evening, wondering whether I should run back into the rundown building I'd been calling home for the past few weeks and change into something less dressy than the Chloé skirt and silk-knit sleeveless top I was wearing. I was also making a mental note to buy a pair of Doc Martens, since the Ferragamo slides I had on, although adorable, definitely weren't the right footwear for what I had in mind. Then I saw the rat, a husky brute that looked as if it could take on Dobermans and win, and all thoughts of clothes and shoes left me.

It was the first time I'd tried what I was about to do, but desperation made me cunning. I held my breath—a trick that's become easier and easier lately—and remained motionless. The rat's whiskers twitched cautiously as he sniffed the air. Then he began scurrying toward the Dumpster. I waited until he was only inches away before I lunged.

I had the sucker, I swear it. I could feel him twisting in my grasp, trying to get his head close enough to my clutching hands to rip some flesh from me. Two red-hot trails exploded down my bare arms and an unearthly yowl split the darkness, startling me so much that I let go.

Mr. Rat streaked toward the hole in the side of the building he'd come out of. I threw myself after him like a baseball player sliding into home plate, my hands outstretched, my silk top shredding on broken pavement and the heel of one of my Ferragamos snapping as I made my leap.

I slammed headfirst into the wall. The mangy tomcat beside me slammed into it at the same time.

"You've killed Bojangles!" The screech startled me more than the yowl had, and the apparition that appeared out of the gloom almost stopped my heart. Then I recognized the figure with the frizzy, waist-length gray hair swooping toward the tomcat as my elusive upstairs neighbor.

"I didn't kill him," I denied, getting to my feet and preparing to beat a hasty retreat. The last thing I wanted was to answer questions about why I was staking out a Dumpster. "I…I tripped over him. I was just walking along minding my own business and I—"

Bojangles chose that moment to prove he was alive by letting loose with another enraged yowl. He sprang from Weird Cat Lady's arms and took off around the side of the building.

"See, he's fine." I gave his mistress a nervous smile. "Well, it was certainly nice meeting you, but I really must be—"

"I should have realized. You were fighting Bo-Bo over a rat." Her voice dropped from its previous screech, and I thought I could hear a note of pity in it.

"Excuse me?" I hoped my laugh sounded suitably incredulous. "Why would I fight your flea-bag cat over a rat?"

"For the same reason I've trained Bojangles and the rest of my strays to catch them and bring them to me," WCL said, the compassion in her tone now unmistakable. "Because you don't want to kill humans to feed your blood hunger. You're a vamp like me, aren't you?"

I opened my mouth to give her a cool brush-off, but the words wouldn't come. Instead, I heard myself utter a choking gasp. Worse, the gasp was immediately accompanied by the wet feel of big, fat tears welling up from my eyes.

Let's get one thing straight—with my baby-blue eyes and strawberry-blond curls I may look fragile and sensitive, and I'm not above batting said eyes and tossing said curls at any hapless male who shows up as an interesting blip on my personal radar screen. I've also perfected the art of instant tears, Swarovski droplets that tremble on my lashes but never get to the point where they smear my Urban Decay mascara. But—and I'll totally deny this if it ever gets out—I'm really as tough as old boots, to borrow one of Popsie's favorite phrases. I've had to be, growing up with Megan and Kat as my sisters. I mean, Meg's beautiful and smart and doesn't take crap from anyone, and Kat simply sizzles with sexiness. They're a hard act to follow, and if I had an ounce of fragility in me my ego would have been completely crushed by now.

Which it's not, thank you very much. Well, not until I dissolved into a weepy pool of tears and clogged nose and embarrassing spitty stuff running from the corners of my mouth as my choked gasps became full-blown howls of misery. I whooped and coughed and shuddered and tried again to speak, but only managed something that sounded like, "Nuh, nuh…nuh fair! Nuh…bell tower! But nuh… nuh chickened out!"

Not my most shining moment. I wouldn't have blamed Weird Cat Lady for thinking she'd run into someone even weirder than herself and leaving me to finish dissolving by the Dumpster all by my lonesome, but she didn't. She hauled me inside and upstairs to her apartment, sat me down at her kitchen table while she brewed some tea and waited until I was vaguely coherent again.

"Firstly, you're not a chicken just because you didn't kill yourself," she said, setting a mug in front of me and bending down to stroke the sea of cats twining around her ankles. "Drink this, it's got goldenseal and Moroccan mint in it. I came up with the basic recipe when I started going through menopause to control my hot flashes, but after I turned vamp I found if I tweaked the ingredients a little it helped with the blood cravings."

I took a sip and tried not to gag. "Nice," I said, still snuffling.

She gave me a grin that made me look past her gray hair to the girl she must have been thirty years earlier. "You lie like Nixon," she declared. "It tastes like hell and I know it, but when my inner thermostat jacks up twenty degrees I'll gulp down anything to get relief. Same goes for the hunger. It's bad enough that a vegetarian like me is drinking rat blood, but after all these years of protesting wars and violence, there's no way Kathy Lehman's going to take a human life just because some dickhead old boyfriend showed up one night and turned me into a vampire. I'll walk into the sunlight before I do that." She frowned. "Which leads me to the question of why you didn't try that route, instead of jumping from a church tower. And how did you manage to get into a church, anyway?"

I choked down another sip of tea. "Vamphood seems to be working differently on me than it does with everyone else. I can still go out in the day without flash-frying and I don't appear to be banned yet from entering a church. I guess it's got something to do with the way I was marked." I saw the question in her eyes and stifled a sigh. "Queen *Vampyr*. I was a baby. The curse was supposed to kick in during my twenty-first year, which it did a few weeks ago, but the hunger only hit me tonight."

"And you immediately wanted to tear your nearest and dearest from limb to limb?" Kathy Lehman said shrewdly. "Been there, almost did that. I fought the impulse and made do with rat blood. But since you're not a crazy cat lady like me, you might have to go a different route." She tipped her head to one side. "There are a few of us around, you know—vamps who've vowed to find any alternative to embracing the darkness. We've even formed our own unofficial support group that meets every Tuesday in the basement of the local union hall. Drop by if you feel the need."

I tried to keep my thoughts from my expression, since my thoughts were running along the lines of, sweet of you to offer, but I think I'd rather stake myself, thanks. "I'll keep that in mind," I said, trying to wipe out the image I'd just had of myself saying, "Hi, my name's Tashya and I'm a vampire," and having a roomful of enthusiastically cheerful strangers chorus back, "Hi, Tashya!"

"You do that." Again Kathy smiled, as if she could read my mind. "But right now I'm guessing you'd like some more concrete help." Rising from the table, she turned to her refrigerator and ripped a page from a cat memo pad hanging from a cat magnet. Scribbling something on it, she handed it to me. "Go to this address. It's a butcher shop and it'll be closed at this time of night, naturally, but old man Schneider does a booming after-hours business in the alleyway at the back of the store. Try to get there as early as possible because he sometimes runs out."

I glanced at the scrap of paper in my hand. "Not that I don't appreciate the grocery tip, but how does buying a couple of black-market T-bones help me?"

"Old man Schneider's after-hours business isn't in meat, it's in pig's blood," Kathy said bluntly. "He sells it in quart bags, like milk, at twenty bucks a pop."

This time I wasn't able to hide my reaction. "Ewww," I said in disgust. "Blood in a bag?"

"Would you prefer it free-range from a human?" she asked wryly. "If you think you can handle the hunger any other way, you're wrong. Sooner or later you're going to kill—" She broke off abruptly as a thump, like something jumping through an open window, sounded from the adjacent room. The next moment Bojangles swaggered into the kitchen, a dead rat in his jaws. With feline pride he deposited it at his mistress's feet.

I realized two things simultaneously: one, I didn't want to see what happened next; and two, the rat didn't look as unappetizing to me as it should. I swallowed the sudden nausea that rose in me and backed toward the door. "I can see you're about to sit down to dinner, so I'll leave you to it," I said quickly. "Thanks for the advice and the tea and for—"

"Good cat." Kathy wasn't listening to me. She scooped the limp gray body from the floor and gave the battle-scarred tom a distracted pat. Her voice sounded thicker and deeper. "I'll save the head for you as usual, Bo-Bo."

Her teeth began to lengthen past her bottom lip as she brought the dead rat to her mouth. I turned and fled, clutching the scrap of paper in my hand.

Chapter 2

It wasn't the scene in WCL's kitchen that night that made me change my mind about buying take-out blood-in-a-bag, it was the realization that if Mr. Bojangles hadn't butted in when he had during our tussle by the Dumpster, it could have been me chowing down on a rat hors d'oeuvre. I take back what I said about standing in line in a garbage-strewn alleyway being rock bottom—the alternative would have been worse.

Famous last words.

"It's okay, Joe, she didn't mean to barge into you like that," a girl's voice behind me called after the old man with the shopping cart. "Hey, Mata Hari, wanna move your butt?" The owner of the voice poked me in the ribs as she asked the terse question.

I lowered my sunglasses at her. "Do you have a problem?" I asked coolly.

She jerked her head at the fast-retreating old man. "Besides the fact that you almost knocked down Crazy Joe? Yeah, my problem is that the line's moving and you aren't. I don't particularly want to get in a rumble with a bunch of wannabes who might think it'd be a hoot to cut in ahead of us."

"Wannabes?" Frowning, I began to close the gap in front of me, only to realize it wasn't there anymore. To be exact, it had been filled by four black-clad figures standing with their backs to me.

"Great. Just fuckin' great." The girl behind me spoke again, her tone bitterly resigned. I turned and studied her in growing irritation. She looked about my age, but that was all we had in common. She was a few inches shorter than my five-seven, and the vintage punk-rock T-shirt and ripped khaki cargos she was wearing didn't hide her compact toughness. Her hair was white-blond with dark roots, carelessly hacked into short spikes that stood up like two-tone chicken feathers around her head. Her eyes glared green at me.

"You gonna tell them to get outta here or do I have to?" She didn't bother waiting for my reply, but stepped in front of me, tapping the nearest black-clad shoulder. "Yo, buddy," she snapped. "Haul your ass to the back of the line and take your friends with you."

Slowly the four figures turned to face her, moving apart so that they flanked us. Four pairs of red eyes stared menacingly out of four dead-white faces, and when the one whose shoulder had been tapped spoke, his lifted upper lip revealed razor-sharp fangs.

"We need blood," he said in a low, emotionless voice that seemed too deep for his Ichabod Crane-like frame. He was older than his companions and it was obvious he was their spokes-vamp. "Force us, and we'll take it from you, human."

"Slice the bitch, Viktor!" The teenaged vamp beside him had skanky black hair extensions falling

nearly to her waist. She carried through her dubious
style sense with a black-and-red bustier that showed
way too much bobbing cleavage, leather boots
climbing halfway up her non-toned thighs and torn
fishnet stockings. The whole ensemble was finished
off with a *Dead and Loving It* tattoo inked on her
slightly pouchy stomach. If I'd been feeling more
charitable I might have taken her aside and suggested she try a few sit-ups or maybe look into
Pilates, but her outburst to Viktor had kind of turned
me off the feeling-charitable-toward-her thing.

It had turned punk-girl off, too, and from her
attitude so far I was guessing she hadn't had an
abundance of charitable feelings in the first place.
She flicked a glance at the teen vamp's soft midriff
and shook her head. "Chickie-poo, I'd find it easier
to believe you were a dedicated blood-drinker if
you weren't flaunting that burgers-and-shakes
tummy at us. Dead and Loving It? I'm Lovin' It
would have been more appropriate."

"Hey, nobody talks to my girlfriend, Cindy, like
that!" The second female vamp had Manic Panic
red hair and a smear of black lipstick on one of her
fangs. She was dressed like her friend and I realized

that their outfits seemed somehow familiar to me, although for the moment I couldn't think why. She turned to Viktor. "I know you said we weren't ready to drink from a human source yet, Master, but if you want to, like, slake your thirst with these vermin, please don't hold back on our unworthy accounts."

"Speak for yourself, Trudy," the second male in the group interjected, his red gaze focusing on me. He had a face like a ferret, if ferrets wore lip studs. And tongue studs, I noted with an inner shudder as he gave Viktor a defiant shrug. "I owe you for turning me, dude, but I don't see why I have to take orders from you forever. Screw lining up for pig's blood—I'm ready for the real thing. I'll drain this bitch and leave the blonde to you." He glanced at punk-girl. "Sorry, babe, but I'm not into dykes."

"My name's not babe, it's Brooklyn," punk-girl said with a cold smile. "And if you meant the dyke remark as a slam, it wasn't. I'm here, I'm queer, and damn glad of it when I run into a primo specimen of the male sex like you." She switched her attention back to Viktor. "Sweet little scam you're running. I normally wouldn't care less that you get your rocks off by playing mentor-vamp to the teen goth set, but you and I both know you don't need what old man Schneider's selling." She glanced past Viktor and scowled. "He's down to the last few bags. I don't plan on letting a line-jumping imposter screw me out of my daily corpuscle fix, so either walk away politely or I'm going to have to go all Lady Dracula on your ass. What's it gonna be, wax-teeth?"

Now, here's the thing: I know that as a vamp myself, other bloodsuckers should hold no fear for me. I mean, the whole taboo about us not being able to feed from each other, right? Except I still think of myself as Tashya Crosse, normal American girl, and when I'm confronted by pointy teeth and red eyes my automatic thought processes go something like, a) damn, where's my stake; b) damn, where's my Daughter of Lilith sister and c) damn, how fast can I run in these frikkin' heels. So while I admired her *cojones,* I wasn't real happy about Brooklyn throwing down the gauntlet to the hungry-looking Viktor, especially since I was pretty sure she'd gotten one vital detail wrong.

"Uh, Brook?" I said, edging closer to her and speaking out of the side of my mouth. "Not to quibble, but they're not wax. His teeth, I mean. If they were, the sharp parts would have gone kind of round and melty by now, no? Just a thought," I added in an undertone.

"Good point, Mata Hari." She rolled her eyes. "Wax, plastic, whatever, he's not one of us. Don't tell me you can't smell the reek of human coming off him and his pathetic posse." She took in my blank look and scowled at me—I was beginning to understand that scowling was her default expression. "Pork barbeque, kind of, with maybe a whiff of mesquite? That's what humans smell like to me, anyway, which might be a partial explanation of why I haven't let myself feed on them yet. When you're raised by a Jewish baba as strict as my grandmother, God rest her, you don't even go for simulated bacon bits on your Caesar salad—and don't even ask how I justify pig's blood, because that's where my dear, departed Baba and I part ways. You really can't smell them?" she asked, raising an eyebrow. "Just what kind of vamp are—"

"What you smell can only be your own wretched humanity," Viktor broke in, "but as tempted as I am to spill your blood in the dust, I will spare your life this time. Restraint is an exquisite lesson to learn, my young friends," he intoned to Trudy and Cindy and Stud-Tongue. "Watch well and learn how we Dark Ones master our impulses."

Beside me Brooklyn made a sound that could have been a snort but if Viktor heard, he chose to ignore it—a further demonstration of his iron control, I supposed. He stepped out of line, Trudy and Cindy falling in behind him, although from their pissed-off pouts they weren't thrilled about their undead leader's decision. The thought crossed my mind that Brooklyn was the coolest vamp I'd yet met—I mean, come on, the woman had that whole funky, don't-mess-with-me aura, plus she was gay. Plus she had those minty-green eyes. Plus under the ratty tee she was wearing, her body looked to-die-for buff and…anyway, despite the fact that I didn't buy her barbeque theory about Viktor being human, I was thinking about how totally cool she was and wondering whether her lips were naturally that Scarlett Johanssonish or if she'd had collagen injections, when something happened that yanked my attention back to the here and now.

Actually, a whole bunch of things happened. But since they all happened at almost the same time, they're lumped together in my recollection as one big near disaster.

In order, here's how said near disaster went down. First, Stud-Tongue decided to skip the impulse-controlling lesson Viktor had decided to demonstrate to his pupil-vamps. Second, he lunged at his chosen blood-buffet—little ol' moi, of course. His maneuver took me by surprise, although not because I was still looking at Brooklyn's lips. A second earlier I'd wrenched my gaze away from her and was idly scanning the alleyway when a movement in the shadows snagged my attention. I realized that while I'd been staring at Brooklyn, someone else had been staring at me. I caught a glimpse of navy-blue eyes under straight brows, a strong mouth curved with amusement and an incongruous froth of white lace against a dark collar and cuffs. But like I said, right then Stud-Tongue attempted to chow down on my neck, diverting my attention from Mr. Tall, Dark and Blue-Eyed lurking in the shadows.

Brooklyn later told me I'd moved so fast that I'd

actually blurred. Then she frowned and said it was more like I'd been in one place one moment and in a totally different one the next, like Sonny Chiba in *The Street Fighter's Last Revenge,* her all-time favorite kung-fu movie. After she dragged me to see *The Street Fighter's Last Revenge* one night, I asked her if my mouth had moved independently from the words that had come out of it, also like in *TSFLR,* and she said no, but that was probably because I was absolutely silent throughout the whole encounter with Stud-Tongue.

"Silent and expressionless," she added, looking away from me. And my eyes had been black, empty holes.

Obviously if I'd known any of that at the time it would have creeped me out, but I didn't. In fact, I don't recall thinking anything in the split second that it took for me to nearly kill Stud-Tongue. All I remember is that I seemed to be looking at the scene that was unfolding as if I was watching through a blood-smeared window. I saw the sleeve of my trench coat slide through a dark-red fog, saw my own fingers close around Stud-Tongue's neck, saw the triumph in his eyes turn to terror. The red stain obscuring my vision darkened to black and my focus narrowed in on the throbbing vein under my pressing thumb.

It beat like a heart. I could hear blood surging through it like ocean waves rising and falling onto wet, black sand. I felt an answering surge come from deep inside me, and as I brought my mouth to that hypnotically pulsing vein and bared my lengthening fangs, the hunger I'd pushed back earlier that evening came roaring back, stronger than ever.

The tips of my fangs pierced flesh. I began to drive them in deeper, anticipating the hotly orgasmic rush of blood flooding into my mouth.

And then I was flat on my back on the pavement, my jaw feeling as if it had been broken and a solid weight bearing down on me. "Leash it!" Brooklyn snarled, bending forward from her squatting position on my chest and thrusting her face into mine. "You're here tonight for the same reason we all are—because you're trying to fight the hunger. Not that I care about this scumbag, but he's not worth losing your soul over! Besides, the freakin' Daughter sometimes patrols this area. I hear she's inclined to stake first and ask questions after, so unless you want a hunk of wood through your heart, you'd better get a grip, Mata Hari!"

Her warning wasn't necessary. The pain from her roundhouse punch to my jaw had broken through the red fog that had surrounded me. Shaking my head to clear it, I saw Stud-Tongue and Viktor and the two females rapidly take their leave and suddenly realized why Trudy and Cindy's outfits had seemed familiar.

"Omigod, they're bad Zena clones," I muttered. "The bustiers, the fishnets—they're practically channeling the bitch. What's that about?"

"Who cares," Brooklyn said impatiently. "All I want to know is whether your hunger's abated. If you lose control—"

"Since her death at the hands of the Darkheart Daughter, the Russian Queen *Vampyr* has become somewhat of a legend, madam. A dark legend, to be sure, but the foolish can be indiscriminate in their emulation. May I help you to your feet?"

In the dust and dirt of the alleyway, the riding boots standing a few inches away from me looked out of place. They were black leather, polished to a mirrored gleam. Still lying on my back, I let my gaze travel upward past the boots, past the dark blue trousers that rose out of them, past the military-cut blue sleeve extended gallantly toward me, lace spilling from its cuff.

Two words: *Yum.* Yes, that's just one word, but I said it twice, as in *yum, yum.* And I'm not sure I didn't say it out loud.

You know those nights when you're lying in bed not sleeping because you just had a fight with your boyfriend and you're thinking all men are jerks? And you decide that if you'd been given the job, you totally could have created a better male sex and you start imagining what that perfect man would be like? And a little later when you've got a clear picture of your perfect-man creation in your mind—for some reason mine always ends up looking slightly Hugh Jackman-y—you kind of glance sideways at the nightstand beside your bed and without really meaning to, you find yourself opening the drawer and reaching for Mr. Love-Bunny, into whom you just put fresh batteries a couple of days ago....

All right, I'm back, and if you're not I'm going on without you. My point is that Mr. Tall, Dark and

Blue-Eyed was even better than any perfect man I'd ever imagined…although he did kind of have the Hugh Jackman thing going on, especially around his mouth. A strand of black hair grazed the straight, dark eyebrows I'd noticed earlier and brushed against thick, spiky lashes I hadn't noticed in my brief glance before Stud-Tongue had embarked on his short-lived career as a working vamp. The afore-mentioned mouth was chiseled and lush at the same time, and just looking at his lips made me want to bite them—not in a fang-girl way but in a nipping-at-them-in-between-getting-kissed-by-them way. Right now they were smiling at me, revealing a gleam of white teeth that seemed dazzling in the shadows of the alleyway.

"My friend doesn't need your help, thanks." Brooklyn yanked me up by my wrist as she rose and brought her face to mine. "Sorry about hauling off and slugging you the way I did, Mata Hari," she said in the softest tone I'd heard her use so far.

I winced as her fingertips gently touched my jawline. "Um, ow," I said on an indrawn breath. "And since we went straight to the hauling off and slugging phase in our relationship, we bypassed the hi, my name is Tashya part, so, hi, my name's Tashya."

"Hi, Tashya. Mine's Brooklyn Steinberg." The corners of her mouth quirked sexily upward as she stepped back. "But I'm not sure Mata Hari didn't go better with the whole incognito trench coat and wig look you've got going on there. By the way, you might want to straighten that happenin' First Lady hairdo before the bangs end up at the back of your head."

I'd forgotten about the damn wig, but now she'd reminded me I realized I might as well ditch it. I'd only worn the thing in an attempt to keep a low profile, and if trying to rip Stud-Tongue's jugular out hadn't turned that into an impossibility, being on the receiving end of a girl-on-girl smackdown certainly had. I pulled off my brunette bob and shook out my own curls, going for a slow-mo shampoo-advertisement effect as I turned to include Mr. Tall, Dark Etc. in our little social circle—merely out of common courtesy, of course, and not for any less admirable reason like wanting to put the moves on him.

"So you think Trudy and Cindy were dressed the

way they were because they're members in good standing of the local Zena-Skank-Mistress-of-the-Universe fan club?" I shook my head again just in case he hadn't caught the full effect the first time. "How do you explain the fangs and the red eyes?"

"Wax, like I told you, and the eyes were colored contacts. The line's moving, Tash," Brooklyn broke in. She directed a cold look at our companion. "I could go into a whole riff on the fact that for someone who's doing a Queer-Eye on other people's clothes you're wearing a pretty weird-ass outfit yourself, stranger, but instead I'll just tell you what I told Vik-baby—move it or lose it."

"My apologies for putting you in the position of not having a name by which to address me, madam." Instead of taking offense at Brooklyn's brusqueness, he obligingly stepped aside. "Allow me to rectify my omission, ladies. Heath Lock-ridge, late of the First New York Muskets." I was concentrating so hard on not going into total meltdown at his adorable English-type way of speaking that I barely took in what he was saying. "Your theory about our hastily departed friends is admirable but wrong, I fear. The cadaverous Viktor is what is called an orthodontist, I understand, recently arrived in town upon the sad demise of his uncle, also a practitioner in the field. I am no expert on the profession, madam, but I have been told 'tis no very great matter for one such as he to outfit himself and other nonimmortals with a set of retractable canines, although he seems to have let his followers believe they received the gift of fangs from his *vampyr* bite."

For a moment I forgot to flirt. "Omigod, he must be Dr. Maisel's nephew. My sis—" I caught myself "—I mean, the local Daughter of Lilith and her Healer sister staked Maisel and his witchy wife after they turned vamp. Not that I was there or anything," I added hastily as I stepped forward into the spill of illumination coming from the open exit door of a building backing onto the alley.

In the doorway stood a stocky older man wearing a stained butcher's apron and holding a clear, sealed bag whose contents gleamed ruby in the light. Suddenly nervous, I passed over the twenty-dollar bill Kathy Lehman had advised me was the inflated price Schneider charged for his disgusting product, but as I reached for the bag a wave of nausea swept over me.

"Sorry, lady, but some precautions I haff to take, ja?"

His breath wafting a withering blast of garlic over me, old man Schneider shrugged in heavy unconcern as my fingers closed weakly over the bag. I felt Heath's grip on my shoulder and took a staggering step away before turning back to wait for Brooklyn, then a different sensation rose up in me. As the hunger flooded through me for the third time that night, I shrugged off Heath's steadying hand.

"I'm okay," I said thickly—and if you're wondering why thickly, all I can say is you try talking when your eye-teeth are in the process of lengthening past your bottom lip. I gave up all pretence of politeness and sunk my canines into the plastic, ripping a jagged hole in one corner. "Just need to take a little nip of the good stuff here—"

"Damn, it's a setup!"

Brooklyn's words sent a chill of fear through me, but the hunger overrode all other emotions. I slurped down a mouthful of blood—

Okay, let's lay down some ground rules here

before I go any further. Yes, I know how totally gross that last sentence sounded, and yes, I know there's no way I can describe the taste or the smell or the exquisite sensations I felt while I was glugging back my happy snack of pig's blood so that anyone who isn't a vampire can understand—and by understand I basically mean not toss your cookies at the very thought. So you're just going to have to take it on faith, the stuff was ambrosia to me. I didn't even want to waste the part that was trickling down my chin, so as I reluctantly lowered my bag o'blood and met Brooklyn's alarmed eyes I used the back of my hand to smear the spilled residue toward my mouth.

"Setup?" I looked quickly about, but I couldn't see anything that might have alerted her. "Who set us up and how?"

Her gaze traveled coldly over me. "Shove the innocent act, Mata Hari, your cover's blown. You shoulda kept the bad wig on, or at least stayed in the shadows. You're Natashya Crosse, the sister of the Daughter and the Healer, aren't you?"

"Yeah, she is, vamp. Wanna make something of it?"

The measured challenge came from behind me. I whirled around, my heart sinking as I saw the two people I least wanted to encounter tonight.

Megan—she was the one who'd spoken—was wearing your basic Daughter of Lilith black and carrying your basic Daughter of Lilith stake. Kat had never bought into the Healer-Nurturing-Soul-Mother look, so she was dressed as she always was, in something slinky and designer and drop-dead sexy. But their expressions as they looked at me were identical, and I suddenly felt like an old wino chugging from a bottle of Woolite.

"Oh, sweetie, no," Kat said, her husky voice breaking with appalled compassion.

"Dammit, Tash, you told us you were controlling the hunger!" Megan accused.

"They didn't know you were here tonight?" Brooklyn's tone lost its edge. She stepped in front of me and whipped out a tissue. "All down your freakin' chin, babe," she murmured as she dabbed at my face before turning to my sisters. "She is controlling it, and if you two weren't such holier-than-thou bitches, you'd realize that," she snapped.

I didn't see Megan's and Kat's reactions. I was

too busy scanning the alleyway for Heath. He'd been beside me only a moment ago, and I hadn't seen him leave.

But he was gone. And at the far end of the alleyway I saw a bat rise swiftly over the rooftops and disappear.

Chapter 3

"Oh, shit. Heads up, Tashya—dude with weapon at five o'clock," Brooklyn said under her breath as a figure detached itself from the shadows and moved to Kat's side. Her eyes narrowed. "And is that a friggin' wolf?"

"Holier than thou?" Megan said ominously as her hand fell to the wolf's silver-tipped black ruff. She kept her gaze on Brooklyn. "I guess we are at that, seeing as how you're about to go straight to hell, vamp. Step away from her, Tash."

I heard a door slam and the sound of a dead bolt shooting into its lock. Glancing sideways, I saw old man Schneider had decided discretion was the better part of valor and had closed up shop for the evening. Which was understandable enough, since his clientele had melted away into the darkness during the past few seconds, leaving only me and Brooklyn and the muttering derelict Brook had called Crazy Joe, who'd returned and was now pawing through a garbage can, oblivious to the drama being enacted a few feet away from him. My humiliation at Megan and Kat finding me here was replaced by anger.

"The dude with the nail gun that shoots silver-tipped nails is Kat's ex-con main squeeze, Jack Rawls. And the wolf's a shapeshifter named Mikhail. Rumor has it Megan lets him sleep on her bed if he's been a good dog," I told Brooklyn, loudly enough for Megan to hear. I switched my attention to my sisters. "No one's going to hell tonight, Meg," I declared. "I hear you've patrolled this alley before, so you know damn well that the vamps who come here don't feed off humans. Take your pointy stick and go home, and tell the rest of your little gang they're not wanted, either. That includes you, Kat."

"There's no such thing as a vamp that doesn't feed off humans." Beside Kat, Jack's finger tightened on the nail gun's trigger. "Only vamps that haven't fed off humans yet."

"Sweetie, you know your killer instinct's one of the things I adore about you, but you're aiming at my little sister," Kat drawled. "If you dust her I'll hunt you to the ends of the earth, so dial it down, *comprendes?* Megan, Tash was just being her usual bratty self with that remark about Mikhail. Lower your stake before Darkheart gets here."

"Grandfather's with you?" I thrust my bag of blood at Brooklyn, almost spilling it in my agitation. "Take this. No, don't just hold it in front of you for everyone to see, stash it somewhere!"

She stared at me. "What's with you? Your big sisters show up and ten seconds later you're emotional wreckage?"

"They're only my big sisters by a matter of minutes," I said distractedly. "We're triplets. Just hide the blood, okay, Brook? Kat, I can't believe you let Megan do this! I'll bet I know what this is about—our Daughter of Lilith sister's decided I'm not pulling my weight at Darkheart & Crosse and she's trying to get me booted from the agency. But since she doesn't have the guts to Trump me herself, she accidentally-on-purpose arranged for Grandfather Darkheart to see how far down Vamp Avenue I've travelled in the past few weeks so he has to tell me I'm fired! All I can say is that when Grammie and Popsie finally come home, you two are going to be in major shit, so there!"

My arms folded across my chest in triumph, I turned to Brooklyn. "Darkheart & Crosse was my brainwave," I informed her. "After Zena got dusted I figured there'd be a need for an agency that specialized in vampire-related investigations, and I was totally right, but since Megan became a Daughter it's all about her. She can't stand that the business I thought up is threatening to overshadow her Daughter of Lilith activities." I waited for Brooklyn's reaction but when it came it wasn't what I'd expected.

"Too bad, babe." In her ice-green eyes I saw a glimmer of something that looked like disappointment. She held out my bag of blood. "I'm outta here."

"So am I," I said, glancing defiantly in Megan's direction. "You want to hit an after-hours club together, maybe see if we can find a couple of interesting guys? Or in your case, girl," I amended.

"I thought I had," Brooklyn said. "Looks like I was wrong. Stay out of the sunlight, Mata Hari." She turned to go, but then she hesitated. "I sometimes wonder why I got vamped, you know? Like why me, a nice Jewish girl who was good to her Bubbe, kind to small children, only bought lattes made from fair-trade coffee beans? Hell, I've got a sister, too—a twin, and except that she's straight the two of us could be clones. Yet I got turned and Xandra didn't. I haven't figured it out yet." She shrugged. "But if life's supposed to be more than just a series of random shitstorms, maybe the reason why you received this fun bonus from fate is because being a vamp is your only chance of becoming a real person. I really hope that happens for you, babe. Vamp or not, the little I saw of who you could be was a hell of a lot more intriguing than the bratty younger sister of the Daughter and the Healer."

In my own defence, I'd like to point out that it

had been a long night, what with chickening out of killing myself, playing tug-of-rat with a cat and nearly getting bitten by Stud-Tongue. Not to mention receiving a wicked uppercut to my jaw from my new best friend, finding and losing the man of my fantasies and having my sisters discover I'd progressed to drinking blood. All in all, I wasn't in the mood to thank Brook for her assessment of me and thoughtfully ask myself if any of what she'd said could be true. I was more in the mood to yell the meanest things I could think of at her as she walked away from me.

Which is what I did, and to this day I wish I could call back the words I flung after her.

"You mean I won't have to think of a polite way to tell you I don't appreciate being pawed on the slightest pretext by another woman, babe?" I gave a short laugh. "News flash, Punk-girl—that's not a tragedy, that's a relief! Even if I were gay, you're so not my type, with that dark-root look you've got going with your hair and that Salvation Army look you've got going with your clothes!" I raised my voice as she slipped into the shadows between two buildings and disappeared from my view without ever having looked back. "And another thing—"

Something brushed against my hair and fell to my shoulders. Startled, I looked down at myself and saw the starry shapes of small, white flowers against the black of my trenchcoat. Then the nausea hit me, ten times more powerfully than it had in reaction to old man Schneider's garlic breath, and I realized what the flowers were.

"Wild garlic!" I choked the words out as I fell to my knees. "Get it off me!"

"Is unfortunate necessity, Granddaughter." As the Russian-accented words reached my ears, my blurred vision made out the bulky shape of a caped figure reeling in the excess length of his wild-garlic lasso as he approached me. "Do not worry, this is not trap to stake you," he said with hearty reassurance.

"Tha's...good to know..." I mumbled as I pitched face-forward onto the ground and lost consciousness at Darkheart's feet.

"It's worse than we thought." As I struggled upward through the fog surrounding me, I heard

Kat's worried voice coming from a long way away. "She keeps her shoes in a plastic garbage bag—Manolos, Jimmy Choos, all jumbled up together in a big pile! How *could* she?"

"What more proof do we need that she's totally deteriorated? And if you think that's bad, take a look at what I found under her bed, covered with dust bunnies." Megan didn't sound worried, she sounded pissed off. "My cream Chanel jacket, the one she swore she hadn't borrowed."

"Refrigerator is disaster area. Bag of stale doughnuts, two cartons take-out Chinese food, old slices pizza. In cupboards are cookies and candy bars." The fog around me lifted enough for me to hear Darkheart sigh heavily. "Is typical symptom. She fights blood hunger but other cravings come upon her."

They'd brought me to my own apartment, I realized, and while I'd been dead to the world my sisters and my grandfather—I couldn't hear Mikhail or Jack, so I assumed they'd been left on patrol—had been searching the place. Outrage flickered in me but I still felt too lethargic to move.

"You mean she gets the munchies?" Kat's tone

went from worried to appalled. "The poor sweetie, she's going to blimp out if she keeps this up. Honestly, Meg, if I can't attempt a Heal on my own sister—"

Her words were like an icy wind blowing the last of my grogginess away. I sat bolt upright, realizing as I did that I was no longer bound by Darkheart's garlic lasso, and the next moment I was racing across the room to the window that looked out onto the metal fire escape. I was steps away from it when I saw the wreath tacked to the sill, its starry white flowers wafting their deadly scent toward me. I changed direction in mid-dash and made for the door, only to see another garlic wreath festooning that escape route. Blindly I headed for my bedroom. The window by my bed didn't open onto a handy fire escape, it looked out over the Dumpster that had been the scene of my embarrassing tussle with Bojangles, but although I hadn't been able to bring myself to jump from St. Jude's bell tower earlier this evening I thought I could manage a three-story drop into a pile of reeking refuse.

Given what the alternative was.

I came to a screeching halt. Megan was standing

in the bedroom doorway, her stake in her hand. "You wouldn't, Meg," I said hollowly.

She looked thoughtful. "Probably not, brat. But do you really want to find out?"

"Sweetie, calm down." I spun around to see Kat advancing on me, her perfect features shadowed with compassion. "As Darkheart said, we're not planning a staking. This little get-together's more along the lines of a—"

"Stay away from me, Kat!" I hissed, shrinking from her. In chagrin I realized my fangs were lengthening, and I tried to keep my top lip immobile—a look that might have worked for Humphrey Bogart, but which I was pretty sure wasn't working for me. "I know what this is! It's an intervention, and you can forget it—I'm not risking an attempted Heal unless you can guarantee it won't go bad, sending me straight to hell and eternal damnation. But you can't guarantee that, can you?"

Kat tossed a swath of silver-blond hair from her shoulders. I could see she was trying to hold on to her I'm-a-Healer-so-I-feel-love-for-all-living-things-even-the-undead serenity and fighting a sisterly impulse to snap at me. "*Merde,* sweetie, that's only happened a handful of times in the whole history of Healing, and when it has it's usually—"

"It's usually been when the prospective Healee bears the mark of a Queen *Vampyr,*" I broke in. "Hmmm…who do we know like that? Oh, that's right—me!"

I was backing away from her as I spoke, but I froze when I felt something sharp in my back, just below my left shoulderblade. I kept my gaze straight ahead. "Stake?"

"Yup," Megan agreed from behind me. "I told you two she'd make a piss-poor candidate," she said laconically to Darkheart and Kat. "Face it, Kat, we've always known our little sister's got a few tiny character flaws, starting with being spoiled, self-involved and immature. Even her punky vamp friend's figured her out. I say we drop this ridiculous plan."

Her character assassination of me aside, I told myself, Megan was arguing my case for me. I should probably keep my mouth shut. Ignoring my own advice, I turned around and glared at her. "Ever since you've taken on the role of a Daughter of

Lilith you've been a royal pain in the butt, Meg. You're the self-involved one!"

"Really?" she said thinly. "Tell me, when you did your midnight flit from the Crosse mansion last week after we got that letter from Cyrus Kane, did it occur to you that we'd be worried sick when we found you gone? We wasted three patrol nights tracking you down to this crappy apartment and when we did I wanted to read you the riot act for scaring us the way you did, but Darkheart—" she nodded at Grandfather, who remained silent "—insisted we give you time to adjust to the realization that you were the one Zena marked when we were babies."

"Of all the ingratitude!" I sputtered. "You're on my case because I left home before I—" I stopped abruptly and Megan's gaze narrowed.

"Before you what?"

Before I killed you and Kat, I told her silently. *Before I slaughtered Darkheart and Mikhail and Jack. Before the hunger became stronger than I could handle, the way it almost did tonight.* Once upon a time I would have blurted out the truth to her, I thought, taking in the firm line of her mouth, the hard steadiness that hadn't been in her gaze before she'd become a Daughter. But now I couldn't know for sure if she'd react to my confession as a sister…or as the sworn enemy of me and my kind.

"Before I went out of my mind with boredom," I said with a shrug. "I mean, things around here are getting so same old, same old. First Zena shows up in Maplesburg and you stake her, then Kane shows up and Kat Heals him—and by the way, Kat," I added in an aside, "Cyrus fleeing to the ends of the earth all tortured with guilt over his evil past and dying in a Buddhist monastery isn't the most reassuring demonstration of the benefits of a Heal. No wonder you don't have vamps lining up to take advantage of the oh-so-special gift you inherited from Daddy Dearest."

"Firstly, Kane didn't die from being Healed, he was murdered," Kat said sharply. "And the vamp that infiltrated the monastery and killed him was the same one he tried to warn us about in the letter the monks forwarded to us after his death—Lady Jasmine Melrose, the bitch who turned him centuries ago right here in Maplesburg. Secondly, what's with the 'Daddy Dearest' *merde?* Finding out that there's a possibility our father didn't die twenty years ago when Zena targeted Angelica should have made you as happy as it did Megan and me, but ever since we read that postscript to Kane's letter—"

"'David Crosse lives'," I quoted impatiently. "And it wasn't Kane's postscript, it was tacked onto the end of his letter by Jasmine, along with her heads-up to us about how she's coming to Maplesburg. But she hasn't shown up here, has she? And if her news-flash about Daddy Dearest was true, why hasn't he contacted us in all these years?"

"That's what *Gospodin* Darkheart has requested me to find out. My family's business contacts in former Soviet Socialist Republic have spent past week questioning peasants in mountainous Carpathian region in attempt to learn what happened to David Crosse after night when Zena left him for dead. Trail is understandably cold after so long and so far is few results, but still is hope we will learn something."

The unfamiliar voice came from behind me, and I turned in quick alarm to see a man standing in the open doorway of my apartment. Under other circumstances I might have let my gaze linger on him, but right now—well, okay, maybe I did let my gaze linger. Not for long, but enough to make a snap assessment of the man's attributes, which included about six foot five inches of tanned, hard-muscled male dressed in jeans and a black T-shirt, close-cropped hair even paler than Kat's platinum shade and icy blue eyes that ignored everyone else in the room and remained fixed on me. He looked to be around twenty-eight or twenty-nine, and from his accent it wasn't hard to guess he was one of the Russians living in New York that Mikhail had called on during our final battle against Cyrus Kane and his vamp army.

All of which didn't explain what he was doing in my apartment and why he seemed to be more in the loop than I was when it came to my family's private business.

One of Grammie's most cherished dictums is that one should always be polite and considerate to guests. Grammie'd never had a massive blond know-it-all Russian dropped on her from out of the blue, I thought wrathfully as I turned on Megan and Kat. "Who's he?" I demanded, jerking my thumb at the Russian. "And what does he mean, his family's been looking into David Crosse's whereabouts? Is Darkheart & Crosse running investigations I don't know about now?"

"Name is Dmitri Malkovich," the blond giant said before my sisters could answer. "Search for *Gospodin* Crosse is not official agency business. Is undertaken by my family in attempt to repay your grandfather for great service he has done us in old country when he saved my sister Anya from *vampyr* attack. Cousins in Mother Russia are *mafya*, have many contacts and ways to find out things." He frowned. "How is said *mafya* in America?"

"Mafia," Megan said briefly. "And it's probably wiser to tell people they're in waste management or something like that." She turned her attention back to me. "You've got no one but yourself to blame for the fact that you're out of touch with what's happening at the agency, Tash. You saw what happened to us when we thought we were the ones Zena marked and isolated ourselves, so why are you making the same mistake we did?"

"Maybe because it's no fun to be around you anymore?" I said, raising my eyebrows at the stake she was still pointing my way. "Gawd, Meg, it's like you and Kat have forgotten how to have a good time. It's all staking and Healing and punching the clock at Darkheart & Crosse—is it such a crime to want to party or go shopping once in a while?"

"I party every night, sweetie," Kat drawled. "As the owner of Maplesburg's hottest club, that's part of my job description, no? You could have dropped by the Hot Box anytime, but maybe hanging out in an alleyway is more your idea of fun."

"Frankly, it is," I shot back. "You just said it yourself—when you're at the Hot Box you're working, not ready to chill with your sis over a couple of cocktails. Besides, I still remember it as it was when Zena owned it. You nearly died there, Kat."

"Yes, but she didn't," Megan said evenly. "Zena did. So forgive me if I don't buy your sudden sensitivity, Tashya. I think the truth is that you're having way too much fun cutting loose for the first time in your life and you don't care that walking away from your family is the price. I guess we should be thankful that you haven't totally embraced your vamphood." She paused. "So far," she added harshly. "I never want to have to hunt you down, sis, so don't do anything that might make that happen. Let's leave, Kat. I told you we were wasting our time trying to talk to her."

I stared at her as she strode to the door, feeling as though she'd just slapped me in the face. Then I looked quickly away, hoping that my blubathon at Kathy Lehman's had depleted my tear ducts for the evening, and realizing it hadn't when I felt a sharp prickle behind my eyelids. Strangely enough, it wasn't Megan's barely veiled threat of staking me that hurt most, it was her attitude. She was trying her hardest to convince Kat and Darkheart that I wasn't worth attempting a Heal.

She was trying too hard, I realized a heartbeat later. Even as I wondered why she was in such a hurry to hustle Kat and my grandfather out before the three of them could attempt what they'd obviously come here to do, Darkheart addressed me for the first time since he'd arrived.

"Is much talk of Queen *Vampyr* among those you meet?" His question was abrupt and his gaze on me was sharp. "Perhaps tonight you hear rumors, *da?*"

"Sorry, *nyet,*" I informed him. "I mean, Zena

was a big deal to us, sure, but after her death the ordinary Joe Vamp in Maplesburg got on with his undead life." I remembered Trudy and Cindy. "Her style sense lives on, though. Does that count?"

"Not Zena, the new queen." Megan turned from the apartment door, her hand slipping from the doorknob. Her voice was low, as if she was reluctant to speak at all. "Lady Jasmine."

"The Cruel," added Kat in the same reluctant tone.

I rolled my eyes. "What's with these queen vamps? Zena billed herself as 'the Horrible,' now Jasmine's calling herself 'the Cruel'—I mean, talk about shameless self-promotion—"

"She does not call herself cruel," Darkheart interrupted. "She has earned that name from others."

"And comparing Zena to her is like comparing a housecat to a saber-toothed tiger," Megan said bleakly. "Except for what Cyrus told us in his letter we don't know much about her, but we know she's one of the strongest *vampyrs* in existence. And from what Kat learned from a vamp she Healed two nights ago, we also suspect she's already arrived in Maplesburg."

"Now I get it." I looked from one to another—Megan, grim and unsmiling, Kat, her eyes shadowed with concern, Darkheart, his expression closed. I was aware that Dmitri's ice-blue gaze was still fixed on me but I ignored him. "That's why you've decided to spring an intervention on me. You're afraid if I run into Ms. SuperVamp I'll go over to her side, me being so immature and self-involved and everything." I divided my glare among the three of them. "The answer's still no. *Nyet. Non. Nada*. I'm not—"

"*Nada* means nothing, not no," Megan said. "And that's not all you've got wrong, brat. We didn't come here to attempt a Heal on you tonight, we—" Her gaze shifted away, but with a visible effort she forced it to meet mine again. "We came here for the opposite reason."

"Only way to learn more about new Queen is to have spy in her camp," Darkheart rumbled. "We need you to stay *vampyr*, Granddaughter. Your sisters are not happy with plan, but—"

"Damn straight I'm not happy with the plan. In case you've forgotten, what's at stake here is Tashya's soul!" Megan exploded, swinging toward

Darkheart. "She's no match for either Lady Jasmine or her first lieutenant!"

"Oh, right, nobody's worthy of going up against the bad guys except you." I loaded my tone with sarcasm. "You seem to have forgotten that I've dusted more than a few vamps in my time, Meggy-poo, including some of Zena's toughest—" I stopped suddenly, a terrible suspicion filling me. "First lieutenant?" I asked in a small voice.

"One of cadre of Revolutionary War soldiers Jasmine turned the last time she was in Maplesburg, over two hundred years ago," Dmitri butted in. "Man is charming, handsome and irresistible, but is big mistake to let that fool you."

His gaze went glacier-cold. "Heath Lockridge is one of most dangerous *vampyrs* in existence. We must kill him soon as possible."

Chapter 4

I nearly blew it right then and there. "What total *merde,* to borrow a phrase of Kat's," I said with a disbelieving laugh. "Heath Lockridge, one of the most dangerous vamps in existence? The man's a dream come true—polite, gorgeous, and that adorable kind-of-English accent he has is a whole lot sexier than some I could mention." I glanced scornfully in Dmitri's direction before returning my attention to Megan and Kat. "Sorry, ladies, you've obviously made a huge mistake. Even if you're right and Lady Jasmine's in Maplesburg, there's no way Heath's her first lieutenant."

"And how would you know?" Megan asked in the new I'm-a-Daughter-so-don't-fuck-with-me tone of voice she'd been using way too often lately.

I gave her a pitying smile. "Because I—" I stopped, choking back the *met him* part of my sentence and realizing I'd just walked into a trap.

Although I suppose if you're going with the definition of a trap being something that's set by someone, it wasn't actually a trap, since a few seconds ago Meg and Kat hadn't had a clue that I'd actually made the acquaintance of the dishy Heath Lockridge. In other words, I guess you could say it was more like me opening my big mouth without thinking first, which is something I've been doing from about the age of eleven months, apparently. According to Grammie, the day her three granddaughters learned to talk, Megan's first word was "Mama," Kat spoke a moment later by uttering "Da-Da" and I went red-faced with rage at the attention being lavished on my sisters and bellowed "Ka-Ka!" at the top of my lungs. And that's pretty much how I've been ever since, Meg and Kat being such tough acts to compete with.

But this time my talk-first-think-later impulse had potentially direr results than usual, like possibly leading Megan and her ever-handy stake to Heath. I had to go into damage-control mode, and fast.

"Because I'm a patriot," I said icily. "I refuse to believe that anyone noble enough to fight for our country's independence would have switched their allegiance to some titled English vamp-tramp."

"Nice save, sweetie," Kat said, her eyes narrowing in suspicion. "But how do you know this Heath Lockridge is gorgeous and polite? Come to that, how do you know how he sounds when he speaks?"

She had me there. I had no alternative but to use my most infallible weapon, the one that always defeats Meg and Kat—my dumb-Tash act. I rolled my eyes in exasperation. "Hello, you saw the movie when I did, right? The one where all the Colonials were sexy and good-looking and wore loose, white shirts unbuttoned down to their six-pack abs, and all the Britishers were haughty and really mean and sweated a lot in red wool? Do you think Hollywood just makes up that stuff?"

The suspicion in Kat's gaze was replaced with amusement. Out of the corner of my eye I saw

Megan's grip on her stake relax, and when she spoke her tone was tinged with exasperation. "News-flash, brat—the movies aren't real life. And just because Lockridge fought on the right side when he was human doesn't mean all bets weren't off once he became undead, courtesy of Jasmine." She turned to Darkheart. "I hate to say I told you so, but I told you so. If Kat or I could pass ourselves off as part of the vamp community and infiltrate Lady Jasmine's inner circle to find out where her daytime lair is, we would, but we can't ask Tash to. We'll just have to keep hoping we run across a vamp informant who can tell us what we need to know."

Kat nodded. "Meanwhile, I think I should attempt a Heal on her. We all agree this situation's gone far enough, no?" Her gaze swept my apartment, taking in the haphazard clutter of shoes, the cream Chanel jacket festooned with dust bunnies that Megan had slung over the back of a chair, the half-devoured box of Mallomars on my kitchenette counter.

"Heal will not work," declared Darkheart decisively. "Is only possible if Natashya has completely turned into *vampyr,* and that is not yet case. *Da,* Granddaughter?" he asked, his salt-and-pepper brows drawing together as he turned his eagle gaze on me. "Liz says she saw you yesterday at mall. You still have no trouble with daylight?"

"None at all," I said swiftly, if not entirely truthfully, sending a silent vote of thanks to Liz Dixon, a fifty-something local art gallery owner who'd become my grandfather's girlfriend when she'd aided us in the fight against Zena (note to self: must try to see Darkheart having a girlfriend as healthy and positive instead of ooky). Liz had obviously neglected to tell him that when she'd seen me I'd been wearing enormous D&G sunglasses that covered half my face, a flowing silk scarf tied Jackie Kennedy-style around my head and neck and a long-sleeved Prada blouse with linen slacks. Not exactly bundled up in multiple layers like the derelict Brooklyn had called Crazy Joe, but I'd certainly made sure that no part of my skin was exposed to the light. Merely as a precaution, of course, and the slight tingle I'd felt as I'd hurried from my car's window-tinted interior to the mall's entrance doors had probably been my imagination.

"You'd tell us if the situation started to change, wouldn't you, brat?" Megan asked, giving me a hard stare. "You haven't always been all that forthcoming in the past, but this isn't like the time you were seeing that hot guy with the Harley and hiding it from Kat and me, or when you tried to change your biology grade on your report card. We need to know how far along Vamp Avenue you've come, because at some point Kat *is* going to have to attempt a Heal on you." She'd switched from her Daughter tone of voice to her big sister one. In the mood I was in, they were both equally irritating.

"I get it, all right?" I said waspishly. "Gawd, Meg, give it a rest. I know I should have told you I was starting to have cravings and I'm sorry you had to find out the way you did, but it's not like you caught me with my fangs sunk into someone's neck. I was buying from a legitimate butcher, for heaven's sake. In some parts of the world they eat blood sausage on a regular basis, so I don't see that my little snack tonight was such a big deal."

"Is true. In Russia is called *krvavica* and many people like taste. My mother used to make often for breakfast." Dmitri had been silent for so long I'd almost forgotten him. I gave him a surprised glance, although I wasn't totally sure whether my surprise was over the fact that he was defending me or because I couldn't imagine him as a little boy with a mother. His blue gaze darkened. "Still, was blood," he said, his chiseled-from-permafrost features tightening in distaste. "To me was disgusting."

"Really? Mikhail loves *krvavica,*" Megan said thinly.

"Is because he is *oboroten,*" Dmitri replied with a shrug of his linebacker shoulders that briefly stretched his black T-shirt over the tectonic plates of muscle that made up his torso. "As you say in America, a manimal, *da?*"

This time my glance locked with Kat's, and I saw she was stifling the same unworthy impulse to laugh as I was. Dmitri couldn't know it, but as far as Megan was concerned he'd just used the single worst term he could have chosen to describe her occasionally fur-bearing boyfriend.

"As we say in America, a *shapeshifter,*" she corrected coldly. "And speaking of Mikhail, if we're finished here I think we should rejoin him and Jack on patrol. Kat, you coming?"

"Yes, but some nights I don't know why I bother," Kat drawled. "When I was a ballbreaking bitch, men were falling over themselves to take me up on my offers, but now I've gone all altruistic Healer-chick and just want to save them from an eternity in hell, most of the time they'd rather take their chances with your stake. Still, a girl's gotta do what a girl's gotta do, no?" She began strolling to the door, but then turned back to me. "Sweetie," she said firmly. "The shoes. Get them out of the garbage bag, okay?"

"And if my Dolce sweater that you didn't borrow is somewhere here underneath all this mess, have it dry-cleaned and give it back to me," Megan added. "Grandfather, do you want to accompany us on patrol for a few more hours?"

"*Nyet,* is late for old man like me. Also, Liz asked me to drop by her apartment tonight for glass of wine. I may stay over, so do not worry if I am not home tomorrow morning," Darkheart said complacently while I tried to forget the Bed, Bath & Beyond shopping bag overflowing with black satin sheets I'd seen Liz carrying when we'd run into each other at the mall. "I will collect garlic wreaths first and then leave."

"You go, *tovaritch.* I will collect wreaths," Dmitri offered, which I suppose was nice of him but not what I wanted to hear. Unfortunately for me, however, Darkheart accepted with alacrity and within minutes I was alone with Russia's answer to Paul Bunyan, watching him de-festoon my apartment of wild garlic while I tried not to breathe in the, to me, nauseating scent of the small white flowers.

"You lie to sisters and grandfather," Dmitri said without preamble as he deftly wound Darkheart's garland lasso around one pumped forearm. His Siberian-blue gaze flicked to me before he turned his attention back to his task. "You have met Jasmine's lieutenant, *da?*"

Now, along with the speaking-before-I-think thing I've developed growing up with Megan and Kat, I also credit them for my ability to lie at the drop of a hat. It's a necessary talent, believe me, when you're saddled with a sister who feels it's her moral duty to force you to confess when you've had some unfortunate accident like breaking Grammie's favorite Lladro figurine, and another sister who doesn't see why she should take the heat for said Lladro breakage when she didn't do it. So if Dmitri had thought he could startle me into the truth with his unexpected accusation, he was sadly mistaken.

"Of course I haven't met him!" I said, putting a hefty amount of outraged virtue into my tone. "I don't *believe* your nerve! What gives you the right to accuse me of lying to my family?"

"This is America, *nyet?* I have right to say truth when is in front of my eyes," Dmitri replied, seemingly unperturbed by my impressive outburst. He finished winding up the garland and set it on the back of the sofa. "Besides," he added calmly, "I cannot stand by and see future *Gospozha* Malkovich take dangerous risks."

It took a moment for his words to sink in and when they did I thought I must have misheard him. "*Gospozha?* Isn't that Russian for the missus?" I said dubiously.

His back toward me, he nodded as he untacked the last wreath from the window frame. "*Da,* is correct. From first time I saw you I had strong feeling inside me that you would lead me to my *sud'ba,* so must be that you and I will be couple one day. These strong feelings that come to me are never wrong," he said, turning from the window and laying the wreath beside the garland. "My *babushka* was *cygan* and from her I inherit gift of knowing future."

I held up a hand. "Whoa, nellieski," I said firmly. "We've got a lost-in-translation situation happening here. I still think I must be wrong on the *gospozha* part, but forget that for a minute. What's a *sud'ba,* who's a *cygan,* and isn't a *babushka* some kind of shawl for old ladies to wrap around their heads?"

"*Sud'ba* is fate. *Cygan* means in America gypsy, and *babushka* is grandmother. You are not wrong on *gospozha.*" His garlic-gathering completed, Dmitri stood facing me, his jeans-clad legs planted slightly apart on the cruddy carpet covering the living-room floor and his arms crossed over his chest so that his biceps came close to ripping the seams of his T-shirt's sleeves. I was so rattled by what he'd just said that for a moment all I could think was that when he stood that way he looked exactly like the

Jolly Green Giant, if the Jolly Green Giant wasn't green, but blond and tanned and wasn't jolly but about to stomp the tiny valley-dwellers by his feet to puree.

Then I got ahold of myself. "So when you first laid eyes on me half an hour ago, you knew you and I would do the till-death-us-do-part thing," I clarified, "because your grandmother was a gypsy and you inherited her crystal ball abilities. Do I finally have it right?" I asked politely.

"*Da,* except first time I saw you was not half hour ago, but night of battle against Kane and his army," Dmitri began, but at that point I dropped my pretence of politeness and let the fury that had been bubbling up inside me boil over in a scalding flood.

"Are you *insane?*" I yelled, striding toward him and grabbing him by his biceps. I tried to give him a shake, but it was like trying to shake concrete. My anger grew. "I don't know you! I don't *want* to know you! The only connection between you and me is that you're using your family's underworld contacts to look for my father and as far as I'm concerned, that's no connection at all! So screw your *sud'ba* and the *cygan* it rode in on, Dmitri—

not only won't I be walking down the aisle with you anytime soon, but I want you out of my apartment right now!"

"Your act is good." With a quick flexing of his muscles he broke my grip on him. "You shout loudly instead of answering my questions, but your anger is enough answer. You have met with *vampyr* called Lockridge. What I need to know now is whether he already has hold over you." His gaze chilled to a subzero blue. "You have slept with him?"

My attempt to slap his face was a purely reflexive action, but his reflexes made mine look like I was moving through molasses. My hand was still inches from his cheek when I felt his grip wrap around my wrist. I glared at him, frustration mixing with my rage.

"Maybe it's different in Russia," I snapped, "but here in the good old U.S. of A. when a man deserves what's coming to him he's supposed to take it. Let go of my wrist, you lug."

"Not until you answer, *l'ubimaya,*" he said evenly. "Is vital I know truth on this matter. Has he had you yet?"

The way he said it made it sound all earthy and raw and uncivilized, and suddenly there was something else mixed in with my anger and frustration.

Dmitri Malkovich was a pain in the butt. I didn't want him in my apartment, I didn't want him poking around in my life and I totally didn't buy in to his crazy assertion that the two of us were bound together by some mystical gypsy fate. But there was no denying it, the man was incredibly hot, I thought as his gaze held mine. Every inch of him was solid muscle. His T-shirt fitted him like a glove, his jeans were taut in all the right places, and even though blond men weren't usually my type I couldn't help but appreciate how sexily his hair and eyes contrasted with his dark lashes and eyebrows and the tan of his skin.

A couple of hours ago I'd been drooling over the delicious Heath Lockridge. Now I was wondering how it would be with a hard, tall Russian. Not only was I turning into a vampire, I was well on my way to becoming a complete slut, I thought in self-disgust, and it was all the fault of the man standing in front of me holding my wrist in his viselike grip.

Comrade Malkovich needed to be taught a

lesson. Luckily, he'd handed me the perfect weapon for doing just that.

"Of course Heath's had me, sweetie," I said, channeling Kat at her most ball-breaking. I widened my baby-blues at him and gave my strawberry-blond curls a careless toss. "Maybe I shouldn't be telling you this, seeing as how you say we're fated to be an item, but he's had me standing up, lying down and every which way in between. One thing puzzles me, though." I tipped my head and scrunched up my nose adorably, as if I were struggling with a problem I couldn't quite figure out. I felt Dmitri's fingers tighten on my wrist, and hid my smile.

"What is this puzzling thing?" His tone was clipped. "Is it that you do not understand how you can find attraction to *vampyr?* Answer is easy. He uses *glamyr* against you to make you think you like being bedded by him. Is usual trick of undead to seduce—"

"Oh, he didn't *glamyr* me into being bedded by him," I said with a husky little laugh. "I practically threw myself at the poor man. I mean, he's totally gorgeous and sexy and dreamy, so why wouldn't I?

No, what's puzzling me is how in the world those Revolutionary War soldiers ever came to be known as Minutemen, because if Heath's any example I think they should have been called Three-Hour Men. Or maybe All-Night-Long Men. Or—"

"Enough talk about *vampyr* who should have been dead two centuries ago," Dmitri said hoarsely. "I show you what it is like having man with heartbeat make love to you, *l'ubimaya!*"

Okay, I know what you're thinking and it goes something along the lines of, *Girlfriend, how skanky can you get? You totally set up this situation so it would turn out exactly how it did,* and to that my answer is, I did not. Not consciously, anyway, although I suppose somewhere in the murky depths of my mind I knew I was striking a match and tossing it into a big, exciting pool of gasoline. I will admit this: when Dmitri pulled me to him with a hoarse Russian oath and his mouth came down on mine, little Tashie Crosse sure wasn't complaining for the first few minutes.

He kissed with the same single-minded determination he probably gave to bench-pressing small cars, and if that doesn't sound all that sexy, just think about it. Here was this strapping hunk of blond male and every fiber of his being was concentrated on bringing me to miniorgasm with just his mouth and his tongue. And when I say his tongue, he didn't use it merely to kiss me.

"First time I saw you, I thought you were warrior princess from Russian fairy tale," he muttered against my lips. "You were staking *vampyr* during battle against Kane's army. Your hair was like Siberian gold and that night you come to me in my dreams."

He broke off to cover my mouth with his again, his tongue moving masterfully into me while his wide-spread hands slid over my arms to the buttoned vee-opening of my sweater. Before I could say, "Don't snag the cashmere," I realized he'd deftly slipped open the first three flower-shaped buttons and was using the same impressive sleight-of-hand to push the pink lace straps of my La Perla push-up bra off my shoulders. I broke off our kiss with a gasp.

"Tell me what happened between us in those dreams," I said breathlessly, my knees turning to jelly and my top teeth sinking into my lower lip as a kaleidoscope of sensations swirled through me.

Call me psychic, but I bet I know what you're thinking this time, too. Yes, asking Dmitri to get me all hot and bothered with the details of his wet dream about me didn't exactly jibe with the fact that I'd been furious with him a few minutes ago.

Confession time, ladies…except if one word of this ever leaks out to Meg or Kat, I'm totally denying this conversation ever took place. So where was I? Oh, right—confessing. Well, the truth is that I've never really seen what the big deal is with sex.

And now I'll give all of you a minute to pick yourselves up off the floor.

Everyone over their shock/hilarity/pity-mixed-with-a-smidge-of-revulsion? Good, because there's an explanation for my lack of enthusiasm for the horizontal mambo, and that explanation can be covered in two words.

Word one: *Todd.*

Word two: *Whitmore.*

Okay, maybe it should be three words: *Dr. Todd Whitmore,* because even as I stood over the dust pile that had been Toddie on the night before Megan's wedding-that-never-happened, holding the bedpost I'd just used to stake him with, I realized I'd never really been in love with him, I'd been in love with the idea of marrying an up-and-coming cosmetic surgeon.

And part of the reason I'd never been in love with him was that he was an absolute yawn in bed. He didn't think so, of course. On the two dismal occasions we did it, Dr. Todd flailed away with all the spasmodic jerking of a landed small-mouth bass on a fishing dock until he sweatily collapsed on me. When he finally rolled off me he shot me a confident smile, told me I was one lucky girl and headed for the shower with an over-the-shoulder observation that he'd heard there were classes in oral sex for women these days, and had I ever thought of supplying myself with a couple of bananas and signing up for one.

Shortly after my second mind-numbingly boring encounter between the sheets with my fiancé, I informed him I'd decided our upcoming union was too sacred to be tainted by premarital sex. I realize now that he only let me have my way on that point because he was dropping his trousers for every nurse and female lab technician under the age of fifty in Maplesburg Hospital, and not getting it from me didn't cramp his style in the least.

So anyway, with the late and unlamented Dr. Todd as my only experience with the wonderful world of carnal knowledge—I'm not counting the few inept episodes in the backseats of cars I had in high school—is it any wonder that lately my most fulfilling sexual encounters involved a vibrating bunny with purple vinyl ears?

Which brings me back to the epiphany I was having while Dmitri's tongue brought me to the edge of something I'd previously dismissed as an urban legend, at least if we're talking without Mr. Love-Bunny. That's right, the Big O.

"Tell me what you did to me in those dreams, Dmitri, and don't leave anything out," I gasped. "I want to hear every X-rated detail."

"X-rated is like *Americanic* movies with violence or sex, *da?*" he muttered as he bent his head to the hollow between my breasts. His tongue left a trail of heat where it touched me.

"*Da,*" I managed to say as I felt myself being swept closer to total surrender. With his head bent in front of me as it was, I could see the muscles of his back rippling beneath his hide like strong under-water currents. A smudge of something dark broke the even tan of his skin just past his hairline at the nape of his neck.

"I understand," he said hoarsely, his breath against me sending minishockwaves through my nerve endings. "Increases pleasure, *nyet?* Is also same with me when I think of dream I had. You and I were in forest at dusk making love. I had taken off all your clothing and was standing over you…"

"And then what?" I panted.

Dmitri lifted his head, his gaze like blue fire. "And then sun went below horizon and horde of *vampyrs* set upon us. I snatched up broken branch and used it as stake against them and when I had chance to look I saw you were doing same thing. Your hair was like gold crown around your head and your naked limbs were like palest Karelian marble, and you staked *vampyr* after *vampyr* with terrible mercilessness. You were magnificent, *l'ubimaya.* I woke up with sheets thrown off bed and great throbbing in—"

"What?" I asked, easing my grip on his shoulders and frowning at him.

"I wake up with great throbbing in my heart from knowledge I must see you again," Dmitri said, his tone low and charged with emotion. He began to bend his head to my breast again, but I yanked up my La Perla bra straps and took a quick step back.

"No, the other part," I said. "*That's* what gets your rocks off about me—that I kill vamps?"

"*Da*." He nodded, his eyes still lit with blue fire as he gazed at me. "You are not ordinary woman. You are brave, you are warrior, you are—"

"I'm a vamp," I said flatly. "Or turning into one, at least. Since you're so much in favor of staking them, I should be the last woman you'd be attracted to."

"When time comes sister can perform Heal on you," Dmitri asserted. "Will not interfere with our destiny, *l'ubimaya*. Is in your blood to kill *vampyrs*, just as is in mine. After we destroy Jasmine and her lieutenant we will look for others to wipe out. You and I will be perfectly matched team—both of us strong, both brave, both great fighters."

"Well-matched, maybe," I informed him, taking another step back. "Not a perfect match, though."

He frowned. "I do not understand."

I widened my eyes. "Well, if the two of us faced off, I doubt the fight would end in a draw. I mean, either you'd beat the crap out of me or I'd beat the crap out of you, right?"

The granite planes of his face relaxed into a faint smile. "We would never be on opposite sides, *l'ubimaya*. But if such impossible thing did happen, would not be fair fight. You are warrior princess, but I am big and strong man."

"I guess you're right, it wouldn't be a fair fight," I said, batting my baby blues at him. "Unless you even up the odds with a stake or some holy water, a contest between a vamp and a big Russian lug never is, but I'm still kind of eager to see how badly I can kick your ass, Dmitri."

Even as his ice-blue gaze narrowed in sudden comprehension, I hauled off and socked him a good one on the side of his chiseled jaw.

Chapter 5

"Fuck!" Dmitri swore as he rocked back on his heels from my blow. I spared a split-second to note that he seemed to have at least one English word down pat before I pivoted sideways on the balls of my feet and slammed my elbow into his solar plexus. "What the *hell* do you think you're doing?"

From the jarring impact I felt in my elbow he'd obviously had time to tighten his abs to steel-plate rigidity, but I could tell from the hiss in his tone that I'd knocked the air out of him. He lunged for me.

"If it was something I said, let's talk, but—" A shutter slammed down behind his eyes. As I dodged out of his reach he went on swiftly, "But this is complete *bezumnyj!* I do not even know what I have done to anger you. Did I misunderstand? Did you not want me to make *l'ubov* to you?"

"Oh, I wanted you to make loo-bov to me, all right," I said tersely, bringing one leg in close to my body and then kicking it explosively toward him in a nifty maneuver I'd learned during the Unarmed Combat 101 classes Darkheart had put Megan and Kat and me through when he'd been teaching us to fight vamps. Sometime in the past few seconds I'd slipped out of my strappy Gina sandals, which was just as well for Dmitri because their wicked stilettos would have turned him into a man-size block of Swiss cheese within minutes. As it was, having my bare foot crash into his ribs like a piledriver merely sent him sprawling to the floor. "But let's not talk about that right now. Tell me, comrade, what happened to the borscht-and-black bread accent a minute ago?"

While I was posing my question I reached down, intending to pull him up so I could take another punch at him, but this time he was ready for me. Bounding quickly to his feet, Dmitri struck my blow aside with one big hand. "I do not understand what you mean," he said, scowling. "Natashya, this is total ridiculous and I will not fight you. Why are you doing this?"

"Good question," I said, feinting a sudden movement to his left. He reacted as I'd hoped. As he stepped quickly to his right I brought my clasped fists up under the point of his chin. His head snapped back, and for a moment I saw anger flash behind the fake bewilderment of his gaze.

And he *was* faking—I knew that as unquestioningly as I'd suddenly known a couple of minutes ago that he was my enemy and had gone into attack mode on him. There was a difference between those two pieces of knowledge, however. The first had come to me when he'd slipped up and dropped his "must kill Moose and Squirrel" way of talking for a fatal second while he'd still been off-balance from my unexpected punch, but I didn't have a clue as to what had set off the sudden alarm bells in my head while he'd been kissing me.

All I knew was that I hadn't been able to ignore them.

"Enough!" When my clasped fists had made contact with his chin Dmitri had staggered backward a couple of steps. Now he steadied himself and his mouth drew into a grim line. "I have told you I will not fight you, *l'ubimaya,* but I cannot allow you to continue this foolish—"

"What does that mean, looby my-ah?" I interrupted. "No, don't tell me, let me guess. Bitch?" My foot lashed out again, this time catching him squarely on the upper thigh. He inhaled sharply. "Is it another word for vampire? Or as you and Dark-heart pronounce it, *wampeer?*" I said sarcastically. "Of course, you only say *vampyr* when you're pretending to have trouble with the language, don't you? Know what, handsome? I wouldn't be surprised to learn you're not even Russian."

"Was born in Stalingrad, city of heroes," Dmitri said stiffly. "Is insult you suggest this is lie, but I will forgive. *L'ubimaya* means sweetheart, and since this is how I feel for you I cannot let you continue doing things you will regret later. I am sorry, Natashya, but this is for own good."

Why is it that when people tell you it's for your own good, *it* always turns out to be something bad? I should have been expecting Dmitri's sudden move but I wasn't, which kind of bothers me when I reflect that *"Shit, why didn't I see that coming?"* is probably the last thought a lot of vamps have before they're swept into the big dust bin in hell.

And even though his plan was to immobilize me, not dust me, when the wild garlic lasso dropped over my head and shoulders and cinched tight around my upper body, pinning my arms to my sides, I still would have been in deep doo-doo…if it had worked.

"Nausea you feel is regrettable but unavoidable," Dmitri said as he began walking toward me, reeling in the slack end of the garlic garland like a cowboy walking toward a roped steer. "In moment you will lose consciousness, so will not be so bad for you. Then I will call Darkheart and he will decide if is time to attempt Heal."

"Is that Plan A?" I asked curiously. "Because if the whole thing hinges on the me-feeling-nauseous-and-blacking-out part, you'd better hope you have a Plan B, comrade."

"What do you—"

I didn't let him finish. Even as he took his next step toward me I grabbed hold of the woven strands of garlic that bound me and ripped them apart. Dmitri froze and his gaze met mine.

"It's not possible," he said tonelessly. "You're a vamp, or near enough. Garlic's your fucking kryptonite."

"I know." Deliberately I took a half step toward him and saw wariness flicker across his hard features. "I can't explain it, either, especially since I felt like I was dying when Darkheart used it against me earlier this evening. But now…" I held up one of the tiny white flowers and inhaled deeply. Wrinkling my nose in distaste, I tossed the blossom aside. "Okay, I still think it smells yucky, but I never was all that crazy about garlic. The point is, it's not kryptonite to me anymore. No wonder you're worried enough to have forgotten to keep up your act, comrade," I added, taking another step toward him.

He held his ground. "There's only one explanation," he said tightly. "Somehow Zena's curse has been lifted and you're not—"

"A vamp anymore?" I shook my head in pretend regret. "I can see how you'd like to believe that, but you're wrong. If I wasn't a vamp, would I have these?" I smiled at him and felt my fangs lengthen past my lower lip. The last shreds of doubt left his expression and he took a step back. I retracted my fangs but left my smile in place as I saw his gaze flick surreptitiously around the room. "Don't bother looking for anything you might use as a stake," I told him in a conversational tone. "I mean, given my condition, how smart would it be to keep stuff around that could be used against me? The coffee table's made out of cheap particle board. Most of the other furniture's plastic. There was some wood trim on the couch, but I pried it off, just in case." I tipped my head to one side. "You know, everyone pegs me as the dumb strawberry-blond Crosse triplet, and that suits me fine. People always underestimate dumb blondes—hell, sometimes I even underestimate myself. The thing is, comrade, strawberry-blondes are as much redheads as blondes, and us redheads aren't dumb, we just have hot tempers. Which probably explains why I'm having trouble hanging on to mine right now." I let my smile fade.

"You're acting a part. Don't waste any more of my time trying to deny it. Who are you really and why are you trying to scam my grandfather and my sisters?"

He hesitated. Then he exhaled, as if he saw no easy way out of the corner I'd pushed him into. "If I told you, I'd have to kill you," he said flatly. "All you need to know is my target on this mission isn't your family."

I stared at him incredulously. Whatever I'd been expecting, it wasn't this. "Mission?" I repeated. "What mission? And if my family's not your target, who—" I stopped abruptly, feeling a chill spread through me that had nothing to do with the temperature in the room. "Oh, shit," I said, swallowing dryly. "I don't know what your real name is or who sent you, but you came to Maplesburg to kill me, didn't you?" His stony silence was all the answer I needed. I swallowed again, this time to choke back the sudden rush of anger that rose in me. "You waited too long," I said thinly. "You should have carried out your damned mission while I was still vulnerable. But as of about ten minutes ago my status changed, jerk, and so did our roles. Now I'm the one with a mission—and my mission is to make you talk!"

Even before I finished my sentence I threw myself at him, but instead of taking the evasive action I expected he met my attack with one of his own. His straight-armed thrust caught me on the shoulder, spinning me sideways. Before I could recover, his booted foot shot out and swept my legs out from under me.

Now, here's the thing: Comrade Dmitri's little maneuver—I had to keep calling him Dmitri since I hadn't gotten his real name out of him yet—should have had me flat on my keister before I could say *hey, tripping's no fair-sies*. If that had happened, the fight between us would have been over right then and there and everything that came after would have turned out a whole lot differently. Sometimes I wish it had, but wishing doesn't change what happened as a direct result of my fight that night with Dmitri.

And wishing won't bring back the two people I loved who died…but I'm not ready to talk about that just yet.

Anyway, having my feet kicked out from under

me should have put me on my butt. I mean, even those of us who barely squeaked through introductory physics have a fairly firm idea of how the first law of gravity works, right? Like old Isaac Newton discovered when he got hit on the head by the apple, things fall down when there's nothing holding them up. People fall down if their legs suddenly aren't beneath them. And vamps don't have to obey that particular law if they don't feel like it.

Okay, that last part wasn't Newton's, it was mine, and I discovered it when I found myself hovering in the air in front of Dmitri with my feet about ten inches off the floor. My first reaction was confusion. My second was a twinge of horror. After all, I'd always thought the sight of a vamp hanging in the air without visible means of support was one of the creepier-looking manifestations of the state of undeadness. But my twinge of horror only lasted about half a second before my third reaction kicked in.

"Omigod, this is so frikkin' *cool!*" I breathed. "I'm practically *fly*—"

Unfortunately, while I'd been busy channeling Tinkerbelle, Dmitri had been channeling Captain Hook. Captain Right Hook, that is. His punch landed squarely on the left side of my jaw, which was when I discovered yet another benefit of my fast-encroaching vamphood.

The punch hurt, but not nearly as much as it should have. It did, however, have the effect of bringing me down to earth both literally and figuratively. As my feet hit the floor I stumbled back into the coffee table, my excitement over my new hovering ability turning into a cold determination not to let him get the drop on me a second time. I heard a splintering crash behind me as the table rammed into the couch and tipped over.

"You're right, I should have taken you out before—" Dmitri managed to say before I picked up the couch and threw it at him.

"Flying? Check. Ability to withstand pain? Check. Superstrength? Yup, looks like little Tashie got that in her Christmas stocking, too," I told him in satisfaction as he leaped out of the way of the couch just before it smashed into the wall. "Sorry, jerk, you were saying?"

"I should have taken you out before tonight," Dmitri grunted as he sprang upward and grabbed on to the ancient brass-and-milk-glass hanging light fixture above him. Immediately it began to pull free of the plaster ceiling, but it stayed intact long enough to complete an arcing swing in my direction. As a chunk of ceiling came down in a cloud of plaster dust, Dmitri dropped to the floor behind me. I whirled around to face him, but the plaster dust obscured my vision.

"If I had, I wouldn't need to neutralize you now," he said as his foot swung toward my ribs.

I moved out of its trajectory, but not quickly enough to avoid being grazed by the steel toe of his military-style boot. "Why don't you say what you really mean, instead of using terms like *take out* and *neutralize?*" I retorted as I wrenched the door leading to my bedroom off its hinges. It came free with a squeal of tortured metal. "I mean, if you're trying to spare my feelings by avoiding the word *kill,* don't bother," I added, propelling the door through the air toward him like a giant Frisbee.

"I've as much as admitted that my orders were to kill you." He grabbed my television set from its corner stand and raised it in front of him like a shield. The door spun into it. Something inside the TV exploded with a loud *pop!* and sparks sputtered from its shattered plastic-and-glass body as he threw it aside. "I also told you everything changed when I met you, so I needed to figure out a way to convince those who sent me that I'd carried out my orders, while at the same time persuading you to let your sister attempt a Heal on you. I thought I had time to come up with a plan before your vampire powers kicked in."

"Un. Frikkin'. Believable." As he'd tossed the television set aside I'd seized his moment of inattention to close the gap between us but his words brought me to a dumbfounded halt, my arm frozen in the act of throwing a fight-finishing right jab at him. "You're still trying to sell me that falling in love with me at first sight crap? And I suppose you still expect me to believe you think I'm your fate, right?" I tightened my raised fist. "In the Men's Lies Hall of Fame, that's right up there with those old classics *Don't worry, honey, I'll pull out in time* and *I'll call you, babe.* What really frosts me is that while you were kissing me I might have fallen for your bullshit if I hadn't seen—"

"If you hadn't seen what?" His question was

sharper than it should have been, given that he was facing my poised knuckles.

I frowned. "If I hadn't seen that black rose tattoo on the back of your neck," I said slowly. "My vamp warning sense must have been the first of my powers to kick in, because even though I didn't know what it was when I glimpsed it, I knew it meant you were the enemy." I met his eyes and saw the shuttered expression I'd glimpsed before. "Does that black rose have something to do with the people who want me killed? What is it, the symbol of some organization?"

"Forget you saw it," Dmitri said in a rasping tone. "*Chernoye Roza* hasn't kept its existence secret for hundreds of years by allowing outsiders who learn about it to live. You're on its death list now, but your friends and family aren't. If you start asking questions, that could change."

"Oh, okay." I gave him my best dumb-Tashie wide-eyed look. "I'm guessing *Chernoye Roza* means Black Rose, so mum's the word on the Black Rose thing. I won't even ask you if your special decoder ring came in a box of Frosted Flakes or if the secret handshake's hard to learn." I took a deep breath and let it out in a bellow. "*Of course I've got questions!* Some mysterious group put me at the top of their hit list and you tell me not to ask *questions?* That's about as insane as everything else you want me to believe! Who are they? What have I ever done to them to piss them off enough to want me dead? And what happened to the real Dmitri Malkovich whose sister was saved by Darkheart years ago—was he killed so you could take over his identity and use his connection to Darkheart to get close to me?"

My fury bubbled over and my fist shot out, making solid contact with his chin. The blow drove him backward, but to my surprise he didn't retaliate.

"The real Dmitri Malkovich came to the attention of certain people who saw possibilities in him. In *me.*" He shook his head as if to clear it. With a wince he dragged the back of his hand across his bottom lip where a thread of blood was slowly trickling. "If you'd hold off on beating me to a pulp for a couple of minutes, I could explain better."

I narrowed my eyes at him. "If this is some kind of a trick, I'll make you sorry you were ever born, jerk. Two minutes. Start explaining."

"I was eight when I witnessed my little sister being attacked by vampires in the forest near our home." A shadow passed behind his gaze and then disappeared as he shrugged. "I rushed at them with a stick, but I wasn't much of a threat to them. If Darkheart hadn't shown up when he did, they would have killed Anya and me."

I tapped my toe impatiently. "Not that I'm not sympathetic for what almost happened to you and your sister, but where does Black Rose fit into all this?"

"Word of the incident reached *Chernoye Roza* and they sent one of their members to my village to investigate the young boy who'd had the temerity to go up against *vampyrs*," Dmitri said in a tone devoid of expression. "He posed as a traveling knife seller, but when he satisfied himself I would be a good candidate for his organization, he revealed himself to my parents. He told them they had the opportunity to give their son to a great cause and although my training as an acolyte in Black Rose would be long and arduous, if I proved myself worthy I would one day be a soldier in the holy war between the darkness and the light. The only catch was, from the moment they handed me over to him, they would never see me again. To prevent them from being able to renege on this condition if they changed their minds, I was to be taken to the U.S. and raised here."

"But that's practically kidnapping!" I said, recoiling at the thought. "No parents would agree to that for their child!"

"Russian parents would," he replied. "Especially if they'd almost lost both their children to the evil that *Chernoye Roza* has opposed down the centuries. I'm not saying that the decision to let me go could have been easy, but they knew what an honor it was that I'd been chosen."

"Honor, shmonor," I said dismissively. "I still don't understand why you had to be snatched away from your parents and not allowed contact with them. No wonder you've turned out the way you have."

"*Chernoye Roza* demands total dedication from all who are accepted into its secrets," Dmitri said stiffly. "Conflicting loyalty to family might weaken that dedication."

"It sounds like they brainwashed you pretty

thoroughly," I informed him. "Too bad there's a major flaw in Black Rose's recruiting philosophy, Malkovich."

"What are you talking about?" His tone was ice.

"I'm talking about the fact that their child-snatching policy doesn't seem to guarantee total dedication in all their acolytes," I said with a mocking shrug. "I mean, if I believe what you've told me, just by letting me live you've already betrayed your oath of service to your masters, right?"

I'd meant my words to be the verbal equivalent of a light jab, but he reacted as if I'd just dealt him a punishing blow. Under those tanned and chiseled cheekbones his skin flushed a dull red and his jaw tightened. "Worse than that," he rasped. "As far as Black Rose is concerned, any member who refuses to carry out a vamp-extermination order has gone over to the dark side. If they find out you're still alive, they'll kill both of us. The only way that won't happen is if you let your sister Heal you."

"Operating on the assumption that at that point I'd have shed my vampness and wouldn't be the enemy anymore?" I said with deceptive calm.

He nodded firmly. "Exactly. In my mission report I'll simply say that before I could carry out my orders, you voluntarily chose to undergo a Heal. They'll probably send someone out to verify that your transformation was successful, but—"

"Your two minutes are up, Malkovich!" I said furiously. "I'll give you thirty seconds to get your butt out of my apartment before I go medieval on it! Read my lips. No Heal. Not now, not ever! You heard Kat—even she can't guarantee that it won't go wrong and send me straight to eternal damnation. I'm not an ordinary vamp, okay? I bear the mark of a frikkin' Queen and as far as Heals are concerned, that's the undead equivalent of a Surgeon General's warning!"

"You don't have a choice, dammit!" Dmitri swore. The hard red had receded from his cheekbones but his jaw was still tense. "Do you think when *Chernoye Roza* realizes I've failed in my mission that they won't send out another exterminator, and if he doesn't eliminate you, that his place won't be taken by a third? You don't understand, you're facing an army! Sooner or later—"

"Oh, I understand everything," I said with an

angry smile. "For instance, I understand that you lied to Darkheart and Mikhail and my sisters. I understand that you came here under false pretences, and when I found you out, you kept up the act with your stupid story about love at first sight and me being your fate. I even understand that all your bullshit was a big smokescreen to hide the fact that you're still lying to me!" I yelled. "You want me scared enough to risk a Heal, even though I'm coping just fine without one! I control my urges. I buy blood instead of going the free-range prey route. Maybe there aren't a whole lot of us who've taken the pledge to stay away from the dark side, but we exist. For your information, Malkovich, this evening I met a woman called Kathy Lehman who's stayed on the straight and narrow for years by eating rats, for Gawd's sake," I added, repressing an internal shudder as I remembered my parting glimpse of Bojangles's mistress. "If she can do that, give me one good reason why little Tashie Crosse shouldn't be able to handle vamphood without resorting to the dangers of a Heal!"

"You said it yourself—you were turned by a Queen," Dmitri ground out. "The powers you exhibited tonight are nothing compared to what they'll eventually be, and the hunger you've felt so far will only increase, too. If I can't convince you of that, then there's only one way I can keep you safe."

Okay, I've got every reason to hate and despise Black Rose and their pseudopriesthood of leaders, but I will say one thing in my least-favorite secret society's favor: they must have a doozie of a training program. If Dmitri was a fair example of the course's graduates, it made Darkheart's sessions with Megan and Kat and me look like a kindergarten jamboree. I saw a flash of movement as he bent down and straightened up again, and the next moment I felt something sharp and pointy sticking into me just below my left breast.

And for those of you who're thinking broken underwire from my bra, good guess, but no.

It was a stake, and from the pungently sappy smell that assailed my nostrils, it was the real McCoy Carpathian yew wood. I took a suddenly nervous breath and felt the stake's point dig more sharply into my skin.

"The ol' stake-in-the-boot trick," I said, trying to

sound cool and unruffled and instead sounding like I was about to wee-wee my panties in fright. I steadied my voice. "This is what you *Chernoye Roza* guys mean when you say you're going to keep a girl safe? 'Cause personally, I'd rather you showed your protectiveness in some other way, Malkovich. Like walking on the outside of the sidewalk, or making sure I have my seat belt on before you start the car, or holding a door open for—"

Dmitri cut across my babbling. "This isn't how I wanted it to end between you and me, *l'ubimaya,*" he said hoarsely. "I lied to you about a lot of things, but not about the fact that when I first laid eyes on you, I knew your destiny and mine were bound together in some way. I just never guessed this was how fate would link us together." His voice got even hoarser, as if he was forcing his words past sandpaper. "The moment you make your first kill, you're damned. I'm not the first person forced to stake the one he loves to save them from an eternity in hell, but somehow that's not much comfort to me right now."

"Me neither," I croaked. "Look, Malkovich, maybe I was a little hasty on the no-Heal thing.

How's about you put the stake down real carefully and we'll talk about this some more?" I saw the implacability in his gaze and went on hurriedly, "On second thought, what's to talk about? Put the stake down and call Kat to tell her her little sister's ready for a big, old Healer hug, why don't you? Because I am. I know I wasn't a minute ago, but that was before you convinced me," I added with gushing sincerity.

But Dmitri was shaking his head. "You and I both know that as soon as I lower this stake you'll be gone, and with you will go my one chance of saving you, *l'ubimaya,*" he said heavily.

Maybe it's just me, but when a man persists in calling me his sweetheart while he's one thrust away from dusting me, I tend to think he's either lying about the sweetheart part or lying about the staking part. If it was the former, I was toast, I told myself edgily. But if it was the latter…

"I'm betting you can't do it," I said with a thin smile. "You're a jerk, Malkovich, but not enough of a jerk to be able to shove your tongue down a girl's throat one minute and drive a stake through her vamp heart the next."

"I can if it's the only way to save you from hell," he answered, his tone even more sandpapered than before. "It's time to make your peace with this world, *l'ubimaya*. If there's anything you want me to tell your sisters, I give you my solemn vow I'll pass your messages on to them."

His gaze was icy, but behind the ice I thought I could see a flicker of burning agony. I made up my mind.

"There is, actually," I said with a thoughtful frown. "Tell Megan her Chanel jacket looked way better on me than on her. And tell Kat I liked her a whole lot more as a ball-breaking bitch than I do now she's turned into a touchy-feely Healer."

I turned on my bare heel and began walking toward the door, half expecting to feel wood sliding between my shoulder blades at any second. But I'd guessed right about Dmitri Malkovich. He'd been lying to himself when he'd said he would stake me.

And it wasn't until I was running down the dark alleyway behind my apartment that I wondered if that meant that Black Rose's hit man had been telling the truth about falling in love with me.

Not that I cared, of course.

Chapter 6

Here's the thing: in the interests of full disclosure, which Megan and Kat inform me is apparently what you're supposed to aim for when you write a tell-all account, I've decided to include the next part. On the other hand, I don't see any reason to dwell on this particular humiliation, so I'm only going to say it once.

I-stole-some-tennis-shoes-from-a-wino-and-wore-them.

Now, where was I? Oh, right, I was just about to

get to the flying part. How it happened was that at some point that night I thought it might be fun to see if I could parlay my newfound hovering skills into actual flying, and I—

Fine, you want to hear the stupid tennis shoes story, I'll tell it. But before anyone rushes to pass judgment on me, keep in mind that I was walking around the grungiest streets in Maplesburg with bare feet, okay? And yes, the aforementioned hovering helped slightly, but I wasn't that good at it yet and I kept having to touch down.

So when I saw the blanket-covered hump lying in a back alley beside a familiar-looking shopping cart moments after I'd narrowly missed stepping into something that should have been stooped and scooped but hadn't been, I wrestled briefly with my conscience, a little longer with my style sense, and then started figuring out how I could relieve Crazy Joe of his deplorable footwear without waking him up.

And in case anyone thinks I'm a complete scumball, I totally was going to return the poor man's shoes as soon as I could. If you'd seen them you'd understand why.

It goes without saying that they were about a jillion sizes too large for me, of course. I take a 36 in Manolos, which translates to a size 6 in sneakers, and as I cautiously approached Crazy Joe—yes, I know how awful it sounds calling him that, but it was the only name I knew him by—I saw he was taller than I'd realized when I'd seen him hunched over his shopping cart earlier in the evening. His feet were about the size you'd expect for a man of his height. That meant his tennies would be boats on me, but I reminded myself that any barrier between my feet and doggie doo-doo was better than none and tip-toed closer to him.

Now, Maplesburg isn't New York or Boston, or even Minneapolis. In the tourist advertising put out by our local Chamber of Commerce, the phrase "Norman Rockwellesque" pops up in every second paragraph. We don't have a high crime rate if you overlook the vamp statistics, you can stop at a red light without scruffy-looking people armed with squeegees attacking your windshield and there isn't a large homeless population. So it's not all that surprising that as I nervously squatted down beside Crazy Joe, being careful not to let the hem of my skirt brush the cracked pavement, I realized that it was the first time I'd ever taken a good look at a street person.

And somehow that excuse doesn't seem good enough.

Whatever Joe carried around in his shopping cart, it wasn't a change of clothes. Despite the warmth of the night, he seemed to be wearing every garment he owned—two grimy flannel shirts over an equally grimy singlet and a pair of too-large, dirt-stiffened corduroy pants cinched at the waist with a large safety pin. At least three pairs of mismatched tube socks, all with holes in them, poked through the slashed toes of the string-laced tennis shoes, and topping the whole ensemble off was the stained army greatcoat I'd first mistaken for a blanket. Snaking from underneath it was a dirty piece of rope, one end tied to the handle of the rickety shopping cart and the other obviously secured around his body.

If his clothes were bad, his shoulder-length hair and snarled beard were worse, but the real giveaways to his social and mental status were what I could see of his gaunt frame under the layers of garments and the constant grimaces that contorted his face even in sleep.

He was a human wreck and my heart contracted in pity for him, but I still needed his shoes.

"The diamonds around the dial are tiny but they *are* diamonds," I said under my breath a few minutes later as with infinite care I eased Crazy Joe's right tennis shoe from his foot and slipped it onto my own. "And the bracelet's fourteen-carat gold, so when you take it to the pawnshop don't let the owner rook you. I totally understand that when you wake up you're going to be upset to see your shoes have been taken, but as soon as you find my watch in your coat pocket you'll realize you got the best of the deal." I eased his left shoe off and tried not to inhale its pungent odor as I put it on and tightened the grubby string that served as a shoelace. "With what you get from it you'll be able to buy yourself a better pair of sneakers, plus have some walking-around money for the next few weeks." I recalled his erratic and unsteady progress with his shopping cart earlier in the evening and murmured, "Although maybe lurching-around money is more accurate, in your case. You'll find it's a lot easier getting around in proper footwear, so in a way, I'm actually doing you a fav—"

A high, thin scream cut across my words. As every square inch of my skin turned instantly to gooseflesh I realized that the thin scream had come from me.

Crazy Joe's eyes were still closed. Under his layers of clothing, his chest still rose and fell in sleep. But the right hand that only a second ago had been concealed under his heavy coat was now clamped tightly around my wrist.

The panic that flooded through me had nothing to do with reason. In my recent fight with Dmitri I'd demonstrated my ability to take on even the fittest and most formidable of opponents, and that description certainly didn't apply to a homeless man who looked as if he hadn't had a decent meal for months. But there was something totally creepy about the way the sinewy hand was locked around my wrist despite its owner's apparent unconsciousness. It was like being clutched by a dead man, I thought with horror as I struggled to free myself and tried to keep a second panicky scream from rising in my throat.

"Let *go* of me!" I whispered, not bothering to reflect on the illogic of issuing a command in a voice that I hoped wouldn't awaken him. Keeping my skirt clear of the ground wasn't an issue any longer. I plopped down onto my butt. Feeling as if I'd been roped into a nightmarish game of tug of war, I dug the way-too-large heels of the tennis shoes into a crack in the pavement for leverage. "It's not as if I was actually *stealing* your stupid sneakers but if you want them back so badly, fine! Let go of my wrist and I'll take the damn things—"

This time my words weren't cut off by a scream, they simply dried up in my throat. At the same time, all the strength ran out of my limbs. Before I knew what was happening to me, I felt myself toppling sideways like a rag doll onto the garbage-strewn pavement of the alleyway.

It felt like red-hot pincers had clamped closed on my insides, and were now trying to drag my vitals out. The pain was excruciating—no, more than excruciating, *unbearable*—but what was worse was the thick nausea that seemed to fill every empty space in me, from my stomach to my head. All I could do was lie there, my mouth open and my wrist still tightly imprisoned in Crazy Joe's grip, and let the waves of sickness flow out of me.

Except what was coming out of my mouth wasn't waves of sickness, I realized in sick confusion. Through my slitted eyelids I could see a pool of blackness spreading outward from me like spilled tar. Obscene bubbles, like fat black flies, moved sluggishly here and there on the surface before popping under their own weight. The slick spread past the broken pavement of the alleyway and flowed onto the edging of quackgrass and weeds bordering it, and just before the pincers inside me turned suddenly into white-hot knives and my vision was blotted completely out with pain, I saw something that sent an icy finger down my spine.

As the tarry pool touched the grass and the weeds, each blade and stem of vegetation instantly shriveled into burned blackness. It flowed toward a bare patch of dirt, and the ground immediately turned scorched and dead-looking. A rank, sulphurous odor hung in the air like the top note of some vile perfume, but under it was layered a worse smell.

It was the smell of death, I realized in revul-

sion…moldering corpses, spilled fluids, unidenti-
fiable horrors. Even as I identified the stench the
pain inside me rose to a crescendo that blotted out
all conscious thought, and I felt my own oblitera-
tion swooping toward me.

Death was a dream. Not just any dream, either,
but my favorite one from childhood, when I'd been
a little girl and Grammie or Popsie had tucked me
into bed. At least once a month when I drifted off
to sleep I would dream of being rocked in my
father's arms as he sang to me. As I grew older the
dream came less often, and I might even have forgotten about it except for something that happened
when I was six.

I'd been absorbed in a spool-knitting kit that had
been a Christmas present from Grammie. My ab-
sorption hadn't lasted more than a few days, but at
the time I was still thrilled with the ever-growing
coil of knitted rope inching out from the bottom of
the red wooden spool and would spend hours
hunched over it, humming quietly under my breath
as I wrapped yarn around the four brass nails pro-
truding from the top of the spool. Anyway, there I

was, knitting away like a little old lady and half humming, half singing a song, when I looked up and realized Grammie was standing in the doorway of the room, her eyes full of tears and her voice quavery with emotion as she completed the verse I'd been singing.

"And there they tied in a true lover's knot
The red rose and the briar..."

When you're a little kid and you see an adult cry, your first thought is that you're responsible. So when Grammie dabbed at her eyes with one of her lavender-scented hankies and asked me where I'd learned the song I'd just been singing, I wanted to lie to her, on the general principle that lying might get me out of whatever trouble I was in. But just like most other times that I thought of lying to Grammie, when it actually came to it I couldn't, and I mumbled something about it being the song Daddy sang to me in my dreams.

I know what you're thinking—*enough with this little trip down memory lane, girlfriend. Get on with the story, will you?* And I will, but I'll just add one more thing. The song was an old one called *Barbara Allen,* Grammie told me, and David Crosse had sung it as a lullaby to his baby daughters…which meant that my dream was actually a memory of my father from the first year of my existence.

And now that my existence was over, I was hearing *Barbara Allen* being sung again, while a man cradled me in strong, protective arms.

"Daddy, is this heaven?" I murmured, snuggling more comfortably into his embrace as his voice, true and low, came to the end of the song. "Because I've got to tell you, even before I began turning vamp I had my doubts that I'd get here. I mean, I haven't been *so* bad, but I might have indulged in one or two of the seven deadly sins, like pride and envy." My eyelids still felt too heavy to open. I shifted slightly, not feeling quite as comfortable as I had a moment ago. I seemed to be sitting on something slatted, I realized as the blanket of wooziness that had been insulating my brain began to recede. Did heaven have park benches? "And I guess anger, sometimes, and covetousness whenever I pass a shoe store. I'd better toss sloth into the mix, as well," I admitted. "Megan always said I was too lazy to live. But I've totally steered clear of gluttony." With an effort I forced my eyes open. "That has to count for something, doesn't it?"

A navy-blue gaze met mine. The corners of Heath Lockridge's well-cut lips quirked up in a smile. "Surely it must, madam," he said, his accent even more to-die-for than I'd remembered. "But those are only six sins. Haven't you forgotten one?"

"Have I?" I said breathily. I didn't know how or why I'd ended up sitting on a bench in Maplesburg's town square with the dishy Lieutenant Lockridge's arms around me, and right now I didn't care. All that was important was that somehow I'd been whisked away from the nightmarish situation in the alleyway. Just the thought made me close my eyes, but that was a mistake. I saw again the blackness pouring from me, killing everything it touched—

Firmly I forced myself to concentrate on Heath—not that that was a hardship. His blue regimental coat fitted him perfectly, accenting his broad shoulders. The pewter buttons marching down the front were unbuttoned and the coat's red facings made a vivid contrast to the white linen waistcoat and drop-sleeve shirt he wore underneath. With the wayward strand of black hair falling across his forehead and those dark, spiky lashes I'd noticed before, he looked dashing and romantic and scrumptiously sexy. I heard a sound like a contented purr coming from the back of my throat. "Oh, right. Lust," I said, unable to take my eyes from him.

"A vice which we weak males struggle in vain against, but your own finer sex is unsullied by, naturally," Heath said, color ridging his cheekbones. "Forgive me, madam, I was not suggesting that you have experience with such base emotions."

He was absolutely serious, I realized as his arm slipped from my shoulders and his jaw clenched resolutely. Lieutenant Heath Lockridge, latterly of the First New York Muskets, might be a vamp living in the twenty-first century but he still held the courtly notions of a gentleman raised in the 1700s. To him, women were fragile and innocent beings to be put on pedestals and adored from afar. Men were rough beasts, tortured by coarse urges to tumble those pure creatures from their pedestals, lift their silken skirts and have their despicable way with them. His attitude was ridiculous, it was outdated, it was…

I had a sudden vision of myself sprawled across a four-poster bed, lacy underdrawers yanked down around my thighs and a ripped bodice revealing me to Heath's hot, blue gaze as he impatiently tore open the buttons straining over the bulge at the front of his uniform breeches.

"Of course I don't," I said huskily. "Experience those base and lustful emotions you're talking about, I mean." Reluctantly I set aside my X-rated daydream and sat up straighter on the bench. "Okay, what happened?" I said, trying to force a coolness to my tone that I didn't feel. "Last thing I remember I was lying in an alleyway certain that I was dying."

He nodded gravely. "Which is where I found you, madam, unconscious and in obvious distress. I brought you here so that when you came to you would be in more salubrious surroundings."

I frowned. "Look, Heath, I'm a twenty-first century girl, okay? Not that I don't adore the way you talk, but do you think you could modernize your vocabulary just a bit? For starters, stop calling me *madam* and call me Tash. And secondly, no one uses words like *salubrious* in modern conversation."

For a moment I wondered if I'd offended him. I glimpsed something that looked oddly like cold reappraisal move behind his gaze, and then humor swiftly slashed the tan of his cheeks. "Your bluntness is refreshing, ma—" he caught himself "—Tash. Do you remember anything of what happened before you fell ill? Some trauma, perhaps, that might have led to your attack of the vapors?"

I stared at him. "Attack of the vapors? Is that eighteenth-century slang for me freaking out over nothing because I'm a ditzy female?"

He looked uncomfortable. "I meant no offense. 'Tis understandable that a lady's nerves might fray, finding herself alone at night in an unsavory area. Possibly a cat startled you or one of the wretched denizens of the street accosted you for a few coins—"

Abruptly I stood up from the bench. "Let me be refreshingly blunt, Lieutenant," I said furiously. "When I first met you earlier this evening, I thought you were a walking, talking wet dream. A moment ago I was willing to chalk your attitude up to old-fashioned protectiveness. But now you're starting to piss me off!"

"Piss you off?" Heath looked taken aback. "Pray, madam, does that phrase mean what I think it—"

"The name's Tash!" I snapped. "And yes, it means exactly what you think it does—frosting my pumpkin, bugging the crap out of me, ticking me off! Women these days don't have attacks of the vapors, okay? Gawd, dealing with a hit man from Black Rose was less irritating than this!"

"Black Rose?" All expression was wiped instantly from his face, leaving it carefully blank. "*Chernoye Roza?* You must be mistaken, Tashya."

I snorted, not caring anymore if my crass modern ways were a turn-off for the delectable but jerky Heath Lockridge. "Read my lips. *Black,* as in the color. *Rose,* as in the flower. *Hit man*, as in the lying bastard I left in my trashed apartment after a knock-down, drag-out fight, which, by the way, means I can kiss goodbye the five-hundred-dollar security deposit I put down when I moved into that dump." I exhaled tightly. "To make a long story short, I ended up almost stepping in a Fido calling card, so when I saw Crazy—" I stopped, my gaze flying to my bare feet. "Wait a minute." I scowled suspiciously at Heath. "Did I have shoes on when you found me?"

"No." His one-word answer was curt. "But I need to ask you more about Black—"

"I don't *believe* it!" I exploded. "The whole pre-tending-to-be-asleep thing was just a ploy to scam me out of my watch! Grammie's going to kill me! That watch was her mom's before it was hers, and when my father married, Grammie told him it would be passed down to *his* daughter." I bit my lip. "Except there were three of us, and then he and Mom died, so it didn't quite work out that way. As a matter of fact, I just happened to come across it the other day when I was looking through Grammie's jewelry box to borrow her pearl necklace, and I thought I'd wear it until she came back. And now some crazy street-person's stolen it!"

To my horror I felt tears rise up behind my eyes. I blinked them back, determined not to play into Heath's old-school preconceptions about emotional females, but since at that moment I *was* an emotional female, the stupid tears kept coming.

And really, why wouldn't they? I mean, within the space of a few hours I'd been busted by my sisters while drinking blood from a bag, made and lost a new friend, and found out I was the target of some murderous secret society. Not to mention sinking to a new personal low by trying to steal the shoes off a homeless man and then having him turn the tables on me by stealing Grammie's watch.

But I knew none of those were the real reason I was blubbing.

I'm the queen of denial, and proud of it. The way I see it, denial's just another term for not letting the crappy stuff that happens in your life get you down, and without it I probably wouldn't have turned out as well-adjusted as I have. Megan has this grim sense of duty that tears her apart at times. Kat used to handle her problems by downing cocktails and using men like Kleenex, although becoming a Healer and taking up with sexy ex-con Jack Rawls seems to have settled her down a little. But my philosophy's always been a simple one: if I don't like something, it doesn't exist. Which is pretty much how I'd been dealing with my impending vamphood until my unpleasant little upchucking interlude in the alleyway.

But denial didn't work anymore. What had come out of me had been death…black, withering death.

I'd been trying to tell myself that becoming a vamp had cool benefits like superstrength and the ability to fly, and that as long as I kept on the straight and narrow, I didn't have a thing to worry about…but now I had to face the truth.

I wasn't Brooklyn or Kathy Lehman. I'd been cursed by a Queen *Vampyr,* and just as my powers would eventually surpass an ordinary vamp's, so would my hunger. I'd taken another quantum leap forward tonight in my metamorphosis—so much so that it had actually made me physically ill—and the blackness that had spilled from me was no more than a preview of my future.

Sooner or later I would kill, and after that first kill, I would no longer fight against my fated role as a bringer of death. There was only one way I could deal with the burden Zena's curse had laid on me.

Dashing the tears from my eyes, I tossed back my curls and gazed up through my lashes at Heath. "Do you think you could teach me how to fly, Lieutenant?"

Chapter 7

Heath didn't seem to hear my question. Instead of answering it, he whipped out an immaculate square of white linen from an inside pocket of his coat and offered it to me with a gallant flourish. "I feared that modern women had become too strong to cry," he said softly. "I cannot help but be glad that your fair sex still has a tender heart, although I would give much to assuage the pain that assails yours. Has anyone ever told you that your eyes look like rain-washed violets when you cry, Tashya?"

"Yeah, one guy I met in a bar once," I said absently, taking his handkerchief and blowing my nose briskly. I felt better now that I'd given in to my urge for a blub-fest, I realized in surprised relief. Okay, I had problems, chief among them being the vamp thing, but going all depression-girl wasn't going to solve them. Getting back Grammie's watch would be a simple matter of finding Crazy Joe and offering him twenty bucks, or if he'd already pawned it, hitting the pawnshops and buying it back that way. Dealing with Dmitri and Black Rose wasn't quite as simple, but until I figured out a better solution, I'd just have to stay away from my apartment. As for what had happened in the alleyway, wasn't it possible that my illness had been nothing more than a violent reaction to my new and gross diet? And wasn't it equally possible that the dying grass, burned ground, yada, yada, yada, had been part of my feverish imaginings before I'd lost consciousness?

You see how easy this denial stuff is? Only moments previously I'd told myself that I had to face the truth, as terrible as it was. I'd taken one look at it and squeezed my eyes shut again as fast as I could…and as things turned out, after that I kept them closed until it was almost too late. But if you're waiting for me to say that the moral of all this is that denial's totally bad, you're wrong.

Because if I hadn't gone into denial just then, I would have missed out on the most magical experience of my life.

"Thanks," I said, handing Heath's handkerchief back to him. His courtly little bow as he took it seemed to lack its usual pizzaz, but I didn't let that curb my enthusiasm. "So, can you, Heath? Tonight I started to hover without even meaning to, but later when I tried to really fly I couldn't get more than four or five feet off the ground. Maybe for vamps who get turned in the normal way flying comes naturally, but all the rules seem to be screwed up where I'm concerned."

"Because you were given the Gift by a Queen Vampire when you were a babe in the cradle?" he asked. He held out his arm and gave me a questioning look. "Shall we stroll as we talk, Tashya?"

I let my hand rest on his arm, wishing I had my cell phone so I could take a discreet pic of me and my tall, dark and uniformed escort to send to

Megan and Kat. Heath wasn't a wolf half the time, and he wasn't a wanted convict. 'Nuff said, as far as I was concerned. I'd just won the boyfriend competition.

"I was turned by Zena. If that's what you mean by getting the Gift, I'd rather she'd given me bath salts or something," I muttered.

Heath's laughter was low and abrupt, as if it had been surprised out of him. I glanced up and saw that he was studying me. "I almost wonder if it is such a bad thing that the rules do not apply to you," he said slowly. "I seem to recall a like example occurring among thirteen rebellious colonies, and their solution was to create their own set of rules." His smile flashed white in the moonlight. "Although the road they chose has not always been smooth or easy, I believe that situation worked out in the end, did it not?"

Okay, here's the thing: from the moment he'd introduced himself to Brookie and me, I'd known Heath had been a soldier in the American Revolution. That fact had added to his romantic aura, but somehow the full impact of who he was and what he'd lived through hadn't hit me until now.

I was holding hands with a man who'd risked everything—his possessions, his liberty, his life—for the ideal of freedom he believed in; an ideal that for the last two and a quarter centuries had been the basis for all that my country stood for. As he said, the path of freedom hadn't always been smooth or easy, and there'd been occasions since Heath's time when it seemed that it grew faint and overgrown for a while, but eventually we always found it again. Men like Heath had marked it with their blood; women of his time had tended it with their tears and their endurance. I swallowed past the sudden lump in my throat and nodded at him.

"I'd say it's worked out pretty well, Lieutenant. But how does that apply to my not being able to fly?"

Something danced behind the dark blue of his eyes. "Would you still prefer bath salts, madam?"

"Huh? I don't get—*omiGAWD!*" My last words came out in a tone that fell somewhere between a squeal and a scream, and under any other circumstances I would have despised myself for it. But the way I see it, squealing's a perfectly understandable reaction when a girl finds herself levitating sixty feet up in the air with the familiar landmarks of her hometown spread below her like a toy village.

And screaming's a perfectly understandable reaction when she realizes that those sixty feet have suddenly become fifty and are rapidly decreasing.

I'd let go of Heath's hand in my excitement. As soon as I did, I began dropping like a rock, my short, tiered skirt blowing upward and snapping like a windsock against my ribcage. As I saw the ground rushing up to make Tashya-puree out of me, I gave full vent to my panic and yelled something like, Heath, I'm falling, how do I pull out of this; except for some weird reason the words came out of my mouth as *Aieeeeeeekkk!*

And then his hand was clasped around mine and my downward descent jerked to a sudden stop. My skirt fluttered airily into place again, my heart slipped back down my throat and into its accustomed position in my chest, and I took a deep, shuddering breath. I looked down. "What would you say—about ten feet between me and planet Earth? Maybe twelve, at the most?" I asked in a voice that seemed way too high and shaky to be mine.

"I beg your forgiveness, Tashya," Heath said

rapidly, his tone low but almost as unsteady as mine. He was doing the resolute-jaw thing again, I saw, except this time it looked like it was carved out of granite. "I am a cur and a swine for allowing—"

"You almost let me get splattered, jerk-off!" I yelled, white-hot fury ironing out the quaver in my voice. "Forgive you? What am I, *crazy?*!" I wrenched my hand from his. The sound of my palm making contact with his cheek a nanosecond later was as loud as a gunshot. *"Damn,* I'm getting tired of men trying to get me killed tonight!"

Although Heath had barely reacted to my slap, at my words he went pale under his tan. He opened his mouth to speak but I didn't give him the chance. "I know Malkovich was working for Black Rose, but what I don't know is whose orders you're following, Lockridge! You deliberately set me up to—"

My gasp drowned out the rest of my sentence. Instinctively my hand shot out to grab Heath's, but my slap had rocked him back on his heels and out of my reach. I didn't need to hold on to him, I realized in dawning wonder. I was high over Maplesburg again—and flying all by myself.

"Oh, Heath, this is *beautiful!*" I breathed, my

gaze moving from the earth below to the velvet-black sky above me. It was strewn with stars, and the big, silver moon that outshone them looked close enough to touch. "You weren't setting me up after all, were you? You knew I could fly, but I just needed a little incentive."

When he didn't immediately reply I tore my gaze from the spangled sky and glanced at him. He was studying me with the same frowning intensity he'd shown before, and as his glance met mine I seemed to see a shadow pass behind the navy blue of his eyes. Swift contrition raced through me.

"I'm totally sorry about slapping you the way I did, and if you don't want to forgive me I'll understand," I said rapidly. "But I hope you do. Forgive me, I mean," I added. "Because I can't think of anyone I'd rather share my first night of flying with than you."

"I had heard that Zena did us no favor when she marked you," he said, ignoring my babbled apology as if he hadn't heard it and giving me the impression he was speaking more to himself than to me. "There was talk that either of your sisters would have been preferable—Megan, for her hard determination, or Kat, who came close to turning to the dark side of her own volition before she chose the way of a Healer. But the whispers about you said you were a foolish child-woman, not worthy of the Gift."

I felt obscurely hurt, even as I realized how illogical the emotion was. I hadn't asked to be marked by Zena and becoming a Queen Vamp was the last thing I wanted, but still, it was like finding out no one wanted to invite you to a party you wouldn't be caught dead at anyway. A thought occurred to me and I narrowed my eyes at him. "Don't tell me. Jasmine's the bitch who's been spreading this crap about me, right?"

Heath stiffened. With a visible effort he forced himself to relax. "So you know of Lady Melrose?" he said, his tone casual but his attitude watchful.

"You might say that," I said coolly. "She had the nerve to announce her arrival in Maplesburg to my sisters in a note, although I notice she hasn't shown her face around town yet. She also thought it would be a hoot to encourage Kat and Megan to think our father's still alive," I added, my coolness evaporating. "Like I said, the woman must be a prime bitch.

And if the Darkheart & Crosse agency's information is correct and you're collaborating with her, then all I can say is you're no better than your former colleague and brother-in-arms, Benedict Arnold."

I waited for him to deny my accusation. When he didn't, my heart sank as thoroughly as my body had a few minutes before. Megan and Kat had been right. Lieutenant Heath Lockridge, as courtly and sexy and gentlemanly as he seemed, had sworn allegiance to a Queen Vamp whose stated intention was to destroy everything and everyone I cared about—a woman so evil she'd earned the nickname of Jasmine the Cruel.

If I'd been standing on solid ground I would have turned and walked away from him. Since I was hovering in thin air, I simply began to let myself drift downward. The night wasn't magical anymore. Flying didn't seem that big a thrill. And men were assholes.

"The lady turned me. By that act she stole my soul and perverted my honor, but she has never laid claim upon my mind and my heart." Heath's tone was jagged. Stopping my descent, I looked him unflinchingly in the face.

"What does that mean?"

"It means that I am bound to serve her," he said hoarsely. "It does not mean that those bindings do not chafe, Tashya…and it does not mean that I do not live for the day I finally gain the strength to break free of them. Yes, it is Lady Jasmine who publicly states you are too weak to bear the burden Zena laid upon you, and until I met you I assumed she was right. Now I wonder if her antagonism is based on fear."

I smiled. Why not, it was funny. "Right, Lieutenant. Jasmine the Cruel is afraid of Tash the Vamp Screw-Up. Let's see. I almost crash-landed while learning to fly, I buy my blood from a black-market butcher and most important of all, I don't want to be a friggin' Queen. I don't see it as a gift, I see it as a curse. Maybe I can't avoid turning vamp, but I can control everything else."

As you can see, I was deep in denial again—so deep that my suspicions didn't kick in when Heath didn't argue with me, but simply inclined his head in acceptance.

"Perhaps you are right, Tashya. As you say, the rules do not seem to apply in your case." He held out his hand to me. "Shall we call a truce and enjoy the rest of the night together?"

Okay, maybe I'm just a pushover for really handsome guys with intriguing accents and shoulders out to here. Or maybe it's just that I'm a total tramp. I mean, I'd already gone at it hot and heavy with Dmitri that evening, but when Heath extended his hand to me I didn't hesitate for a second. Somewhere in the back of my mind my X-rated fantasy of me and him getting naked together kept playing in a continuous loop, and although I didn't intend to let things go that far on our first date, I was perfectly willing to entertain the possibility of losing my kissing-my-first-vamp virginity with the scrumptious Lieutenant Lockridge.

But he had something else in mind.

I think I've already said it was the most magical evening of my life, but that doesn't come close. I haven't really described what it felt like to fly, but take it from me, there's nothing like it—not bungee-jumping or parasailing, both of which I've been talked into by Megan, and not parachuting or gliding, which she couldn't pay me to try. Flying's like…well, like being on the swoopiest rollercoaster ride ever, except instead of being strapped into a seat you're absolutely free. Now that I think of it, maybe that was the main sensation I felt: that I was totally free of all the worries and constraints and restrictions that are part and parcel of being earthbound. And I felt free of Tashya Crosse, too.

Growing up, everyone gets tagged by their family pretty early on, right? You're the smart one or the artistic one or the wild one, and once you receive your tag, it seems like you have to live up to it. Well, with triplets it's three times worse, because without our tags we'd just be *theCrosse-triplets*—all one word and all one entity. And Megan and Kat and I *hated* being *the Crossetriplets* in people's minds. So Megan became the bossy and brainy Crosse triplet, Kat lived up to her reputation as a heartbreaker and a flirt, and I…

Well, I became the brat. The ditz. The tattletale, the irritating youngest triplet, the pain in the ass sometimes. I learned early how to toss my curls in the exact way that would set Megan's and Kat's teeth on edge, and how to bat my baby blues in the exact way that would make them roll their eyes and write me off me as an airhead. Then I would go ahead and do just what I'd wanted to do in the first place, leaving my brainy sister and my sexy sister with the feeling that the brat had just performed an end run on them but they didn't quite know how she'd done it.

As a schtick, it had worked pretty well right up until two months ago when everything started to change for us.

Megan was the first to carve out a new and real identity for herself when she became the Daughter, and Kat followed soon after when she discovered her Healer powers. Which left me holding the crappy end of the stick. Big surprise—*not*—the brat turned out to be the one Zena had marked when we'd been babies. Irritating Tashie Crosse was doomed to go all fang-girl. I couldn't rise to the occasion as Megan had or rise above my nature as Kat had done, so I just kept on being what everyone expected. The only thing was, sometimes I got just as sick of Tashie Crosse as my sisters did.

Flying gave me the chance to be someone else. And being with Heath gave me the chance to be someone else, too.

I loved the way the dark air felt rushing over my skin and streaming my hair back. It was like being poured through black silk. I didn't have to flap my arms or anything, thank Gawd, because how uncool would that have looked. No, I just *thought* about moving through the air and there I was, doing it. This'll sound dumb, but the only comparison that even comes close is the way otters play in water. When we were about six, Popsie took Megan and Kat and me to the Bronx Zoo, and when it was time to move on from the otter exhibit I threw a tantrum. I could have spent the whole day watching them swirl and frolic in their stream and slide down their mudbanks. Even at that age, I knew I was watching something absolutely perfect—living beings moving rapturously through the element they'd been designed for.

"Which star do you wish me to pluck for you, madam?" Heath asked at one point. We were hanging motionless high above the steeple of Maplesburg First Episcopalian—an irony I chose to ignore. What I hadn't been as able to ignore was the way Heath hadn't accompanied me as I'd circled the steeple, rousing sleepy and flustered pigeons.

He'd kept his distance from the church, only rejoining me when I'd soared high enough that it looked like a featureless speck.

"That one," I said, unhesitatingly pointing at the biggest, most blazingly bright star I could see. "The blue-white one that's to the left of that big bunch of stars. See it? Just above that other bright one."

"Lyra," Heath said with a mock frown. "'Tis scandalous how modern schooling has degenerated since my time. The 'big bunch of stars,' as you would have it, madam, is the Milky Way, and the bright star below Lyra is Altair. Do you know the legend?"

He had his arm lightly around my shoulders and although I was gazing upward, I was all too aware of the wry smile he turned my way. Suddenly I felt as if at any moment gravity could claim me, sending me tumbling head over heels through the enveloping darkness without any chance of breaking my fall. I tamped down the fluttering in my stomach and tried to sound nonchalant.

"Even if I did I'd say I didn't, Lieutenant, so you could show off your superior knowledge of astronomy."

His smile was rueful. "I confess, identifying the heavens' starry denizens was always a favorite pastime of mine. Lyra and Altair were secret lovers who were found out. As punishment they were separated by a river of stars, and it is said that the dew on a summer's morning is their tears." His tone lost some of its lightness. "A romantic story, but knowing the whereabouts of Lyra in the sky was of more practical use to me during the bloody night following the Battle of Long Island, when we were forced to retreat from that butcher Howe's redcoats. I and the remnants of the company I was leading were cut off from the rest of Washington's troops, and only by calculating our relative positions with the help of Lyra and her banished lover, Altair, was I able to keep us from being captured." His smile reappeared, widening into a grin that made him look suddenly boyish. "I'm a poor excuse for an escort, am I not? Here I am with the most beautiful woman I have laid eyes on, and I drag out old war stories to entertain her."

"I don't mind," I said honestly. "I learned about some of those battles in school, but I never thought much about the real people who lived and died in them." I looked up at him through my lashes. "Although as a change of subject, that 'most beautiful woman' line was pretty smooth, Lieutenant."

"It is no more than the truth." His arm was still around me. He moved slightly, turning toward me and clasping me lightly by my shoulders. "I was a soldier, Tashya, and soldiers are not known for their celibacy. Before I joined the fight for my country I was a landowner—wealthy and well-favored enough by the ladies that I seldom had to sleep alone. What I am trying to say is that I was far from inexperienced when I was turned, but when I saw you this evening I felt as callow as a boy who had not proved his manhood yet." A muscle tightened at the side of his jaw. "It is foolish-sounding, I know. After all, I have fully embraced the pleasures of the dark side. There are few indulgences I have denied myself, few debaucheries I have turned down." He drew me closer, until his lips were nearly touching mine. "Yet when I saw the golden fire of your hair, for the first time since I left my humanity behind me I felt heat…and when you turned those crushed-violet eyes on me, I remembered what springtime had once felt like."

Why I didn't dissolve into a great, big puddle of meltiness right then and there, I'll never know. I mean, no man had ever said anything so fabulously and extravagantly romantic to me in my whole life unless you count Peter Schneider, who played Romeo to my Juliet in a high school drama club production, and he was just quoting Shakespeare. The best I'd ever gotten in a non-Shakespeare-quoting situation was the occasional "You're so hot in that dress I'm getting a hard-on just looking at you, babe," from my late and unlamented fiancé, Todd.

But Heath thought my hair looked like golden fire and my eyes looked like violets. He could have been five foot six, skinny and with glasses, and I still would have felt all swoony at his words, although I have to admit they sounded even better coming from a gorgeous hunk of uniformed male.

I swayed toward him, not in an I'm-so-desperate-for-a-kiss-I-think-I'll-just-launch-myself-at-your-lips kind of way, but in a move I'd practically patented by the time I was fifteen. It was designed to let a man know that if he wanted to lock lips with little Tashie Crosse, now would be a good time, and I'd never known it to fail.

Heath bent his head closer to me. I let my lips part slightly. Through my half-closed lashes I saw Lyra and Altair wink out above us, and a thin line of pale gold rim the horizon as his mouth began to come down on mine. And then I noticed the flicker of flame running along the sleeve of his jacket where the first watery beam of sunlight was falling.

In my experience, there's nothing that can break the mood faster than the realization that the man you're getting ready to kiss is seconds away from turning into a pillar of fire. I jerked backward from Heath as if I'd been stung, slapping vigorously at his sleeve with one hand and pointing frantically at the horizon with the other.

"Dawn!" I croaked. My throat felt like it had closed to a pinhole. "Heath, the sun's coming up!"

He began to glance over his shoulder, but didn't complete the motion. "Shit," he said, and despite my panic I wondered how he could make even that word sound courtly. "This is not how I wished to leave you, sweet lady," he said rapidly, "but I fear 'tis the swiftest way for me to seek refuge. The light is not yet your enemy, so you will be safe descending in a more leisurely manner."

I didn't understand what the hell he was talking about. I looked past him again and saw that the thread of gold on the horizon had inched upward. Wrenching my gaze back to him, I felt all the breath slam out of me in a horrified scream.

The enormous bat hanging in front of my face flapped its creaking, leathery wings once and was gone, speeding through the dissipating shadows. A heartbeat later, the hollow realization struck me.

I'd just lost the boyfriend competition.

Big-time.

Chapter 8

"Even if he'd said something like, 'Heads-up, madam, I fear I shall be turning into a big-ass bat momentarily,' I might have handled it better," I said, sitting up and reaching for the broken trowel I'd used earlier. Disconsolately I scraped at the hard-packed dirt, trying to pile it up in the spot where my head had been resting. "But oh, no. One minute I'm about to kiss the hottest guy I've ever seen in my life and the next minute I'm nose to snout with something that looks like it came straight out of a

Stephen King movie. No wonder I went into free fall, for Gawd's sake. If my sweater hadn't snagged on the church steeple, I wouldn't have pulled up in time to save myself."

From Brooklyn's corner by the massive boiler that squatted like a dinosaur in the cobweb-festooned apartment basement came a deep and even snoring sound. Too deep and too even. I tossed the trowel in her direction. "I know you're awake, Brookie. So what do you think—if he shows up again tonight should I go out with him or get a rabies shot?"

It was about noon, although I couldn't be sure of the exact time because of the handing-my-watch-over-to-a-double-crossing-street-bum thing. It felt like ten hours had passed since the abrupt end of my date with Heath, but I knew it only seemed that long because I was bored out of my mind.

Which made me an ungrateful bitch, I told myself guiltily. After all, when I'd finally unhooked my ruined sweater from the steeple and planted my bare feet on good, old Mother Earth again, I'd suddenly realized that I had a more immediate problem than the fact that Heath had metamorphosed into a vampire bat. For all I knew, Black Rose's lying creep of a hit man was waiting for me at my apartment. Even if he wasn't, he was probably watching the place. I was wearing a cashmere sweater that was ready for the rag-bag and no shoes, and pretty soon the good citizens of Maplesburg would begin stirring. I had to get out of sight before they did, but thanks to Dmitri, I was temporarily as homeless as Crazy Joe.

And for some odd reason, the first rays of sunlight shooting over the horizon felt a whole lot hotter than they should have.

"Psst! Mata Hari—over here!"

I whirled around at the low-voiced command, but the sidewalk by the church was deserted. I looked farther, my gaze scanning the storefronts and small businesses that made up downtown, but I still saw no one. Then a shadow detached itself from the art deco-style architecture of the Rialto, an eyesore of an old movie theater that Maplesburg's beautification committee kept promising to restore when the town found enough money.

"Hurry up before I flash-fry!" Brooklyn called

in a hoarse undertone. She was bundled up in an old blanket, but even as I gaped at her the part that was swathed around her head began to slip downward. With a gloved hand she hastily yanked it up again, winding it around her face like a burka so only her furious eyes showed. "Fuckin' move your *ass,* Crosse!" she snarled. "It's almost full daylight and we've got to get to ground, pronto!"

Her tone more than her words broke through my stupefied paralysis and I did as she said—moved my ass. As I reached her, however, she set off down the still-darkened laneway between the Rialto and Suzanne's, the dress shop next door, without even glancing over her shoulder to see if I was following.

I was, but at a hobble, not a run. "Ow!" I exclaimed, wincing as I set my bare heel down on one of the sharp pieces of rock that covered the lane. "Brook, wait up! Where the hell are we go—"

Something snaked out of the shadows near my feet and hooked my ankle. I stopped just in time to avoid sprawling face-forward on the gravel and looked down angrily.

I was standing by a weed-covered window well that obviously let onto the basement of the old

movie theater. Brooklyn's T-shirt-clad torso protruded out of the well, the rest of her disappearing
into the basement. She tugged at my ankle again.

"Come on, Crosse," she said impatiently. "Get
inside before a rummy stumbles down this
laneway looking for somewhere to take his first
leak of the day."

As her head and shoulders moved out of sight
into the basement, I reluctantly clambered into the
window well, hoping there weren't any stray shards
of glass lying around. I let my legs drop into noth-
ingness, yelped nervously as I felt Brooklyn tug at
them and lost my precarious balance and landed in
a heap in a dark void.

"Hold on, I've got to replace the security bars,
such as they are," she muttered from somewhere
above me. I heard a clank of metal against stone,
and then the sound of a wooden window frame
swinging shut with a soft thud. "Okay, now we can
get comfortable," her disembodied voice said.

Before I could ask her what her definition of
comfortable was, since it obviously wasn't the same
as mine, I heard a rough scratching noise by my ear.
I jumped, the equation *scratching + basement = rat*

immediately going through my mind. Then a warm, golden teardrop of flame flared into life in front of me, and I let out a relieved breath.

"This society is going to hell in a handbasket," Brooklyn said, shaking her head as she touched the flame of the wooden match she was holding to a half-used candle in a glass jar. "I found this in someone's garbage can the other night, can you believe it? It's French so it must have cost an arm and a leg, and some spoiled, rich bitch who probably drives an SUV and doesn't bother to recycle just threw it out. *Figoo*," she mused. "I don't know what that means, but it smells great."

"*Figue,*" I muttered, pronouncing it without adding an *oo* on the end. "It's French for fig," I added, recognizing the Diptyque candle I'd tossed in the trash a few nights ago when I'd accidentally snapped the wick down below the wax. After finding it in my garbage can Brooklyn had obviously taken the time to dig the wick out and salvage it. Hurriedly I changed the subject. "What a dump," I said, looking around at the dirt floor and damp walls that were now illuminated by the candle's glow. A massive octopus-armed shadow in the corner had to be the furnace, but there were other bulky outlines I couldn't readily identify. One looked vaguely like a pair of theater seats, still joined together; another could have been a folded-up display easel. I gave an exaggerated shudder and turned back to Brooklyn. "What *is* this place?"

"My home," Brooklyn said coldly. "And even if it's not up to your standards, Crosse, there's plenty of vamps in Maplesburg who go to ground in the daytime in way worse places, so just count yourself lucky that I stuck around when I saw you bouncing off that steeple. You can also count yourself lucky that no one else saw you," she said, setting the candle carefully on an upturned metal bucket that was covered with what looked like the ripped bottom half of an old lace-trimmed slip.

Her shoulders set stiffly under her retro Violent Femmes T-shirt, she walked over to the theater seats and flipped one down. Parking her khaki-clad butt on the seat, she grabbed a comic from a stack beside the chair and began leafing through it.

I'd been a total shit, I realized, so I'd have to be the one to make the next move. I cleared my throat. "Love the tablecloth," I said tentatively.

"Screw you, Crosse," Brooklyn replied without raising her eyes from her comic book.

I looked around for something else to compliment and then gave up. "I'm sorry, Brookie. I mean, I know I totally owe you for letting me hide out here for the day, especially after the stupid stuff I said last night."

"Stupid stuff?" she said, her voice coolly distant and her gaze still intent on the comic. "You mean what you said about me pawing you on the slightest pretext? Or are you talking about your comments on my hair and my clothes?"

"I'm talking about all of it," I said uncomfortably. "If you must know, I was trying to get back at you for what you said about me acting like a brat, except I guess my little performance only proved you were right."

With a sigh Brooklyn tossed her comic book aside. "No, I'm the one who was out of line, Mata Hari," she said, running her fingers through her chicken-feather hair so that it stood up in ice-white spikes. "At first you seemed like such a cool babe, but as soon as a man showed up you started in with the girly games. Then your sisters appeared on the scene and it was like you regressed to kindergarten. But who am I to judge? Maybe if I'd been able to get along better with my sister, I wouldn't be living in this dump now." A corner of her mouth lifted. "It *is* a friggin' dump, isn't it? But it's got one major advantage—there's an old stairway no one seems to know about that leads up to the theater. Sometimes I sneak in and catch a matinee." She shrugged. "You wanna go tomorrow, they're running a Sonny Chiba double bill."

I didn't know who or what a Sonny Chiba was, but I nodded anyway. "Sure, sounds fun. What's this about your sister, though?"

She got to her feet and walked over to a ramshackle cabinet propped against the wall. "That's a long story for another time," she said over her shoulder as she opened the cabinet's upper doors. "I'd rather hear how you ended up nearly impaled on a steeple. Ding Dong?"

"Huh?"

She held up a cellophane-wrapped object. "I don't know about you, but ever since I became a vamp I'm a fiend for snack cakes. Let's see, I've got Ding Dongs, Little Debbie Swiss Rolls,

Hostess Twinkies—oh, and my fave, Moon Pies. Take your pick."

"I've never had a Moon Pie," I said dubiously.

"Babe, you don't know what you're missing." Brooklyn grinned, tossing one my way. "Okay, take it from the top. Last I knew, you were doing the nya-nya thing with your sisters. What happened after I left?"

Three Moon Pies, two Swiss Rolls and one Twinkie later, I finished the saga of Tashie's Big Night and waited for Brooklyn's reaction. She frowned and pointed a half-eaten Ding Dong at me. "This Black Rose hit man—what's his name?"

"Dmitri Malkovich," I said, wishing we were talking about Heath instead.

"Yeah, this Dmitri dude." She popped the other half of the Ding Dong in her mouth and spoke around it. "Mmmph nnd hnph, wnt?"

"Swallow, then talk," I suggested.

She gulped down the mouthful. "He had the drop on you and let you walk away, right? He better watch his back. If Black Rose finds out he fucked them over, he's a dead man."

"How are they going to find out?" I said with a shrug. "I'm not going to tell them."

"You're telling me," she pointed out. "All I'm saying, this guy cut you a break. Maybe you don't trust him all the way, maybe you don't even like him, but if you don't want him to pay with his life for what he did for you, you better keep your mouth shut about it. And that means from your sisters and your Zaidy Darkheart, too." She saw my blank look. "*Zaidy*'s Yiddish for Grandpop, you *shiksa*."

"I knew that," I said unconvincingly. "Anyway, I doubt I'll be running into Meg and Kat in the next little while. It wouldn't be a bad idea to steer clear of Darkheart, either, since he'll probably trot out his nifty idea about me spying on Jasmine again."

Brooklyn opened her mouth as if she was going to say something. Then she closed it.

"What?" I asked.

"Nothing." She got up from the theater seat and went over to the cupboard again, this time opening one of its lower doors. "My wardrobe doesn't consist of designer duds like yours, babe, so you'll probably be disappointed with the selection, but you can't go around in a shredded sweater. That skirt's not real practical for living on the street, either, so pick out a pair of pants. They'll be too short for you, but us beggars can't be choosers."

"You think I should do it, don't you?" I demanded, not moving toward the cupboard. "You think I should offer myself up as the sacrificial lamb in Darkheart & Crosse's insane strategy of infiltrating Jasmine's inner circle."

"This tee should fit you and I always have to roll up the legs on these cargos, so they shouldn't look too bad on you." She tossed the two garments to me. "It's your call, Tash. If it were me, yeah, I'd do it. But you've obviously got your reasons for turning Darkheart and your sisters down on this."

"Frikkin' right I've got my reasons," I said vehemently, peeling off my ruined Beth Bowley sweater with a pang and skimming the black T-shirt over my head. I pulled my hair out of the neckline and squinted at the upside-down writing on the tee. "What's it say?" I asked suspiciously. "These look like characters, not words."

"*Namaste,*" Brooklyn said, pronouncing it *namastay.* "I think it's a yoga thing, but for all I know it's Sanskrit for "I'm With Stupid." How do the pants fit?"

I shimmied out of my silk tiered skirt and pulled on the cargos. "Fine," I said, privately vowing to figure out a way to sneak into my apartment and retrieve some of my own clothes as soon as possible. "You know what Jasmine's nickname is?"

"The Cruel," Brooklyn answered. "You don't have to explain yourself to me. Like I said, it's your call."

I ignored her. "Megan even admitted my chances of keeping up the deception weren't good, so why did they ask me in the first place?"

"Maybe because the situation's worse than they're letting on," Brooklyn said evenly. Her mint-green gaze held mine. "Your sisters might be major pains in the ass, but it's pretty obvious they love you, and so does your Zaidy Darkheart. My guess is they wouldn't ask you to take a risk like this unless you were their only hope."

I looked away from her and scowled at the cargos. "What's up with all these pockets?" I demanded. "They totally ruin the lines of the pants, and if you actually loaded them up with stuff they'd be too heavy to walk in. Talk about a design disaster!" I looked up and saw that Brooklyn was still watching me. "I know I'm their only hope," I said unsteadily. "That's why I turned them down."

"Run that by me again, babe?" Brooklyn's tone was uncharacteristically gentle.

Those minty eyes saw too much. I picked up my discarded skirt and began folding it as an excuse not to meet her gaze. "I've got a sister who's a Daughter and another who's a Healer. That makes them a pretty tough act to follow…but the thing is, they always have been. Ever since I can remember, I've been waiting for them to tell me they need my help. Now that they have…"

"Now that they have, you're scared shitless you'll let them down?" Brooklyn asked.

I shook my head. "No, I *know* I will. I'll screw up somehow. Last night Heath tried to tell me that Jasmine was afraid of me, but that's crazy. I'm no match for her."

"You did pretty well against the lying prick who's her first lieutenant," Brooklyn said sharply.

I stared at her. "Heath?"

She gave me a tight grin. "Come off it, Crosse.

Yeah, Heath—the murdering vamp bastard who tried to kill you. Hell, you told me you accused him of it to his face, so don't pull that starlight and romance shit with me now."

"You're wrong," I said firmly. "*I* was wrong, and I realized that almost right away. If Heath was trying to kill me on Jasmine's orders, why did he save me at the last minute?"

"That's what I mean about you holding your own against him. You *glamyred* him somehow, right? I mean, you must have." She grinned. "Maybe you didn't even know you were doing it, but trust me, Mata Hari—the guy hooked up with you with the deliberate intention of killing you. Instead, he ended up staring into your baby blues for so long that he nearly got killed himself. I've got to hand it to you, Crosse—you're one tough chick under that fluffy society-girl exterior."

Nothing I said could persuade her she'd misjudged Heath. I finally convinced her I hadn't deliberately *glamyred* him, but I didn't feel a whole lot of satisfaction over winning that argument, since as soon as Brook realized I was telling her the truth her eyes went flat and her mouth went tight.

"So you really *did* buy in to the old starlight and romance crap with him," she said, running a hand through her hair. "What was it, babe, the fact that he wears a uniform? That he's tall, dark and handsome and talks like some jerk out of a historical romance? Or was it that the whole time you were with him, you were thinking about showing him off to your sisters?" She glared at me. "You won't be able to, you know. He's a vampire, and not one who toes the line, like us. He might have fed you a line about wanting to break free of his bitch mistress, Jasmine, but has he done it yet? Take it from me, if he ever runs into Megan or Kat, they'll recognize him for what he is—their enemy. And they'll send him to hell, one way or another." She tossed a blanket on the dirt floor and jerked her head in the direction of the cupboard. "I'm getting some shut-eye. There's extra blankets in there if you want to do the same. My supplies don't run to pillows but heaping up some earth under your head works almost as well."

That had been over an hour ago—again, give or take, since I didn't have a watch anymore. I tossed down the broken trowel I'd been using to make a dirt-pillow—okay, I totally can't believe I just said that—and stood up.

This blew. Why was I skulking around in a dingy basement in the middle of the day? More to the point, why wasn't I shopping? I looked down at my borrowed clothes and repressed a shudder. Brooklyn had meant well, but I really wasn't the weird T-shirt and baggy pants type. Unfortunately, I'd left my credit cards and checkbook back at my apartment along with everything else that made life worth living, like clothes and makeup and shoes.

However, there *was* a solution....

"Brook, is there another way out of here besides crawling through the window well?" I walked over to her and shook her shoulder. "Okay, here's the deal. I'll stop talking about Heath and you stop pretending to be asleep, okay? The reason I asked about another exit is I need to go shopping and I'd rather not walk into Suzanne's Fashions looking like a chimney sweep, especially when I intend to ask her to send me the bill instead of paying upfront. My sisters and I are some of her best customers so there won't be a problem, but—" A soft but distinct snore cut off the rest of what I was going to say. I sighed impatiently and shook her shoulder again. "I get it, okay? You don't trust Heath. I promise I'll think about what you said—"

"'Zit nighttime awready, babe?" Brooklyn squinted sleepily up at me. "Duzznt feel like it."

She hadn't been faking, I realized contritely. I squatted down beside her. "It's not, but I didn't think you needed to do the traditional sleeping-all-day vamp thing. Didn't you say you took in a matinee sometimes?"

With what seemed like an immense effort, she forced her eyes fully open. "I know, but lately I've been getting sleepier and sleepier during the day. If I didn't know I hadn't touched human blood, I'd think I was turning to the dark side." Her slurred words trailed off, but then she roused herself. "You wanted to know about another way out. The door at the top of those stairs on the other side of the furnace opens onto an old storeroom no one uses anymore. The storeroom exits to the lane running beside the building, but it locks from the inside, so you won't be able to use it coming back." Her eyes drifted closed again. "You are coming back, aren't you, Mata Hari?" she said drowsily. "'Cause it's kinda fun having company. I think the thing I hate most about being a vamp is not having any friends anymore...."

"You've got me," I said, standing up and looking down at her. She was already snoring again, and the chill that had gripped me a moment ago intensified. I believed Brook when she said she didn't drink human blood, but that didn't seem to matter. She was dead to the world—not merely sleepy but unconscious, just because it was daytime.

But what chilled me even more was that when she'd opened her eyes, they hadn't been mint-green...they'd been blood-red.

Brooklyn was going over to the dark side and there wasn't anything she could do about it. And that meant that maybe I was, too.

Chapter 9

I've never understood why people go to shrinks when they could just go shopping. Think about it: you buy a new dress that looks fabulous on you, that takes care of any self-esteem issues you might have. Feeling depressed? A dreamy pair of Jimmy Choos or Manolos are guaranteed to lift any girl's spirits. And if you're having a problem dealing with your rage over catching your boyfriend sleeping around, the most satisfying way to handle it is to drop a bundle on the sexiest lingerie you can buy and when you kick him out on his cheating ass, tell him it'll be a cold day in hell before *he* gets to see you in it.

Shopping is therapy, plain and simple. So when I ducked out of the laneway beside the Rialto and scooted next door into the yellow and Provençal-blue awning-covered entry to Suzanne's, my mood automatically brightened. I entered the store and took a deep breath, inhaling the unmistakable scent of indulgence—a mingling of Milan leather, French perfumes and the massive bouquet of white roses that Suzanne had delivered daily from the florist.

I was home. And whoever it was who said you can't go home again was obviously a man, because—

"You! Out! *Venez vite, mademoiselle!*"

I blinked in shock. Suzanne herself, her elegantly thin figure clad in one of her signature little black dresses, was bearing down on me, her bony hands making furious shooing motions in my direction. Her perfectly *maquillé* face showed no expression at all, but that wasn't due to any Zenlike composure on her part. Botox and her third face-lift had ensured that she always looked eerily calm, even at a moment like this when she was obviously agitated.

As Kat once thoughtfully noted, Frenchwomen might not get fat, but they sure get scary after a certain age.

"Zis is not Ze Gap, mademoiselle! You will find nozzing to interest you here, so please leave immédiatement!" Her arched eyebrows looked as though they were trying to rise in hauteur, but since they'd already been surgically lifted to within an inch of her hairline they couldn't go any higher. She compensated by flapping her hands at me again, a disdainful gesture that seemed to take in my T-shirt, my multipocketed cargos and the Doc Martens I'd borrowed from Brook before I'd left the basement. "Out! *Out!*"

I gathered my wits. "Suzanne, it's me—Tashya Crosse." I gave her my best Gallic shrug in an attempt at solidarity. "I know, right? These pants and this shirt are *so* not me. As for the shoes…" I smiled at her while my mind raced frantically to come up with an explanation for my out-of-character mode of dress. I had a brainwave. "*L'amour, toujours l'amour*…but isn't that always the way? You're a Frenchwoman, Suzanne, so you understand."

"Tashya?" Her features overpowered the Botox long enough to register a faint flicker of confusion. "What has *l'amour* to do with those awful clothes you are wearing?"

"A new boyfriend." I sighed. "Except now he's my new *ex*-boyfriend. I mean, at first I thought he was totally adorable in a save-the-rainforest, buy-third-world-goods, vegetarian kind of way, and of course when he told me he disapproved of our consumer society, I tried to dress down to make him happy. But after our relationship moved to a new level last night and I found out that he couldn't make *me* happy, I ditched him. And now I just want to go back to being the real me."

I'll say one thing for Suzanne: she can smell money better than French pigs can scent out truffles. Immediately she became all business, her gimlet gaze scanning the nearest display and her scarlet-tipped fingers (strange but true: French-women never seem to have French manicures, have you noticed?) plucking three dresses on padded hangers from the rack. "Strip," she said briskly, nodding toward one of the two change cubicles at the far end of the store. "And *les chaussures, aussi,*" she added, barely repressing a shudder as her disapproving glance took in my borrowed Doc Martens.

Two minutes later, clad only in my La Perla push-up bra and matching panties, I was sitting on a dove-colored velvet chair in one of the tiny but elegantly appointed rooms, levering off Brook's clunky boot from my right foot. It fell with a solid thud beside its mate on the pale-carpeted floor. The door to the cubicle flew open.

"Arrange the feet in these first," Suzanne commanded, thrusting a pair of red-soled high heels at me. "They are a size 38.5," she added, "so they should fit you perfectly, *non?*"

When I'd first started shopping at her store, I'd been disconcerted by her custom of barging into the fitting rooms without warning while her customers were semi-naked and at their most socially vulnerable. Now I was used to it. I smiled in cool amusement at her. "Your fabled memory for your clients' measurements slipped up in this case, Suzanne. I'm a thirty-eight. My feet would absolutely *swim* in those, as yummy as they are."

And the Louboutins *were* yummy; the very sight

of them had sent my saliva glands into overdrive. They had five-inch stiletto heels, the undersides finished in the fabulous Monsieur Christian's trademark vermilion, and the shoes themselves were a beautiful midnight black, sexily pointed and with cut-away sides. The inners were creamy peach leather stamped in gold.

Suzanne made a French-type noise, something between a snort of impatience and a derisive laugh. "Thirty-eight and a half," she said implacably. "You always try to wedge your feet into thirty-eights, but *enfin* you always take a half size larger. *I* wear size thirty-eight shoes, mademoiselle. *You* do not."

Before I could come back with a cutting rejoinder she shoved the shoes into my hand and left, which was probably just as well, since the only cutting rejoinder I could come up with at such short notice was a muttered, "Yeah, well, at least I don't have espresso breath." But my disgruntlement vanished as I tried on the Louboutins.

They slid onto my feet like *buttah,* damn their decadently seductive little shoe souls—pun not intended. Obviously this particular style fit a tad smaller than usual. Wearing Brook's Docs had felt like walking around with concrete blocks strapped onto my feet, but the Louboutins felt like my heels and my arches and my toes were being gently but masterfully caressed by the genius from Brittany who had created them. I gave a little sob of pure joy and stood up to check them out before remembering Suzanne's decree of no mirrors in the fitting rooms. It was her way of ensuring that she had a part in the decision process, especially if a customer was torn between an expensive dress and a blow-the-budget one. No prizes for guessing which one La Suze always swore looked better on you.

The door flew open again and she brushed past me to the ornately old-fashioned gold-and-porcelain hooks on the back wall of the room. She hung up the three dresses she'd chosen for me, her red fingertips stroking invisible creases from their fabric.

"Galliano, Rodriguez and Valentino. Try the Rodriguez on first," she informed me, glancing over her shoulder in the direction of the store's front window. Following her glance, I saw a gleaming black limousine with discreetly tinted windows pull up at the curb under the store's yellow-and-blue striped awning. The driver's door opened and the black-suited chauffeur got out, his Ray-Bans scanning the street before he reached for the passenger door handle and opened it.

An elegantly silk-sheathed leg appeared. The Manolo-shod foot it was attached to stepped onto the sidewalk under the store's awning. Beside me Suzanne came to quivering attention, like a bird-dog scenting quail.

Rich quail, I thought wryly. Maplesburg wasn't in the same league as Martha's Vineyard when it came to a summer influx of well-heeled visitors, but we got our share. Local business owners like Suzanne saw them as walking dollar signs, and since this particular dollar sign came with a limo and a personal chauffeur/bodyguard, my guess was that I'd just been demoted to customer number two.

"I will return *dans un instant,*" Suzanne said, bearing out my prediction and hastily exiting the fitting room. I closed the door behind her and dutifully reached for the Narciso Rodriguez, but then I hesitated.

It was a beautiful dress, with a darling empire waist flaring out into floaty pleats, but it was a fiery cranberry color. With my strawberry-blond hair, I'd look like an exploding Stop sign in it. The Valentino's melty rose pink was a better color for me and the semitulip-cut hem was adorably retro, but it was just too…too…

Well, actually there was nothing wrong with it. It was me, right down to the brocade florals in the fabric and the demurely rounded neckline that just cried out to be filled by Grammie's pearls. And that was the problem.

I didn't want a dress that was me. I wanted a dress that was as unlike me as possible. I wanted a dress that would force me to be someone else in it.

But most of all, I wanted a dress that would make Heath's jaw drop if he saw me in it tonight…and the Galliano was just that dress, I thought, catching my breath as I lifted it from its hanger.

It was little more than a wisp of tulle the color of cobwebs in the moonlight, but the fragile-looking fabric looked like it had been thrown into a plundered treasure chest and then brought out again, haphazardly strewn with cloudy diamonds and tarnished coins, and dripping with blackened silver lace. Of course, the Divine John is known for his romantic decadence, but this dress practically *reeked* of corrupted innocence.

Even before I tried it on I knew I had to have it.

The neckline looked as if Galliano, in a fit of creative pissiness, had ripped it open to the waist and then regretted his outburst too late to resew it. A barbaric metal medallion sunk cruel clasps on either side of the plunging tulle at about ribcage level, holding the dress together. My La Perla bra would definitely have to be ditched, I thought, unsnapping it and tossing it aside impatiently before dropping the dress over my head and shimmying it down over my body.

Even without the benefit of a mirror, I knew at once that it had been made for me. The cobwebby fabric clung to my skin like fog. I moved slightly, and the wafer-thin metallic coins shivered against each other, giving out a faint clanking sound that seemed to die as soon as it encountered the air. For some reason, the sound reminded me of something I'd seen once when I'd helped Grammie and her Maplesburg Beautification Society friends spruce up the graves in an old cemetery. Beside one of the crumbling and lichen-covered markers had been the rotted remnants of what looked oddly like a wooden pulley—although that wasn't so odd, one of the older ladies had informed me, since that was exactly what it had been. With the hoe she was holding, she parted the weeds beside the rotted wood and when the hoe struck audibly against something metal, she reached down and picked the object up.

It had been a small bell, now eaten by rust and with its clapper missing. A coffin bell, Grammie's friend had told me—a signaling device that consisted of a rope, a pulley and a bell, with one end of the rope disappearing under the freshly turned earth of the grave and into the casket of the recently dead-and-buried, and the other end hanging from the pulley and attached to the bell. The object of this whole contraption supposedly being that if you were buried alive and woke up to find yourself six feet under, you could ring the bell to let everyone know they'd made a big boo-boo.

That was the last time I went grave-beautifying with Grammie, believe me.

But although the coffin bell story had grossed me out—okay, it didn't just gross me out; for weeks afterward I had nightmares in which I woke up in a padded satin enclosure that smelled of dirt and realized I'd been buried alive. In my nightmare I grabbed frantically in the darkness for the coffin bell rope, but when I finally found it I realized in cold horror that it had come free in my hand and wasn't attached to anything. But as I say, although learning about the existence of coffin bells had creeped me out, the dull tinkle of the tarnished metal paillettes on the dress sounded eerily beautiful to me. I moved again, closing my eyes, and this time when the faint ringing shivered the air it seemed to translate into a vision behind my closed lids.

I was gliding through a mist-shrouded landscape. Around me, the twisted limbs of autumn-bare trees rose out of the mist like tortured souls, and the grass beneath my feet was faded and brittle with frost. Lifting my hand in front of my face, I saw that my skin looked as pale and insubstantial as smoke, as if the fog had seeped the color out of everything, even me. Then a strand of my hair drifted across my vision like that of a drowned woman twisting slowly in an underwater current, and I realized that it was a burning red, richer and darker than the strawberry it had been.

The dead and blasted landscape should have been repellent to me. Instead I felt supremely at home in it, as if my life in Maplesburg had been spent trapped in someone else's body and I had awakened with relief to find myself back in my own skin and my own place.

"This *pochette* is an amusing trifle, *n'est-ce pas?*" I opened my eyes, feeling slightly disoriented as Suzanne's voice carried from the main part of the store to break through the weird daydream I'd been having. "It is made in Milan, *naturellement,* and the stitching is masterful, especially here, where the lilac suede merges into the gold kid leather." Her voice dropped. "Unborn kid, you understand, madam. That is why there is not even the most minute of blemishes on the leather, *comprenez?*"

"I'll take it." The other woman's tone held the languid boredom of someone to whom money was no object, or maybe her upper-crust drawl was simply a trace of an accent. "You're sure it's unborn kid?"

Susanne's laugh was edged. "*Mais oui.* I suspect that is why such an exquisite clutch has not been snapped up by my regular customers before now. As soon as I tell them what it is made of—*poof!*—their interest suddenly disappears. I find Americans do not understand that the stylish woman cannot afford squeamishness, *non?* Now, this makeup case is truly outstanding. Observe the pebbled finish, the steel-gray sheen? Stingray hide, madam, one of the most costly and coveted—"

"Unborn baby goat?" I muttered under my breath. "Yuck. I'm not a card-carrying member of PETA or anything, but that puts a whole new and unpleasant spin on the term fashion victim." With a tiny shudder that set the paillettes on the dress faintly tinkling again, I opened the door of the fitting room and headed for the mirrored wall on the far side of the shop.

"Ah, Tashya…please excuse me, madam. This will only take a moment." As Suzanne made her hasty apology, her customer gave a negligent nod and turned away, examining the sumptuous selection of leather goods on display. My guess about price being no object for her was obviously right, I mused. Mrs. Moneybags was wearing a divinely simple Chanel suit the color of a Starbucks double latte and the interlocking *C*s on the jacket's gilt buttons matched the ones on the huge black sunglasses she wore. But it was her hat that I coveted. If my eyes didn't deceive me it was a Philip Treacy and, like all his creations, heartbreakingly gorgeous—an Audrey Hepburnish confection in tan sinamay with flirty black polkadots, finished off with an outrageous pink ribbon that shouldn't have worked but looked perfect.

"*Non*," Suzanne said decisively, stepping in front of me and holding one hand up like a *gendarme* stopping traffic. "No, no, no and *no*. The Galliano is not right for you, I see that now. You have a fresh attractiveness, Tashya. This dress is not *convenable* for a young woman." She clapped her hands together. "Try the Valentino on."

Now, here's the thing: in the past I'd always let myself be swayed by Suzanne's dictates. I mean, she's French, she's bossy, she has classic taste…and on the other hand, I've been known to commit more than a few fashion *faux pas,* as both Kat and Megan have kindly pointed out to me. Or not so kindly pointed out—they still snicker over one of the outfits I chose to go vamp-hunting in when Cyrus Kane was the big bad in Maplesburg. Kat says when she saw me in my boots and diaphanous tunic and enormous gothic cross, she simply assumed I was channeling Cher.

So anyway, when Suzanne laid down the style law, I usually complied. But this time I didn't.

"I really think this is the one, Suzanne," I said smoothly. "Of course, I'd like to see myself in it. Do you mind?"

I gave her an unwavering look. Her gaze flickered. Shrugging, she stepped out of my way.

"But it is your choice entirely, Tashya," she said with a tight smile. All her smiles were tight, though, so that probably didn't mean anything. "Since you are not interested in them I shall retrieve the Valentino and the Rodriguez."

Nope, I'd been wrong. Her tight smile meant she was pissed off, and so did her stiff demeanor as she left me to take the all-important mirror test without her hovering around me. But that suited me just fine, because I didn't want my first impression of myself in the Galliano to be colored by her opinion. I moved to the mirror and realized that it seemed to be angled slightly away from me.

"Personally, I think the famous French chic is

damned overrated, but what can you expect from a country that produced an egomaniac like Napoleon?" The languid, faintly English-accented drawl came from directly behind me as I moved in front of the mirror. I spun around, startled by Mrs. Moneybags's silent approach. From under the coffee-and-cream brim of her hat, her shadowed eyes behind her sunglasses flicked appraisingly over me. "It's exquisite on you," she murmured thoughtfully. "Truly exquisite. Take a look, Miss Crosse."

"Thanks," I said, recovering my composure and turning to face the mirror. "Coming from someone who's obviously a style expert herself, that's quite a complim—"

My words died in my suddenly dry throat. I stared into the mirror and saw the rack of clothes I was standing beside, the arrangement of white roses beside the cash register farther back in the store, the gilt-and-dove-gray chair I was resting my hand on.

But there was no reflection of me in the mirror. And there was no reflection of the woman standing behind me.

"How do you know my name?" I asked, barely

able to hear my own voice over the terrible roaring, like a hurricane-force wind, that seemed to be rushing through my head. I reached out a trembling hand and touched the surface of the mirror. As if by magic, a faint imprint of my fingertip appeared on it, but the glass threw back no image of my finger or my arm or any part of me, and the store reflected behind me appeared to be empty.

"La, madam!" The cool tones were tinged with laughter, and now the English accent was more discernible. I felt suddenly sure that if I turned around, I wouldn't see a twenty-first century woman dressed in Chanel with sunglasses obscuring her amused eyes and an elegant chignon pinned up under her hat, but a woman from the court of a mad king whose excesses had lost him thirteen colonies; a beauty with powdered and piled hair, hiding her cruel smile behind a fan. "'Tis no wonder, is it? I dare to say you know mine, do you not?"

"Yes." My own voice seemed to lack all strength. Slowly I turned, but my supposition had been incorrect. There was nothing about the fashionably dressed woman facing me that made her seem out of place in Suzanne's shop, nothing at all to suggest that she—

But there was, I saw as my gaze froze on her Manolos, floating several inches above the carpeted floor. And the reason I hadn't noticed at first was because I wasn't standing on the floor anymore, either.

"Lady Jasmine, I presume?" My throat felt like it was clogged with gravel. Perhaps it was, I thought, closing my eyes dizzily as the room began to spin around me. Maybe I'd died and hadn't known it. Maybe even now I was lying in my own grave, grasping for a rope that wasn't there, a rope that was supposed to set a coffin bell's frantic, pealing alarm to ringing but that would now remain silent, leaving me alone in the darkness forever—

"Mon Dieu!" Suzanne's shocked exclamation was thick with horror. I forced my eyes open and saw her staring at me from a few feet away. Her glance flicked wildly to Jasmine, and her face went white under her *maquillage*.

"Exactly, madam—your *dieu,* not mine," Jasmine drawled. "I discarded my faith long ago. How amusing it would be to find out that you had, too."

"Suzanne, run," I said in the rusty tone that

seemed to be my new way of talking. "Don't tell yourself you're not seeing what you're seeing, because you are. She's a—"

"*Une non-morte,*" Suzanne said through bloodless lips, backing away as Jasmine advanced on her. "An abomination. Something that should be dead and damned but walks among us. When I was *une petite,* the old women in my village used to whisper about such evil things, but I thought their talk was the clacking of foolish tongues." Suddenly her hand flew up to fumble beneath the neckline of her black dress. She drew out the object that was secured by a fine gold chain around her neck and held it up to Jasmine as she came closer.

Jasmine halted as if she had been turned to stone.

"As you see, I did not lose my faith, vampire," Suzanne said, her manicured fingertips pressed tightly against the small crucifix. "I may have come a long way from the poor village I was born in, but I never turned away from the church. You will let me pass."

"It seems I have no choice, Frenchwoman," Jasmine said, her lips curving into a smile that didn't match the quiver of fury in her voice. "But one victory does not win a war."

Suzanne edged by her, the crucifix still held in front of her like a tiny shield. She paused by the counter, reached behind it, and retrieved a black leather handbag. "*C'est vrai,*" she said with a barely perceptible nod. "But me, I am not interested in fighting a war that could cost me my immortal soul. I am leaving this town now. I will never return."

She meant it, I realized as she walked shakily but purposefully toward the door. With only a handbag and the clothes on her back, Suzanne was walking away from the business she had built up from nothing. My first thought was that she was crazy.

My second thought was that the former dress-shop owner just might be the sanest person in Maplesburg.

The door swung closed behind her. Through the plate-glass window I saw her walk by the limo's Ray-Ban-wearing chauffeur, her posture stiff and her heels clicking a staccato beat against the sidewalk. As soon as she was past him, however, Suzanne did something I was willing to bet she hadn't done since she'd been a young girl in a village somewhere in France.

She ran like hell.

"La, such a dreary creature!" The skin around Lady Jasmine's nostrils was still white with anger, but her tone was deliberately dismissive. "Prattling about the church like any peasant washerwoman! I had thought she might be an interesting addition to my circle, but it seems I misjudged—"

"You might be a Queen but you're still a vampire," I said through numb lips. "How can you be out and about in the daytime without bursting into flames?"

Jasmine's lips curled up in a tiny smile. "How can you?"

"You know I'm still safe in the sunlight because I haven't fully turned yet," I said tightly. "I haven't experienced a lot of the symptoms that go with being a vamp, like—"

"Like having no reflection in a silver mirror?" she asked silkily. "Perhaps you are changing more quickly than you realize."

Okay, I admit it: I'm not exactly proud of the way I'd wimped out up until that point. Granted, the no-reflection thing had shaken me badly and finding myself face-to-face with Lady Jasmine—excuse me, Lady Jasmine the *Cruel*—had shaken me even more badly. But that was no excuse for turning into a big bowl of Jell-O. After all, Jasmine wasn't the first vamp I'd gone up against. Heck, she wasn't even the first Queen Vamp. Although my sisters and I hadn't become intimately acquainted with Zena before her brief sojourn in Maplesburg had been tragically cut short by Megan staking her, we'd learned a thing or two about the way her twisted mind worked.

And one of her favorite tricks was to go on the offense whenever she wanted to divert our attention from something. I had the feeling that Jasmine's last comment had been made for the same reason, and I suddenly knew why.

I gave her the same thin smile she'd given me. "Now I get it. The whole object of your showing up here was to make me think you weren't affected by the sunlight like ordinary vamps. Maybe you even hoped I'd tell Megan. After all, a Daughter who doesn't feel she can relax her vigilance in the daytime is eventually going to make mistakes, right?" My smile tightened. "Your limo's got black-tinted windows. When your driver pulled up, he made sure to stop right under the awning. You can only function in the daytime if you make sure to stay out of the sun."

"You've found me out," Jasmine said lightly, but behind her sunglasses her eyes flashed with quick anger. "Have you found yourself out yet?"

"What do you mean?" She was using the same trick, I warned myself, only this time she was trying to throw me off balance with cryptic comments.

"You avoided the light just as I did. You passed through the laneway, did you not? A wise move, to choose a fully shadowed passage between two buildings, and to then step directly under the fabric shade that shields this establishment." She held up a hand. "Pray do not deny it, for I know much more than you think I do. La, I even know that you went to earth this morning with that pitiful female who yearns not for the touch of a strong male lover, but for the softness of another woman. I wonder, will she still be as enamoured of you when she learns that those who aid you can expect no mercy?"

My heart seemed to freeze in my chest. I could ignore her ridiculous insinuation that I wasn't invulnerable to sunlight, but not the veiled menace in her voice when she'd spoken about Brook. "That better not have been a threat against my friend," I said, rage hoarsening my voice. "Because if you hurt her in any way I'll find you and send you to hell, even if it takes me the rest of—"

"Such vehemence!" Jasmine laughed lightly, stepping back from me in mock fear. "And so misplaced! No, I have no immediate plans for your tomboyish companion, madam. My thoughts were running in an entirely different direction indeed." She turned slightly to face the counter behind her. "Pale flowers are so insipid, do you not agree? To my mind, they only look appropriate on a casket."

"What are you talking about?" I snapped. Then I looked past her to the vase of flowers that sat beside the cash register. My breath abruptly left my lungs as I finally understood the reason behind Lady Jasmine's smile of triumph.

The roses that had been white only a moment ago were now withered and dead…and totally black.

"Black roses," I said unsteadily. "You've found out that *Chernoye Roza*'s hit man is here in Maplesburg. You don't care about Brook or me…it's Dmitri Malkovich you're after."

Chapter 10

"Oh, 'tis too unfair!" Jasmine's lips formed a disappointed pout. "Now that you have guessed my secret, surely you would not warn him? Be assured, madam, that the members of the murderous society he has sworn fealty to do not warn *us* before they attack."

"You better believe I intend to warn him," I said tightly. "I know Black Rose wouldn't extend the same courtesy, but we're not talking about Black Rose, we're talking about a human being. Maybe

I've turned enough so that silver doesn't reflect my image anymore, but I haven't turned enough to stand by while a vamp attacks a human." I advanced toward her, my muscles tensed, but to my surprise she stood back to let me pass.

"Go, then," she said with a shrug. "Perhaps I shall regret my graciousness later, but I find myself unwilling to engage with you over such a trifle."

I paused in the doorway. "Really? See, I kind of thought that the reason you're chickening out is because you find yourself unwilling to flash-fry," I said with a flicker of satisfaction at her predicament. "I mean, we both know how risky it is for a vamp to get into a knock-down, drag-out fight when a few steps in the wrong direction could burn you to a crisp. But hey, if you want to pretend you're doing this out of the goodness of your heart, be my—what the *hell?*!"

A friggin' *bee* had stung me, I thought as I jerked my arm in toward my body. And it had friggin' *hurt,* not to mention it had ruined my triumphant little speech to Jasmine. I examined my forearm, but instead of the tiny red puncture wound I expected, I was shocked to see a raw, red wound about the size of a dime. The edges of the wound looked seared and bubbly, and from the center a wisp of smoke rose. It disappeared into the pin-size shaft of sunlight coming through a minuscule rip in the awning above.

I heard the sound of a lock falling into place behind me. I spun around to see Jasmine on the other side of the store's iron-grilled door. She flipped the Open sign around so that it read Closed, and took her sunglasses off to reveal irises as red as blood.

But I was too busy kicking myself to care that she'd dropped her Mrs. Moneybags mask. Smoke and mirrors—those were her tools and she'd used them to the hilt. And I'd been stupid enough to fall for them. From the start she'd kept me off balance by one means or another; first with Suzanne, then with her veiled threats toward Brook, and finally by her trick with the roses to make me think Dmitri was her target. But all along she'd been maneuvering me into the very position I was in now. It was no use asking myself how she'd known before I did that I'd become as vulnerable to daylight as any other vampire. That didn't matter. Getting out of here without turning into Tash-on-the-barbie did.

And that wasn't going to be as easy as I'd…well, actually I hadn't thought it was going to be easy. I still didn't. Time had flown while I'd been in the store—I'm a girl, I was shopping, so sue me, okay? But time *hadn't* been the only thing that had flown; the sun had, too, across the sky. And instead of a blessedly dark chunk of shade under the awning, now there was only a slice of shadow where I was standing by the door.

And I was sharing that meager safety zone with Jasmine's vamp chauffeur, I realized as he stepped away from the wall of the building and came toward me.

"She's locked the door," I informed him. "Here's the deal. She wants me to burn and you're expendable. Got any bright ideas about how we can—"

His foot came up in a swift, arcing kick that caught me under the chin and sent me reeling backward. My hands flew out instinctively to break my fall and pain seared across my left palm.

There was no mistaking it for a bee sting this time. Agony slammed into me with all the force of a freight train, and I felt myself pitching farther backward toward the glare of the midafternoon sun. Pure adrenaline raced through me, giving me the strength to twist out of the fall and throw myself forward onto the sidewalk by chauffeur-vamp's feet.

I can hear you asking now: hey, girlfriend, where were all the normal people? You know, the ones who don't have problems with their teeth going all sharp and pointy at inconvenient times, the ones who actually *like* strolling around on a sunny afternoon, window-shopping or walkin' to the soda shop to share a cherry coke with their gal or just pausing by the hardware store to pass the time of day with—

Hold on a minute. I said Maplesburg *looked* like a Norman Rockwell painting, I didn't say that it was one. As I threw myself forward I saw a businessman across the street frowningly check his watch and hasten into the entrance to an accounting firm. A couple of teenage girls were heading toward me, totally focused on their giggling conversation. An immaculately turned-out übermommy wheeling a massive Mac Stroller down the middle of the sidewalk with all the arrogance of a trucker barreling a semi down the freeway cooed perfunctorily at her matched set of Ralph Lauren-ad twins and went back to talking on her cell phone.

And there you have it: a charming slice of life in my hometown. But I didn't have time for warm and fuzzy, because chauffeur-vamp's booted foot was coming toward me again. I tried to roll sideways, but the floating gauze of my brand new Galliano gown impeded me. I closed my eyes and waited for the impact I knew was coming.

Except it didn't. I opened my eyes enough to squint through my lashes at the situation and saw C-Vamp's kick whizz through the air six inches or so to the left of me.

Half a heartbeat later I realized what I'd done. I'd *shimmered* sideways, in the same eerie way I'd seen one or two vamps do in the past when I'd been trying to kill them. One second they'd been in line with the business end of my stake and the next moment they'd been out of harm's way, without appearing to have moved at all. I'd always thought it was a nifty maneuver, and now I was doing it.

Floating free, my dress wasn't an impediment anymore. Better yet, the Louboutins had become a deadly weapon. The chauffeur's forceful kick into thin air had thrown him off balance. I took aim with a spike heel and let him have it in the kneecap, driving him backward, but just as it had done with me, fear gave him an acrobatic agility. He wavered precariously on the sharp dividing line between the awning's shadow and the full blaze of sunlight on the sidewalk before he reversed his fall through sheer muscle and will. He crashed to the ground, and at first I thought he'd landed safely on the shadowed side of the demarcation line.

"…told her, 'Carmela, the nanny-cam doesn't lie. It doesn't matter that it was more convenient for you while you cleaned the nursery, the upstairs bathroom is for our personal use only.' And then of course when Tyler and Pomme realized this morning that she was gone they started crying—"

I didn't hear what came next in Übermommy's cell-phone conversation because of the high-pitched scream coming from the chauffeur. My attention jerked back to him, and I've got to tell you, I really, really wish it hadn't.

He hadn't totally avoided the sunlight. A bright, golden ray fell on the side of his face, and where it had touched him, his flesh had burst into flames.

"—to get an English nanny to replace her, but the ones I interviewed last year had all kinds of outrageous minimum wage demands—"

Übermommy shot me a dirty look as she was forced to make a minute adjustment to her trajectory to avoid mowing me down. The wheels of the stroller passed within an inch of the chauffeur's writhing body, but she seemed totally oblivious to him.

She *was* oblivious, I realized. And so was everyone else in the vicinity. It was in Jasmine's best interests to keep Maplesburg's residents complacently disbelieving when it came to a vampire infiltration of their town, so she'd cast a general *glamyr* over the passersby. As an example of her power, it was impressive…and terrifying.

But I had an even more immediately terrifying situation to deal with. I'd made the fatal error of taking my attention from Chauffeur-Vamp for a moment, and before anyone goes all what-were-you-*thinking?* on me, I'll tell you: I was thinking that a vamp with half a head was pretty much down for the count. I was wrong. Out of the corner of my eye I saw his black-suited figure rise up, and I just had time to wonder why the Fates had picked little Tashie Crosse's life to turn into a clichéd horror movie before he lurched toward me. I flexed my newly discovered shimmering muscles and slipped sideways to avoid him, which nearly turned out to be fatal error number two in as many seconds.

Imagine a fireplace poker. Now imagine a blast furnace—stay with me here, there's only one more step. Imagine said poker being shoved into said blast furnace for as long as it takes it to turn cherry-red, then being thrust into my arm just above my elbow and plowing a furrow of liquid fire all the way up to my shoulder.

The pain was so intense that it blotted out everything. Blackness rose up in front of my eyes, and my knees began to buckle. The furrow of fire hacked lower, now plowing its way downward into my forearm.

"Dammit, Crosse, don't pass out! You're falling into the sunlight!"

The desperate shout coming from the direction of the laneway penetrated my consciousness. My blurred vision took in the sight of my right arm, ablaze now from wrist to elbow. The artfully slashed sleeves of my dress had fluttered aside and were only singed, but the tinkling metal coins were melting into my sizzling flesh. I swayed slightly, and as an innocent-looking shaft of sunlight fell onto the back of my hand, the skin there began to smoke and bubble.

Shimmering was out of the question. The most I could manage was a stagger, but that was enough. As soon as my arm was out of the sun the flames instantly extinguished themselves, but the damage had been done. My arm was one long burn, the skin flaking away in black flakes and the tissue underneath raw and seared. No visible flames remained, but I had the feeling that just below the surface of that raw, red furrow I was still burning and that if I plunged my arm into a tub of ice water I would hear a sound like wet embers hissing.

I suddenly wanted to be sick. I fought down the nausea with difficulty, and then nearly tossed my cookies anyway as I saw Chauffeur-Vamp in his final death throes.

His failed lunge toward me had evidently been his swan song. He lay on his back where he had finally fallen, half-in and half-out of the last scrap of shade thrown by the awning. His right side was nothing more than a heap of soot-blackened bones, his ribs twisted by the heat into strange and fantastical shapes, like a turkey carcass painted by an abstract artist, and his right leg drawn up in a last spasm of agony. But as awful as his body looked, his face was worse.

The Ray-Bans had melted at the bridge, and on the unmarked side of his face the left lens still crookedly shielded his eye. He didn't have a right side to his face anymore; just a skull, the jawbone stretched wide in a silent scream of agony and an eye socket that would have been empty except for the pool of melted plastic that gave me the sickening feeling he was still watching me with a liquid-black gaze.

Was he?

"Not for long," I said in a hollow, whistling voice that didn't sound like mine. I bent unsteadily and slipped off my shoe. Crouching over him, I drove the Louboutin's spike heel deep into the unburned left side of his chest. A moment later he was dust.

"Good thinking, Mata Hari. I'm pretty sure I saw him twitch when you staked him." Shoe in hand, I

whirled around to see Brook standing behind me.
She was swathed from head to toe in the old blanket
I'd seen her wear earlier, and bundled under her
arm was another one. She held it out. "Wrap
yourself in this and let's get back to my place so I
can look at your arm." Shakiness threaded through
her peremptory tone and her mint-green eyes
suddenly took on a sheen. "I thought I was going to
see you burn to death. I raced back into the
basement and got these blankets, but I was sure that
I was going to be too late. Warn a girl the next time
you decide to turn yourself into a one-woman
wienie-roast, will you?"

"I hope there never is a next time." My tone was
just as unsteady as hers as I nodded at the pile of
ash that had been my would-be killer. "He worked
for Jasmine. Somehow she knew I'd lost my invul-
nerability and she locked me out of the store. She's
still in there."

"You sure?" Brook jerked her head at the door.
I followed her glance and saw it standing ajar.
"Maybe she left while you were preoccupied with
staying alive."

"Left to go where? It would make more sense for

her to stay here until the sun sets." Cautiously I pushed the door farther open but before I could enter, Brook stepped in front of me and into the store. She cut off my protest.

"You're in no shape, Crosse, and I need something to restore my macho pride after just standing there like a dummy while that vamp was trying to kill you."

I didn't agree with her second point, but I couldn't muster the strength to argue with the first. I *wasn't* in any shape to risk running into Jasmine, and besides, it seemed obvious Brook's guess was right and she was gone. The interior of the store was empty. The fitting room doors stood open, and as Brook returned from the storage room at the back of the store, she shook her head. I sank down on one of the dove-gray chairs, feeling suddenly shaky with reaction.

The store didn't just seem empty, it seemed to have shrunken somehow. Some vital spark had gone out of it. The same racks of luscious clothes still lined the walls, the same small but exquisite displays of shoes and leather goods and perfumes still stood here and there about the shop, but it had the air of being long abandoned. I didn't realize I'd shivered until Brooklyn gave me a sharp-eyed look.

"You feel it too, huh?" she asked, her tone flat. She went to one of the racks and pulled out a white linen Jil Sander shift. From an adjacent belt rack she selected a butter-soft leather Prada belt.

I shook my head weakly. "I never thought I'd hear myself say it, but I'm not in the mood to try on clothes right now."

"Who said anything about trying on?" With a quick tug, Brook tore a strip of linen from the shift's neckline to its hem. She caught my appalled glance and gave me her tough-girl grin. "This is going to be gruesome, Mata Hari, so don't look."

I averted my eyes. "I know you're not into fashion, but I didn't realize you had a hate-on for designer dresses," I protested. "Do you make a habit of sneaking into stores and ripping up the merchandise?"

"Only when I need to bind up a wound." She reached into one of the capacious pockets of her cargo pants, scowled, tried another pocket. "And only when I know the owner's never coming back. Where the hell...oh, here it is."

She was holding a plastic jar shaped like a bear. I raised my eyebrows. "Got sugar cravings again?"

"Honey's the best thing for a burn," she replied, uncapping the pour spout on the bear's head. "My Bubbe swore by it, so I always carry some with me in my vamp first aid kit—which, by the way, is one of the reasons I wear these *schmattah* pants you fashionistas seem to think are beyond the pale. That dress you've got on is gorgeous, but hardly practical."

"But I've got you to take care of me," I retorted.

My words had been light, but I regretted them when I saw a dull brick color rise under Brooklyn's skin. Her gaze dropped swiftly to my arm. "Yeah, babe, you've got me," she said, obviously trying and failing for the same light tone I'd used. She squatted down beside my chair, her shoulders squaring. "Okay, this is going to hurt," she said, her briskness sounding forced. "Anything would hurt on flesh as raw as this, so bite down on this."

As I reached for the Prada belt she held out to me, the coins on the unsinged left sleeve of my dress shivered and a faint tinkling like icy bells rang out from them. I let my hand drop. "I don't need it," I said abruptly.

"Don't be a hero, Crosse." She kept the belt extended to me. "Believe me, you'll want—"

"Can we just get this over with?" I snapped.

Brook gave me a searching look. "Yeah, sure," she said evenly. "Hold out your arm."

I felt ashamed of my outburst. "Shit, Brookie, I'm sorry," I said, tightening my jaw in anticipation of the pain to come. "I know I'll probably wish I'd taken you up on the belt offer, but I can't help thinking that Jasmine would tough it out without a crutch. If she can—" I drew in a hissing breath between my teeth as her fingertips, dipped in honey and surprisingly gentle, brushed against my arm. "If she can, I can," I said, clenching my teeth. "But talk to me to take my mind off this, okay? What did you mean when we walked in here and you asked me if I felt it, too?" A wave of agony overtook me as honey dribbled stickily from Brooklyn's fingertips onto my burned flesh. The room swam around me for a second and I forced myself to focus on what she was saying.

"Remember when you asked me about my sister and I told you it was a long story?" She didn't wait for my reply, which was fine by me since my teeth were clenched so tightly I couldn't have gotten a word out. "I lied," Brook went on, her gaze fixed on my arm. "It's not a particularly long story, it's just one I don't like talking about. But maybe it's time I did—and maybe you're the only person I can tell it to. Brace yourself, I'm going to smear some honey on this bad part by your elbow."

Bracing myself didn't help. The pain came toward me in a wave, towered over me, then crashed down on me, burying me under its weight. I hung on to Brook's voice as if it were a life belt.

"Xandra and I are twins, like I told you. You'd think we'd get along—well, maybe you wouldn't make that assumption, since you're a triplet." She smiled briefly, her attention focused on her task. "Anyway, we didn't. From the time we were little, we fought like cats and dogs. I'm not saying that I wouldn't have gone to the wall for her, or her for me—hell, I'm not saying the two of us didn't do exactly that whenever someone else said or did something against our twin—but although we loved each other, we couldn't seem to be friends. It got worse when we were teenagers. It got worse still when I came out of the closet."

"She…she was ashamed you were gay?" I managed to ask as Brook ground more broken glass into me. Actually she was applying more honey, her touch featherlight. It only felt like broken glass.

"I think it was more that she saw the difference in our sexual orientation as a betrayal of our twinship. That wasn't me, that was the bottle," Brook said with a quick grin that didn't reach her eyes. "It's empty. Now I'm going to bind your arm." She picked up a strip of linen that had started life as a Jil Sander dress and was now being demoted to a big Band-Aid. Carefully she laid the end of the strip on my sticky skin and began winding it around the burn. "But whatever her reasons, she distanced herself even further from me after that. I went punk, she went preppy. I fixed motorcycles out of Bubbe's garage and rode a Harley, she was working toward a degree in art history and got around in a second-hand Volvo. Then came the biggie—she got the opportunity to study for a couple of years in Italy and she couldn't leave Smith's Falls fast enough. That was the final break between us."

Gently Brook pressed the end of the strip against the honey. I sucked in a hoarse breath. "I've got the no-reflection thing, the sunlight thing and the fang thing," I ground out. "I'd trade them all for the superhealing thing regular vamps have. Smith's Falls is the name of your hometown? I've never heard of it."

"Most people never will, now," Brook replied, her eyes suddenly shadowed. "But I'll get to that in a minute. The fight between Xandra and me before she left was mostly my fault. Bubbe'd had a stroke the previous year. Not a massive one but after she had it she wasn't as independent as she'd been. When Xandra informed me she was going to Italy, I blew up. I told her she was being selfish, that it was time she helped out with Bubbe, that I'd been thinking of doing some traveling myself, maybe going out west on my Harley. It was all bullshit. I was just jealous—jealous that she was being offered the chance of a lifetime, jealous that she knew what she wanted in life and was going after it. Mostly I was jealous of her being straight." She reached for the last linen strip and grinned wryly at me. "Yeah, I know. Totally fucked up, right? But small towns aren't the easiest places to grow up in when you're gay and Xandra seemed to have it so easy compared to me. None of that matters now, anyway. Short version is, we both said stuff we couldn't take back, she left, things started going weird in Smith's Falls—just little things at first, like people who'd always been around suddenly dropping out of sight. Then Bubbe had another stroke and this time she didn't pull through. *Baruch dayan emet,*" she added softly. She met my gaze. "Blessed be the one true Judge. It's what Jews say when hearing about a death, but in this case the words have a special meaning for me. I'm just thankful Bubbe didn't survive to live through the nightmare Smith's Falls became. As it was, hers was one of the last natural deaths that occurred there."

Looking down, Brook resumed winding the bandage around my arm. "I phoned Xandra in Florence, of course. In our religion, the body has to be buried as soon as possible, so there was no way she could get back in time for the funeral, but even if there had been, she didn't have the money for a plane ticket. Poor art students usually don't," Brook added with a shrug. "She said she wanted to come home to sit shiva for Bubbe—that's a period of mourning after the burial—and asked me if I'd loan her the money for the flight. I said she should have thought of that when she'd taken off and left me with the responsibility of staying with our grandmother. Part of me will never forgive myself for refusing her. But a bigger part of me is grateful that I was such a bitch." She smoothed down the tail end of the linen strip. "I shoulda been a doctor, babe. I don't know if that'll heal without leaving a scar, but it'll heal, and that's the main thing. How much longer to sundown, do you think? Fifteen, twenty minutes?"

About to argue her estimate, I glanced toward the window and saw long shadows falling across the town square on the other side of the street. I'd been so absorbed in Brooklyn's story that I hadn't noticed how much time had passed, I realized. I nodded. "About that, I'd guess. Aren't you going to tell me the rest?"

Her smile was tight. "Not much more to tell, Mata Hari. I sat shiva for my Bubbe, a week or so later I went back to fixing motorcycles and wondering why there seemed to be fewer and fewer people around in the daytime and a couple of nights after that some fuckin' clownshoes whose bike I was fixing bit me and I turned vamp myself. I realized I'd never be able to fight off the hunger if I stuck around in a place where killing and draining humans had become the town's regular pastime, so one night I saddled up my trusty Harley and got the hell out of Smith's Falls. The town had died by then, anyway."

I frowned. "What do you mean, the town had died?"

She shrugged. "No one ever came right out and said the word *vampire,* but a lot of people suspected what had happened to sleepy little ol' Smith's Falls. Some of them packed up their families and left without looking back. That's what the owner of this store did, right?"

"Suzanne." I nodded. "Everything she had was tied up in this dress shop, but she didn't think twice about walking away."

"Smart lady," Brook grunted. "Others in my town weren't so smart. They told themselves it was crazy to leave without trying to sell their house, pack their belongings, let the kids graduate with their class—never mind that by then the school only had a handful of students and three or four teachers. They kept their eyes closed because they were afraid of what they might see if they opened them. Some of them, the lucky ones, were killed. The others became the reason why tourists get a bad feeling when they drive through Smith's Falls—a bad enough feeling that most of them don't stop. Those who do—well, if the boarded-up diner and the empty pumps at Davie's Sunoco and the stains on the sidewalk that they try to tell themselves are rust but that look a whole lot more like blood—if all those aren't enough to hustle them back into their cars before the sun starts to set, they sure give it the old college try when they see the hordes of vamps coming at them through the dusk. I saw a traveling salesman once who—" Her lips tightened. "Nah, let's not get into that. The thing is, when I stepped through the door to this store I got the same feeling I had in Smith's Falls before I was turned. This town might still look okay on the outside, but it's dying, Crosse. Parts of it might be dead already."

I looked away. "I know. I think I've known for a while. I've just been keeping my eyes shut, like the people in Smith's Falls, but what happened today made me open them." I made myself meet her gaze.

"I'll see Megan and Kat tonight and tell them I've changed my mind about infiltrating Jasmine's inner circle. I'm going to bring the bitch down."

Standing up, I took a deep breath. "Or I'm going to die trying."

Chapter 11

"If you think I'm leaving my weapon at the door you're crazy, vamp." Jack Rawls, Kat's rough-trade boyfriend as Megan had once called him, secured his grip on his specially modified nail gun—specially modified because it shot silver-tipped nails—and gave Brook a junkyard dog grin. She gave him one back.

"Then you don't sit in on this meeting. Tash's orders."

"Since when did the brat start laying down rules

when it comes to Darkheart & Crosse?" Megan, Mikhail one pace behind her as always, narrowed her eyes at Brooklyn. "Have we met?"

"No," Brooklyn lied. "The stake gets stashed, too, Daughter."

It was several hours after my conversation with Brook at Suzanne's store. In the interval I'd phoned Kat and asked her to arrange a council of war for that evening.

"A council of war, sweetie?" she said cautiously. "I assume you mean the war between vamps and humans, no? Not to be tactless, darling, but which side will you be representing?"

"My own," I said shortly. "Just do it, Kat. I want everyone there—Grandfather, you and Megan, right down to Ramon."

"No can do," she said immediately. "I run a business, remember? If I'm not going to be at the Hot Box tonight, my manager has to be there to keep an eye on things."

"Ramon's fought with us. He's earned the right," I said, more sharply than I'd intended. "This is important, Kat."

On the other end of the line I heard her draw in a

breath. "I'll temporarily promote Jean-Paul from bartender to manager for the night," she said, her drawl no longer in evidence. "Where do we meet you?"

"I'll phone you back in a couple of hours and let you know," I replied. "No offence, sis, but the last time we had a family get-together I seem to remember garlic lassoes and stakes being part of the festivities. I'd prefer not to be set up this time."

I hung up. Brook, who was standing beside me at the public pay phone outside the Rialto, gave me a crooked smile but all she said was, "You aren't anyone's little sister anymore, are you, Mata Hari?" She glanced up at the movie theater's marquee. "Did I hear you say something about a couple of hours to kill? 'Cause it just so happens that that all-time classic, *The Street Fighter,* starring the incomparable Sonny Chiba, starts in five minutes. We might even get in the first fifteen minutes of *Return of the Street Fighter.*"

"Be still my heart," I said wryly. "Okay, but I reserve the right to throw my popcorn box at the screen if it's as schlocky as I think it's going to be."

"Nuh-uh, Crosse," she said, linking her arm

through my uninjured one as we headed for our secret and non-paying entrance to the Rialto. "Like I said, it's a classic. And who knows, you might even pick up some pointers for the next time Jazz-baby sics one of her thugs on you."

The movie *had* been schlocky and I *had* thrown my popcorn box. I'd also laughed my head off—the dubbing was truly horrendous—jumped out of my seat twice and closed my eyes more than once. And every so often I'd glanced over at Brook, sitting transfixed in the seat beside me and shoveling popcorn into her mouth like a little kid, and I'd felt a wave of love wash over me.

Okay, I know what you're thinking. And guess what—I don't care. Maybe it's like Kat says when she's feeling particularly Healerish: labels don't matter. The only important thing in this world is love. Brook was gay and I wasn't, but those were just labels. They didn't change the way I felt about her then, and they don't change the way I feel about her now.

And no label is adequate to describe her love for me.

But to get back to the night in question: when

we left the Rialto, Brook and I took a short stroll up the street to the offices of Darkheart & Crosse. I figured no one would expect me to hold the meeting there, which made it the perfect choice. I was still wearing the Galliano, partly because I didn't want to disturb the bandages on my arm by changing outfits, and partly because…well, I don't know, exactly. The best I can explain it is that it didn't feel like a dress anymore, it felt like armor. It had come through my fight with Chauffeur-Vamp and my subsequent Joan of Arc imitation with only a singe or two and a few melted coins on the sleeve. The way I saw it, the damage only enhanced its decadent allure.

So the stage was set. I looked drop-dead undead, Brooklyn looked toughly sexy, and although this was long before I started studying Sun Tzu's *The Art of War,* I'd already stumbled upon two of its prime precepts: *appear where you are not expected,* and my personal fave, *the one who first occupies the battlefield awaiting the enemy is at ease.*

Sonny Chiba couldn't have done better. In fact, with my vamp abilities I had him beat, because while Brook was checking everyone at the door, I was watching from a shadowy corner of the corridor at ceiling level (see *The Art of War: defend where the enemy cannot attack*).

And Megan was definitely acting like the enemy right now.

"My stake is my right hand," she said coldly, and I thought pompously. Brook evidently thought so, too, because from my vantage point near the ceiling I saw her roll her eyes.

"Then I hope you weren't planning on taking notes, because your right hand's staying here," she informed Megan. "Unless…"

"Unless what?" Megan's gaze narrowed in suspicion.

Brook shrugged carelessly. "Unless you want to swear on your stake that you won't attack Tash or me."

I'd told Brook to offer her this alternative. I watched Megan's expression, hoping I hadn't miscalculated.

She gave a brusque nod and brought the hilt of her stake to her lips. "I swear by Lilith, Mother of the First Daughter, that I shall not use my weapon against Tashya or you. While we're in this meeting," she added with a humorless smile that faded as she stared more closely at Brook. "The alleyway where the brat was buying blood," she said with a flicker of disgust. "I knew I'd run into you—"

"Her name's Tashya." Brook's hand was wrapped tightly around Megan's bicep, her reaction so quick that I hadn't even seen her move. Megan stiffened, and beside her Mikhail's form seemed to become less solid.

"Tell your boyfriend that if he starts shapeshifting, you'll be dead before he can say woof," Brook said evenly. Megan flicked a glance at Mikhail and his form solidified again. "This is a council of war," Brook said softly to Megan. "Your sister's meeting with you because she thinks she can help you. You got out of checking your weapon, but leave the attitude outside. Are you hearing me loud and clear, Daughter?"

Very deliberately, Megan put her hand on Brook's and lifted it from her arm. "Five by five. But if you ever touch me again, all bets are off," she said curtly. "Do you hear *me* loud and clear, vamp?"

Without waiting for Brook's reply, she stalked through the doorway, Mikhail behind her. At a nudge from Kat, Jack scowlingly handed his nail gun to Brook and they went in, too. Ramon had been the first to arrive and he was already in the office, which left Darkheart and Liz Dixon to bring up the rear of the procession. They had their backs to me, so I couldn't see Darkheart's expression as he paused by Brook.

"Strange days, when *vampyr* and human come together," he rumbled as Brook finished patting down Liz for weapons and took a step toward him. "Stranger still when *vampyr* and human mingle in the same body, *nyet?*" Although he couldn't have seen me, he half turned in my direction. "My granddaughter will confirm that I carry no threat to her."

He knew I was watching him. The small discs of silvery metal on my dress shivered, their tinkling so faint that it might have been my imagination. Of course he knew. Megan was all about vengeance; Kat, about forgiveness. And Darkheart—

A Daughter's power comes from bone and sinew and a Healer's from her human heart, but Seekers do not pursue power, only knowledge. Underestimate him at your peril, for knowledge is

*the most powerful weapon of all. The old man may
prove to be your greatest ally...or your most formidable foe.*

It had been a long day, okay? I'd almost lip-
locked with a bat, a Queen Vamp had amused
herself by fucking with me, and my immunity to
sunlight had chosen a *really* inconvenient time to
break down. Plus my arm was throbbing. And I'd
overloaded on sugar this morning and hadn't eaten
anything else all day except for a couple of kernels
of popcorn before I hurled my box at Sonny Chiba.

So the cold voice that had just spoken in my
head had to be a result of my overstressed imagination, right?

I knew it wasn't.

Megan had once confided in me—this was when
we were confiding in each other—that before she'd
grown into her full powers as a Daughter, she'd
wondered if she was going crazy. Only when it was
almost too late did she realize that the voice she'd
been channeling in her subconscious had been the
spirit of Lilith. Kat's experience had been similar,
although it had been her inner Healer who had come
to her at the most dangerous time of her journey

toward her heritage. But who was I channeling? Zena? Dracula? Elvira, Mistress of the Dark?

I felt the floor beneath my feet and realized I'd allowed myself to drift silently down from my position near the ceiling. I walked out of the shadows toward Darkheart and wasn't surprised when he turned to watch me approach, his hooded gaze sharply assessing under his salt-and-pepper eyebrows.

"Has been many changes for you since we last meet, Natashya," he said, not wasting words on preliminaries.

"Our last meeting was only an evening ago, Grandfather," I reminded him.

"*Da.*" His answer was terse. I decided to skip the social niceties, too.

"When you came into our lives a few months ago, you told Megan and Kat and me that we had destinies to discover, roles to fulfill," I said, choosing my words with care. "But you never told us what your role was, Grandfather. Are you what they call a Seeker?"

His gaze on me didn't waver. "Was not my intention that granddaughters should know this yet, but *da,* is correct. How did you know?" He raised a heavily veined hand before I could reply. "*Nyet,* do not answer. The changes I spoke of are evident. You are more *vampyr* than human now. I see it will be harder to keep secrets from you, Natashya."

He put his hand on the small of Liz's back and they started to enter the Darkheart & Crosse office. Brook stepped in front of him and shot me a questioning glance.

"I haven't searched him yet," she said to me.

I shook my head. "It's okay, Brookie, let him pass."

She stepped back. As Darkheart began to follow Liz through the doorway I spoke again, my tone harsh enough that he turned to look at me. "You say I'm more *vampyr* than human now. That may be so, Seeker, but let me ask you this—am I now more *vampyr* to you than granddaughter?"

Behind Darkheart's gray eyes something seemed to flash brilliantly. Then it was gone, and his gaze on me was steady again. "*Nyet,* Granddaughter. Not yet."

"Whoa, what was that all about?" Brook asked, letting out a tense breath as Darkheart and Liz entered the office. "For a minute there I thought I was going to have to cap your Zaidy, babe."

"I'm not really sure." I gave her a shrug and winced as the burned flesh on my right arm tightened painfully. "Go on in, Brook. I'll be with you in a minute."

"Aren't you going to wait for Malkovich?" She scowled. "Not that I wouldn't prefer we hold this meeting without Black Rose's local Johnny-on-the-spot."

"He'll be here in a second," I told her. "And don't ask me how I know that, either, because I don't have a good answer."

"Yeah, you do, babe," Brook answered quietly. "You're changing over, and the change is getting faster now. That's where all this heightened awareness is coming from." A corner of her mouth lifted in a wry smile. "I thought we could stave it off by not drinking human blood, but that doesn't seem to be working out for either of us, does it?"

"For you it is," I began, but with a quick gesture she waved my assertion away.

"Don't kid a kidder, Crosse. I've started sleeping in the daytime, just like any other undead freak.

And my eyes…" She tried to maintain her smile, but she couldn't. "Hell, I could tell by the expression on your face today when you looked at me. You could see the blood-hunger, couldn't you?" Abruptly she jerked her head up, like an animal scenting danger. "You're right. *Chernoye Roza*'s killer is here. You sure you don't need me to watch your back?"

"I'll be okay." I let my glance linger on her for a second as she passed through the doorway, but then I turned my gaze on the man pushing open the door at the end of the hall that led to the stairs. Dmitri's expression was unreadable as he came closer. I hoped mine was, too.

"Glad you could make it. I want my apartment back," I said by way of greeting.

"That might be a problem. Apparently there was something wrong with the rent check you gave the building's owner," he replied. "I made good on it and told him to switch the name on the lease to mine, so for all intents and purposes it's my apartment now. As a *vampyr,* you won't be able to enter unless I give you permission."

I raised an eyebrow. "You might want to keep

some holy water on hand just in case I show up one night and shoot your theory all to hell, Malkovich."

"You've saved me the trouble by calling this—" His Siberian-blue eyes widened briefly and his quick step forward closed the gap between us. "What happened to your arm?" he asked, the harshness in his tone underlaid with concern.

The slashed sleeves of the Galliano had parted to reveal Brook's neatly wrapped bandage, I saw as I glanced down. I looked up at Dmitri again. "I got up close and personal with some sunlight."

He let out a measured breath. "Then what I was about to say is even more relevant. You're almost completely vampire, Tashya. It's time you let Kat perform a Heal on you." His jaw tightened. "You know what I feel about you. Hell, you gambled on it yesterday when you bet on my not being capable of staking you. I can't stand by and let you cross over to the dark side—"

"You're going to stand by and let me do whatever I have to, Malkovich," I cut in. "In return, I won't blow your cover with Darkheart."

Damn, the man was good-looking, I thought with regret as his gaze iced over. He was in his usual uniform of jeans and a muscle-fitting tee, and he'd obviously had a shower before he'd come here, because his pale, close-cropped hair was still damp. Looking at him through half-closed lashes, it didn't take a whole lot of imagination to see him in my shower, his tanned biceps bulging as he braced himself against the walls and let the pounding spray run down his broad shoulders, his washboard abs, his—

"I'll tell Darkheart myself," Dmitri said flatly. "I probably should have before now. I need to tell him something else tonight, anyway, and I might as well dump all my bad news on him at once."

"What other bad news do you have for him?" I asked sharply.

"My *mafya* contacts finally came up with solid information on David Crosse." Dmitri's gaze lost its iciness. "Your father was killed only weeks after Zena attacked your parents and left her mark on you. A Carpathian peasant who was shown a photo of Crosse confirmed that he'd been the man he'd witnessed being overpowered by three *vampyrs* in a forest one night, and the peasant saw enough before he fled to tell my investigators that the

Americanic put up no resistance at all. It was as if Crosse wanted to die, the old man said."

I closed my eyes briefly. "Yes, that fits with a man who'd just lost the woman he loved to an unimaginable evil."

"If you can understand that, you should be able to understand why I'd rather break my cover than let that same evil overtake you." Dmitri's tone was low and urgent. "I told you, the first time I saw you I knew you held my fate in your—"

"Don't say it!" I opened my eyes, anger pushing aside my grief for a man I'd never known. "I don't want to hold your fate in my hands! I'm having enough trouble dealing with my own fate—and I'm having even more trouble getting your help in dealing with it!"

I glanced toward the open door where the rising sound of conversation signaled a growing impatience with my nonarrival. It was probably thanks to Brook that no one had actually left yet, I thought, but how long she could keep a lid on things was anyone's guess. "I don't intend to go over to the dark side, but I can't allow Kat to perform a Heal on me yet," I said rapidly. "I'll make a deal with you. I won't say anything to Darkheart about you. In return, you walk into that room and listen to my proposal before you bring up the subject of a Heal." I met his eyes and saw indecision flicker behind them. "It's important, Dmitri. When you hear what Brook has to say about her hometown, you'll understand just how important."

He held my gaze for a moment without replying. Then he gave a tight nod. "I'll hear you out, but nothing you could tell me will change my mind."

"No? Ever hear of a town called Smith's Falls?"

He frowned. "No."

"You're about to." I smiled without humor. "After you do, then you can tell me whether you've changed your mind."

I didn't wait for his reply. Turning from him, I walked into the office of Darkheart & Crosse and prepared to fight the battle of my life.

"Forget it." Megan stood up from the conference table. "This meeting's over, as far as I'm concerned."

"After what the gay chick just tol' you about what happened to her hometown?" Ramon, the manager of the Hot Box Club and Kat's best friend, looked around the table with a pugnacious scowl that didn't match his dissolute cherub's features. "I don't know a whole lot about this procedure Tash's willing to try, but I do know she's got *cojones* for even suggesting it. We should talk this out, people."

"There's nothing to talk about." Beside him, Kat spoke up, her tone uncharacteristically strained. "Megan's right, the risk is insane."

"What about the risk to Maplesburg?" Liz Dixon demanded. "We're talking about hundreds of innocents, including children. I'm with Ramon. If Tash is willing to volunteer for this, I think we should at least consider it."

"I'll ramp up the nightly patrols," Megan said as if Liz and Ramon hadn't spoken. "Mikhail and Jack will put in more hours, too. Every vamp we find, we question before we stake them. I know it's always been priority one to find Jasmine's daytime lair, but as of tonight it's our only priority."

"Will not be enough." Darkheart had been looking down at his hands. Now he raised his head, and I found myself flinching at the pain in his eyes as he looked at me. "A Binding is very obscure ritual, Granddaughter. How is it you learn of this?"

"Uh, I snooped in some of your books when you were training us?" I said apologetically. I heard Megan give a snort of disgust, and I turned to her. "Okay, I know it was totally sneaky of me, Meg, but that was before we knew which of the three of us was the Daughter. I thought if I could get an edge over you and Kat, I might tip the scales in my favor."

Two things happened at the end of my little speech. The first was that the coins on my dress struck dully and discordantly against each other, although I would have sworn I hadn't moved a muscle.

And the second thing that happened was that Brook looked across the table at me as if I were someone she didn't know.

"You never change, do you, brat?" Megan said dismissively. "When we were kids I had to keep my diary under lock and key to stop you from snooping through it and now you riffle through Grandfather's personal possessions. Maybe when you grow up a little you'll be ready to take on some responsibility—"

"I thought this council of war was supposed to include all of us. Someone shoulda told me it just included the straight members of Darkheart & Crosse." Ramon folded his arms across the front of the trendy bowling shirt he was wearing. "Darkheart seems to know what this Binding thing is, and so do you, Megan. Kat seems to know, too, but since she never tells me anything I guess I'm not surprised she don't fill me in. Anybody want to let me in on the secret, or should I just get back to the Hot Box?"

"It's not a slam, pal," Jack growled. "I never heard shit about this, either."

"Ditto," Brook said. "Seems like quite a few of us have been kept out of the loop. Even those of us who thought they were in it," she added, her gaze nailing me.

I looked away from the accusation in her eyes, but I knew it was justified. She'd known I intended to infiltrate Jasmine's inner circle. What I'd chosen not to tell her was that I'd come to the conclusion I couldn't penetrate that circle without undergoing a Binding…and the reason I hadn't told her was because I was afraid that she'd be as opposed to it as Megan and Kat were.

I'd taken the coward's way out by trying to put off the inevitable, and even now I was trying to think of some way I could shift the onus onto Dark-heart or Megan to explain to the others what I intended to do. But in the end I didn't have to.

"Binding is exactly what is said," Dmitri stated to the table at large in the Russian accent of his cover identity. "Lesser *vampyr* exchanges blood with more powerful one. Can be several results, all bad. Shall I list, *Gospodin?*" he asked Darkheart.

"Don't bother. I know them off by heart," Megan said, her tone dangerously edged. "Let's see. The brat Binds with Jasmine and doesn't survive. That happens occasionally, especially if the more powerful vamp's an ancient. Which, of course, Lady Jasmine is," she said with a smile that belied the anger in her eyes. "Or there's scenario number two. Tash Binds with the bitch and becomes the living undead. Now *that's* an interesting one, especially to someone like Jasmine. What happens is after the ritual, the Bound vamp—that would be you, brat," she added as she looked at me, "—falls into a comalike state. You never wake up from it, but being a vamp, you never die."

"Is thought by some scholars that vital force from Bound *vampyr* transfers to one who Binds her," Darkheart confirmed heavily. "A Queen such as Jasmine would believe is way to gain more power. Would be very tempting for her."

"The final and most likely possibility is even more tempting for Jasmine," Megan said, her words sharply clipped. "Tashya undergoes the ritual and it works the way it's supposed to. She enters fully into the dark side, Bound for all eternity to serve and obey Jasmine. As if that's not one hell of a life sentence, get this—there's no time off for good behavior, no chance of parole. Because a vamp who's stupid enough to let herself be bound to a Queen—" She stopped abruptly, her eyes a glittering gray-blue in her pale face. "Why don't you take it from here, Kat?" she asked. "This is your area of expertise."

"A vamp Bound to a Queen becomes a special case when it comes to Healing," Kat said, her voice hoarse with emotion as she stared at me. "A *very* special case. If you undergo a Binding with Lady Jasmine, Tashie, you'll forfeit your chance of ever being Healed."

Chapter 12

"I know," I said into the silence that followed Kat's words.

"Well, isn't that just swell for you, babe." Brook was half-out of her chair, her palms flat on the table between us as she thrust her face toward me and gave one of her tough-girl grins. "You know the risk and you're willing to take it. Ever think of asking me whether *I* was on board with you risking your everlasting soul? Because I'm not, Crosse! And if I'd had a fuckin' clue that this was what you were going to spring at this damned council of war, I'd never have backed you up!"

She wrenched her gaze from me to Darkheart. "We haven't heard too much from you, old man. What do you say, are you willing to go along with this?" Her eyes flashed green fire at him. "From what Tash told me, getting her to infiltrate Jasmine's inner circle was your idea in the first place, but right from the start you must have known Jasmine would have to be convinced of her loyalty. No Queen Vamp would be gullible enough to welcome the sister of a Daughter and a Healer without some pretty drastic proof that she's turned her back on her family for good. You were counting on Tash to figure that out, and then you were counting on her to do the right fucking thing and volunteer to be Bound to the bitch!"

"Those stars in your eyes when you look at my little sister must be blinding you to reality, vamp," Megan interjected. "Darkheart wasn't counting on Tash to do the right thing, for the simple reason that we never do. You think she's called this farce of a meeting because she's suddenly gone all noble and altruistic?" Meg gave a harsh bark of laughter.

"Think again. If I know Tash, this is just another childish ploy to get attention. Well, it worked," she said, swinging her coldly furious gaze to me. "Now if you'll excuse me, I've got to get back on patrol. Don't worry, brat—I'll be waiting with bated breath for your regretful revelation that you couldn't manage to talk Jasmine into Binding—"

"Don't call me that anymore, Meg."

The coins on the Galliano rang softly as I rose from my seat. But the dress I was wearing wasn't a Galliano, I knew. It might look like one, it might by fastened by his signature side-buttoned closing, and when it had been hanging on the rack in Suzanne's boutique, it might even have been an ordinary designer gown. But it had changed into something else when I'd tried it on. Deep down, I'd known that all along—just as I'd known that I'd changed. If Meg didn't realize that yet, I had no one but myself to blame. I'd tried to slip back into my old role with her and Kat tonight; tried as hard as I could, because stepping out of that role meant leaving the comforting past behind. And she felt that, too. That was why she was fighting so hard to hang on to her picture of me as her bratty little sister.

Megan was afraid for me. And a tiny, unac-knowledged part of her was afraid *of* me.

So be it. Pain swept through me as I gave silent voice to the decision that would swing a door shut between me and my sisters forever. No matter how this turned out, we could never go back to the rela-tionship we'd had. Megan and Kat were on parallel paths, both leading toward the light…and to reach my goal, I had to plunge into the dark.

"Don't call you what—brat?" Megan said with a tight shrug. "What are you going to do, wait until Grammie comes home with Popsie from their cruise and then run to her like you did when we were kids and I got mad at you for breaking my Barbie? Burst into tears like the time when Kat got crowned queen of the Christmas dance in our senior year and you were first runner-up? Or maybe you'll throw a hissy fit, the way you did when you first began to suspect that you weren't this generation's Daughter. What's it going to be, Tash? Personally, my money's on the hissy fit, because that seems to be your style these day—"

"If I have to, I'll fight you, Megan," I said

flatly. "I don't want to, but you're not leaving me much choice."

"*Nyet!*" Darkheart's fist crashed down on the table. "This I will not allow!" He got slowly to his feet, his expression thunderous. "Megan, as Daughter, you should keep cooler head. Natashya, if you intend to go up against *vampyr* as powerful as Jasmine, you must learn restraint." His eaglelike gaze swept the room. "We will meet here again tomorrow, when tempers are calmer," he said in a tone that brooked no argument.

He didn't get one from anybody there. Swiftly they filed out of the office. Kat exited close behind Darkheart and Liz, Jack's hand on her elbow and Ramon on the other side of her. Her shoulders were hunched, as if she was trying not to cry, and I felt a stab of regret for causing the pain she was attempting to hold in. Megan stalked out next without looking at me. At her side padded a massive black wolf with silver-tipped fur, and I realized with a small start that sometime during the confrontation Mikhail had shapeshifted. It seemed my sister had managed to smuggle a usable weapon into the room despite my restrictions, I thought wryly.

That left only Brook and Dmitri, and Brook was already at the door. Ignoring the big Russian, I moved quickly to intercept her.

"I should have told you," I said baldly. My words surprised me. I'd gone to her with the intention of making excuses, but somehow I couldn't get them past the tightness in my throat. Brook's face was hard and set, but her eyes were suspiciously shiny. She jerked her arm from my touch.

"Yeah, Mata Hari, you should have," she said huskily. "But you needed my help in setting up this meeting, so instead you played me for a patsy. I thought we were on the same side but you treated me the same way you did your sisters. You treated me like I was the enemy."

"*No,*" I said with urgent emphasis. She started to turn away from me and I grasped her again, forcing her to meet my eyes. "I screwed up, but that's not why. The truth is that I didn't have the courage to tell you. I was prepared to oppose Megan's and Kat's objections, but I didn't know if I'd be able to say no to you if you asked me not to do this."

The shininess in her right eye ran together into

a single tear. It sat stubbornly on her lower lashes, reflecting the green of her iris and refusing to fall. Raising my hand to her set face, I used the ball of my thumb to smear it into a gleaming silver track across her cheekbone. "Just one word from you and I would have lost it," I said. "And I can't afford to lose it. You know better than I do what hangs in the balance here, Brook."

She stared at me, and for a moment I didn't know if I'd gotten through to her. Then she nodded, a brusque and frozen jerk of her head. "*Yes.*" Her whisper was harsh and thick with the tears that hadn't made it to her eyes. "But why does it have to be *you?*"

I let my hand fall to my side. "Remember what you said about asking yourself 'why me?' when you got turned? You told me you hadn't figured out the answer yet. Neither have I. But maybe part of the why in my case is the other thing you said—that becoming a vamp might be my only chance of becoming a real person."

"Me and my big mouth," Brook said with a bitter little smile. "My Bubbe always told me it would get me into trouble one day." She shoved her shoulders back, her momentary vulnerability once more papered over with her customary toughness as she glanced in Dmitri's direction. He was on the other side of the room and apparently engrossed in a relief map of the Carpathian Mountains—Russian decor left a lot to be desired, my sisters and I had agreed when Darkheart had hung the violently colored map on the wall. Brook lowered her voice. "What your sister said—*Bound for all eternity to serve and obey Jasmine*. That sound like anyone you know, Crosse?"

I'd been waiting for her to bring the subject up, but her words still twisted like a knife thrust in my heart. Brook wasn't the only one capable of putting on a mask, though. "Heath," I said without hesitation. "The moment Jasmine did her trick with the roses in Suzanne's shop I knew he'd betrayed me. I told him about Dmitri last night. He must have gone straight to her with the information." I attempted a smile. "I should have known he was too good to be true, Brookie. Tall, dark, handsome— and Bound for all eternity to Lady Jasmine Melrose. But I can use him to get to her."

The skin on her face tightened, her features

standing out in sharp relief. "And when you do, then what? I know what you're counting on, even if your sisters don't...but what if you're wrong?"

"I can't be wrong," I said in the same tone my grandfather had used when he'd terminated the meeting. I hesitated, not sure how to bring up the other topic that was on my mind. "You hate being a vamp, Brook. Why haven't you ever asked me to talk to Kat about performing a Heal on—"

"Fuck off, Crosse." The tight grin was back on her face. "You wanna break up with me, have the balls to be straight about it. Until then, as long as you're a vamp, I'm a vamp." Her grin slipped. "I don't have the kind of power you're already exhibiting, but you might need a vamp friend in the next few days. After this is all over, I'll ask Kat for her help." Her green gaze flicked sideways to Dmitri. "He's waiting for me to go. I think I'll disappoint him."

"No, let's give him what he wants," I said in the same undertone she'd used. "If Black Rose's hit man has something to say to me in private, I'd better know what it is. Wait for me outside the building."

"How did I know you'd say that?" She grimaced

as she began to turn to the door. She looked back, a corner of her mouth lifting wryly. "He's not my type, with the *XY* chromosome thing going on and all, but the dude's hot, I'll give him that. Don't let your hormones get the better of you like you almost did the last time, Mata Hari."

"Fuck off, Steinberg." I grinned back at her, feeling a faint blush touch my cheeks. She raked her hand through her hair, making it stand up like the feathers of a slightly punk-looking baby chick, and blew me a kiss before heading down the corridor toward the fire stairs at the end of the hall. The two of us were as different as night and day, I thought wryly. Brook was gay, I was straight; she was punk, I was a spoiled shopaholic—or at least I had been, until recently. In our former lives we wouldn't have had two words to say to each other, but now... I smiled as the door to the stairs closed behind her, Brook waggling her fingers in a "toodles" gesture at me without turning around. Now she was my best friend; so much a part of me that I wished I'd met her years ago.

And for the rest of my life I'll regret I never told her that.

I stepped back into the office where Dmitri was waiting and got straight to the point. "So what's the verdict, Malkovich? Do you understand now why a Heal's out of the question?"

"No more than your sisters do," he said, folding his arms across his chest and glowering at me. "There's a gaping hole in your plan of battle, Tashya."

"Darkheart didn't seem to think so," I pointed out.

Dmitri nodded slowly. "Which makes me think that *Gospodin* Darkheart knows something your sisters and I don't. You're volunteering to undergo a Binding with Jasmine to allay any suspicions she might have about you, so she trusts you with the knowledge of where her daytime lair is. The gaping hole is that once you're Bound to her, your loyalty will be to her, not Darkheart & Crosse. You'll be incapable of betraying her."

"From the way you spoke up during the meeting, it seems you're an expert on the subject. How did you put it—'*lesser* vampyr *exchanges blood with more powerful one*'? With the end result that the vamp who's not as powerful is Bound to the one who is." I met his frowning gaze. "What makes you think that I'm going to walk away from that ritual Bound to Jasmine, instead of the other way around?"

For a moment Dmitri just stared at me. Then he exploded. "*Nyet!* That's totally *bezumno!* She is a *koroleva,* a *drevnih!*—shit!" He strode toward me and grabbed my shoulders. "A queen and an ancient, dammit," he ground out. "And you're a—"

I wrenched myself from his grasp, the tension I'd been holding back all evening spilling from me in sudden anger. "I'm a what? An ordinary vamp? I don't think so, Malkovich! My mother was a Daughter and my father was a Healer. I didn't get turned in the usual way, I got marked by Zena, a queen and an ancient in her own right!" With an effort I reined my anger in. "Most important of all, I belong to the Darkheart line," I said tersely. "We're more ancient than Jasmine is or ever could be, and for all the centuries of our existence we've been battling vampires—battling them and surviving, since we're still here. When Zena marked me, she created something that's never existed before. I'm a mongrel, Malkovich—a Heinz 57 mutt. And mutts are always stronger than the breeds that went into them. I'm a cross between a vamp who hasn't had the strength of her humanity taken from her and a human with the power to survive the dark side."

I stepped back from him. "I'll admit I'm not ready to take her on just yet. I need a day, maybe two, before my power outstrips hers."

"How can you know that?" His frown had disappeared. There was no expression on his face, and his eyes were as unreadable as chips of ice. "Even if what you say about your destiny is true, how do you know you'll be ready to confront Jasmine so soon?"

"Because I can feel it happening in me," I snapped. "Things are changing, and the change is getting faster by the hour. Yesterday I could barely defeat gravity. Today I can do this." I walked toward the wall that separated the office from the hall outside.

Okay, I might have left out a tiny detail when I was describing myself hovering near the ceiling and watching Brookie divest everyone of their weapons when they arrived. And the tiny detail I left out was that at some point I realized that the right side of my body had disappeared.

Which freaked me out so much that I almost went crashing to the floor. Since at that very second Jack Rawls was telling Brook it would be a cold day in hell before he handed over his nail gun, my career as a vamp might have been cut humiliatingly short by the hair-triggered Mr. Rawls if he'd suddenly heard a crash behind him and whirled around to see me dropping from the ceiling.

Luckily for me, I managed to get past my initial moment of shock long enough to realize that the reason why I couldn't see half of my body anymore was because I'd drifted too close to the wall…and right through it.

I count it as a mark of my growing maturity that when I demonstrated my newly discovered talent to Dmitri, I refrained from backing up to the wall until only my grin remained visible to him, like the Cheshire Cat in *Alice in Wonderland*. Instead, I simply walked through the wall into the hallway on the other side. And for those of you who want to know how it felt to pass through a solid object, sorry to disappoint, but it didn't feel any different than walking through a patch of fog or a drift of smoke. Which isn't to say that it wasn't a thrill, because it was. I mean, part of me might have been evolving into a supervamp who intended to go up against a Queen Vampire, but part of me was still Tashie Crosse and I couldn't help thinking what a total blast this new talent was. But when Dmitri strode through the open doorway into the hall to find me waiting there for him, I simply lifted an inquiring eyebrow at him.

And then I spoiled it by letting my face split into a big, goofy grin. "Come on, Malkovich, admit it— you've never seen a vamp do that before, right? Want me to show you again? Watch." I stepped to my right and stopped halfway through the wall. "Impressed? Because I am. I mean, I'm totally going to wipe the floor with Jazz-baby when I go up against—"

His movement was a blur. Before I knew what was happening, he'd grasped my left arm to prevent me from slipping through the wall any farther and his stake was piercing the flesh just below my left breast.

"You're no match for her! You still think this is some kind of game!" he rasped, his face thrust close to mine. "Understand this—Jasmine doesn't play games. She's old and she's evil and she's won every battle she's ever engaged in, some of them against better opponents than you! Have you studied her history?"

"*Get that stake out of me!*" I said, fury turning my voice to a harsh whisper. "If you don't, I'll—"

"You'll what?" he said grimly. "Before you could move a muscle I could shove this so deeply through you it would come out the other side, *l'ubimaya*. And as good as I am at what I was trained for, I'm only a human, with a human's reflexes and speed. If you can find yourself a heartbeat away from death at my hands, what do you think will happen when you go up against a Queen *Vampyr* like Jasmine? I'll ask you again, what do you know of her history?"

"I know she turned Cyrus Kane and then killed him," I shot back. "Kat figured that out from his final unfinished letter to her after she Healed him. If that's supposed to scare me, it doesn't. Cyrus may have been a Master Vamp at one time, but after his Heal he was just a tortured old man who could have been just as easily killed by a human thug."

"Do you know how many Daughters she's killed over the centuries?" Dmitri's look hardened even further. "Too many to count. One was an Ethiopian princess named Mahtsente, a Daughter so skilled and experienced that some thought she was an incarnation of Lilith herself. Jasmine drained her body of blood and left it hanging on the palace gates, where it was found the next morning by her sister, Desta."

The image his words conjured up sickened me, but I forced my voice to remain steady. "If you're trying to discourage me, you're doing just the opposite. I'll be avenging Mahtsente as well as all the others when I bring Jasmine down. Now let me go!"

He went on as if my words had meant nothing to him. "At her sister's funeral, Desta swore to avenge Mahtsente's torture and death. She disappeared from public life, dedicated herself to learning all she could about Jasmine, and put herself into the hands of a Healed vamp who trained her mercilessly in the ways of his former kind. Knowing that her soul would be tested as cruelly as her body, she made sure that her spiritual training was just as rigorous and after six years, she was finally ready. Deliberately allowing herself to be turned by a vampire, she arranged to have herself presented to Jasmine, ostensibly to swear allegiance to her new Queen but really to kill her. As dawn broke the next morning, Desta was found hanging on the palace gates. Before the guards could save her, the first rays of the rising sun touched her and she died screaming."

Just as suddenly as he'd grasped me, Dmitri released my arm and withdrew his stake. I stepped fully into the hallway, my legs feeling almost too shaky to support me. "I appreciate the history lesson, but it hasn't changed my mind," I said, hoping my cold tone disguised the horror his story had aroused in me. "Now, if you don't mind, Brook's waiting outside for me."

I stepped around him and began heading for the stairs. As I reached the door leading to them, a heavily muscled arm brushed my shoulder as Dmitri pushed it open. I spun around, my anger at the boiling point, but at the look in his eyes my anger died.

For once his gaze wasn't shuttered, and I suddenly realized why *Chernoye Roza*'s assassin normally took such care to shield his expression.

Without those precautions, the blue eyes blazing out of the hard angles of his tanned face were open windows to his soul. Fear shadowed them—fear for me. And burning behind the fear was an even stronger emotion.

He'd been telling the truth, I thought with an odd flicker of dismay. Dmitri Malkovich, the hit man who'd been sent to kill me, had instead violated every vow he'd sworn to Black Rose and had fallen in love with his assigned target. He truly believed what he'd told me: that our lives were so closely intertwined that I held his fate in my hands, for good or for worse. And I cared for him, too, I realized as I placed my hand lightly on the tense muscles of his arm.

Just not in the same way.

"Don't say it, *l'ubimaya*." His words came out jaggedly, as if each one were a shard of glass piercing his heart. "I know it, but don't say it. Just show me."

Slowly he bent his head to mine. His mouth brushed against my parted lips, and then his restraint was replaced with a fiercely desperate passion.

I wish I could say that I returned his kiss with nothing more than compassionate tenderness, I really do. I mean, I'd just come to the regretful conclusion that the eminently hot and sexy Mr. Malkovich and I were never going to be an item, so if I'd had an ounce of moral fiber I should have clamped a lid on the purely physical reaction that boiled up in me as soon as his mouth came down on mine. But hey, I'm only human. Well, actually human with a hefty dash of vamp, I guess, which is an even better excuse for the way I practically melted into Dmitri's hard embrace and dug my nails into his T-shirted back when he took his kiss deeper.

But before it had barely gotten started, the party came to an abrupt end. Dmitri's mouth left mine and he pulled back. "We'd be great in bed together," he said, the half smile that ghosted across his lips at odds with the bleakness in his eyes. "And that's all it would ever be for you, *l'ubimaya*. So much for my inherited gypsy gift of knowing where my future lies."

The rawness in his tone made me feel like the shallow bitch I'd just proven myself to be. "You wouldn't have had much of a future with me," I said, forcing my gaze from his mouth and my imagination from wondering whether I could persuade him to use it on me again. "Everything else aside, Black Rose wouldn't allow it. I'd have been the biggest mistake of your life."

"Maybe you're right," he said evenly. "But I would have gone ahead and made that mistake, anyway. What worries me is that you might make the same dangerous decision."

"You mean with Heath." I drew away from him. "You couldn't be more wrong, Malkovich. He betrayed me. I'll admit I had a little thing for him, but I don't need it spelled out for me that he's bad news." I gave him a cool smile. "So don't worry about me and the divinely decadent Lieutenant Lockridge when we have bigger problems on our plate, like where you're going to sleep tonight after inviting me and Brookie to stay the night at my apartment. She and I can share the bed. You can have the sofa unless I totally broke it when I threw it at you yesterday."

It's my firm belief that mindless chatter has its uses and one of those uses is to ease a girl out of an awkward situation, like when a man makes it plain that he's going to suffer unrequited love for her the rest of his life. But as useful as my nonstop conversation was as we headed downstairs to the lobby of the building, I was glad when we exited onto the street where Brook would be waiting for me. It was definitely a case where three wasn't a crowd, I thought as I looked around for her.

I turned to Dmitri, my mild exasperation not directed at him. "Okay, where is she? If I find out she snuck into the Rialto to catch the second showing of—"

His face was frozen in horror. Even as I followed his gaze, he pulled me to him, his hand spreading wide over my eyes. "Don't look!" he commanded in a voice hoarse with shock.

I wrenched myself free. The next moment I wanted to bury my face against his chest again and let him block out the terrible sight in front of me forever.

The Maplesburg Beautification Committee had arranged for baskets of flowers to be suspended from the top of the old-fashioned swan's-neck lampposts that cast a faux-gaslight glow in this part of downtown. But what hung from the lamppost across the street wasn't a graceful cascade of petunias and trailing ivy, I saw as a sudden, terror-filled keening split the night and built to a crescendo of pain.

It was Brook's body. And the figure screaming below her on the sidewalk was the homeless man she'd called Crazy Joe.

Chapter 13

When Kat had been toying with the idea of moving to New York a year or so ago, one of the main reasons for her restlessness was her disgusted declaration that Maplesburg was the original town that rolled up its sidewalks at night. That wasn't strictly true, but in the small downtown office district her assessment came close. So although Crazy Joe's screams were decibel-shattering enough to attract attention, there was no one around at this time of night to hear them.

Except me and Dmitri.

"*Shut him up!*" I snarled over my shoulder at Dmitri as I raced across the deserted street to where Brook's torn body hung from the lamppost. In my side vision I saw Dmitri stride over to the scream-ing man and, with more gentleness than I would have been capable of at that moment, put his arm around Joe's shoulder to turn him away. Joe's screams choked off into terrified moans, but I'd stopped listening.

On the other lampposts the heavy baskets of flowers were secured by black iron-link chains. The chains had been left in place on this one, and used to secure Brook. One looped her ankles tightly to the main part of the post, but the chain that wrapped her wrists together behind her back was affixed to the post's horizontal cross-member and obviously bore most of her body's weight. Under her slashed Violent Femmes T-shirt her shoulders stuck out at an impossible angle, and with a fresh wave of horror I realized that her arms had become dis-jointed.

Her injuries would have killed a human. But Brooklyn was a vamp. She was alive and in agony.

"Going to get you down from there, babe," I said thickly. I began to move around to the back of the post but before I could take more than a step her bloodied lips parted.

"Don't come any closer, Tash!" Her whisper was more of a rattle and as my gaze jerked upward toward her again I saw that her throat bore the imprint of a boot sole. "They—they've got me wired."

"No, sweetheart, the bastards who did this to you used chains," I said, trying to keep my voice soothing and probably failing miserably. "I'm coming up there to snap them, and Dmitri will break your fall when you're released. I know you're in terrible pain, Brook, but we have to get you down—"

"No!" Her right eyelid was swollen to twice its size, but amazingly, she managed to open it. A slit of mint-green gleamed desperately at me. "You don't understand—they *wired* me. I'm a damned bomb, Tash, and the slightest movement on my part could set off the explosion!"

"Fuck." At the muttered oath from behind me I turned to see Dmitri. Beside him stood Crazy Joe, his matted hair pushed back to reveal the empty, uncomprehending fear on his face.

"Get him out of here!" I barked. "Dammit, Dmitri, I don't need any distractions right now!"

"He won't leave," Dmitri said flatly. "I think he knows Brook."

"Yeah, I know Joe," Brook rasped. "Hey, Joe, tell you what—why don't you go on over to the Ming-Lee's Restaurant, see if you can scrounge us a couple cups of coffee. Remember when I first met you I told you I'd call you Joe, 'cause you drank so much of the stuff? By the time you get back, I should be down from here." Her mouth quivered in an odd way. My heart contracted painfully as I realized she was trying to smile. Even at such a moment she had compassion for a frightened homeless man who didn't know what was happening.

Or maybe he did. Tears spilled from his confused eyes, running down his grimy face into his tangled beard. Before I knew what he intended to do, he reached up to touch a gaping wound on Brook's torso. I heard Dmitri's swiftly indrawn breath, but I was incapable of even that much.

"Joe, take your hand away from me very carefully," Brook said in a voice tight with strain. "A bad thing's going to happen to me, and I don't want you to get hurt, too."

Crazy Joe looked up at her, his eyes dull with pain. "Not...not...so bad now. All...over soon." Slowly he lowered his hand and took a step backward.

"You've been holding out on me," she said in a soft rasp. "You could talk all along, huh? You're right, Joe, it'll all be over soon. Go now. I don't want you to see this." She waited until he'd turned from us. As he shuffled into the night she spoke again, her voice no longer soft but sharply urgent. "And that goes for both of you. The thing's strapped across my chest with a leaf-spring detonator, and when my arms give way a little more and I sag forward, it's going to go off." Her face twisted. "The payload's got silver in it, Tash, I can feel it eating into me. Even if there were some way to get me out of this, it's already too late. Jasmine didn't leave anything to chance."

"She didn't count on me finding you," I said tightly. "Look, if I can somehow support you while I deal with the chains we might—"

"The bitch didn't even show up herself. She sent a bunch of gay bashers who probably got plenty of practice doing this kind of thing long before they became vamps," Brook said with weak anger, a fresh gout of blood spilling from between her broken teeth. "They had a high old time putting the boots to me, and an even better time telling me how this thing was rigged so that when my girlfriend— that's you, babe," she added, "—showed up, you'd be faced with a lose/lose choice. Don't fool yourself, Tash. Jasmine didn't just count on you finding me. This whole setup was designed to tear you apart—either with silver, if you were crazy enough to try to save me, or with guilt if you saved yourself."

"I'm willing to risk the first one." I turned to Dmitri. "Take cover. If everything goes bad, tell Megan and Kat and Darkheart what went down here tonight—"

"If you can get her down safely, I might be able to defuse the device," he interrupted. "I'm no bomb squad expert, but I've had some experience. I don't intend to hide behind the nearest building, *l'ubimaya.*"

"Maybe you're right." There was a thread of tired laughter in Brook's fading voice. "I guess there was something Jasmine didn't count on, like my having a couple of *meshuggeneh* friends with more loyalty than brains."

"When this is all over, remind me to get a Yiddish dictionary so I know when you're insulting me, babe," I said with a small smile. "Okay, Dmitri, as soon as I release the chains get ready to—"

"I finally figured out why I got turned, Tash. If I hadn't been, I wouldn't have met you and been given the two happiest days of my life." Through the mask of blood on Brook's face her undamaged eye blazed mint-green as she looked at me. "Love you, Mata Hari," she said softly.

"Get *down!*" Dmitri's forearm slammed against my chest, knocking me toward the sidewalk, but before I hit the concrete I felt his arms wrap tightly around me, hugging me to him and covering my body with his. As we crashed to the ground, the night suddenly lit up behind us with a painful brilliance.

The blast that immediately followed sounded

like a freight train running at high speed into a mountain.

"Oh, God, Brookie, *no!*" My scream was lost in the explosion. I tried to get up, but something heavy slammed between my shoulder blades, driving me down again.

"Cover your face!" Dmitri's shouted command came from within inches of my ear, but I could barely hear it. I was in a world of noise and chaos that seemed to go on forever, and none of that mattered.

She'd been a tough girl right up to the end. She'd sacrificed herself by deliberately detonating the bomb, rather than let me risk my life in trying to save her.

The pressure on my shoulder blades eased. I felt the weight of Dmitri's body move off me, and I clumsily raised myself to my knees and started to turn around.

He dropped a warning hand on my shoulder. "You don't want to do that, Tashya," he said in a low, strained tone.

"Yes, I do." My own voice sounded flat and dead. That was good, I thought as I got to my feet and slowly swung my gaze toward the lamppost. I didn't want to soften this moment with emotion or dilute it with tears. I needed to burn the image I was looking at into my heart like a brand so it would stay with me forever, as fresh and as raw as it was now.

"You said I treated my fight against Jasmine like it was a game." As I spoke, I kept my gaze on the horrific sight in front of me. "You were right, I did. Some part of me saw it as a competition, a way of proving my powers. Jasmine made a big mistake when she did this to Brooklyn."

Just for an instant I let myself close my eyes, and saw a wickedly amused mint-green gaze topped by spikes of hair that looked like ruffled chicken feathers.

Love you, Mata Hari....

I opened my eyes and turned to Dmitri. "It's not a game anymore," I said tonelessly. "Even if I have to go down with her, I'm sending the bitch to hell."

"You and I have been on opposite sides a lot lately, Tash, but I want you to know I'm truly sorry about what happened to your friend."

"Her name was Brooklyn, Meg," I said, staring out of the living room window in my apartment. "Brooklyn Steinberg. And spare me the fake sympathy, because I know that if you'd run into her on the street after dark, you would have staked her without a qualm."

"That's not quite fair, sweetie," Kat demurred. "Whenever possible, Meg gives vamps the option of undergoing a Heal with me. But she *is* a Daughter, after all. If they refuse, it's her duty to stake them."

In the dark glass of the window I saw my sisters exchange glances behind me, and just for a moment I felt an unhappy sense of isolation from them. Then the feeling died, replaced by the cold detachment that had settled over me since I'd turned away from Brook's torn body an hour ago.

On our way back to my apartment Dmitri had used his cell phone to contact Darkheart, and when we'd arrived, Meg and Kat, accompanied by Darkheart, Jack and Mikhail, had been waiting. My grandfather's attitude had been sympathetic but firm as he'd told me he wanted the Darkheart & Crosse contingent to return to the scene and remove all signs of what had happened there.

"Is best if *policiya* do not become involved, Natashya. They would have questions for you and you cannot give answers they will accept." He'd frowned. "Is strange they did not arrive on scene immediately. Such an explosion must have been heard and reported."

I'd looked at him without interest, barely taking in what he was saying. "I didn't want a crowd of thrill-seekers showing up, so I dark-sparkled the area. No one reported anything. Even if someone drove by the scene after Dmitri and I left, all they'll think they see is a perfectly normal lamppost with a basket of flowers hanging from it." The shell of detachment around me had cracked momentarily. "What…what do you intend to do with—"

I hadn't been able to continue. Darkheart had put his hand briefly over mine. "She was *yevrejskij, da?* Jewish? I have rabbi friend who knows something of what I do. He will arrange proper procedures." He frowned slightly. "This word you say…dark-sparkle. It means you were able to *glamyr* every person in area who might have noticed tragedy?"

I shrugged again. "Yeah, dark-sparkle. That's how I think of it in my mind when I need to do it.

But I guess I didn't just do the area, I threw a *glamyr* over all Maplesburg. It seemed simpler to do it that way."

"Simpler," he'd repeated in a carefully neutral voice. "That is interesting, Natashya. We will talk more of this later." He'd turned to go, but then swung back to face me, his gaze fixing on my right arm. "Why have you removed the bandage you wore earlier?"

"I didn't need it anymore." I lifted my arm so that the sleeve fell away, revealing the thin white scar that ran jaggedly to my wrist. "I guess my healing ability finally kicked in, although I didn't think us vamps were supposed to scar," I said listlessly, letting the sleeve fall back into place.

"*Da,* I have always believed that *vampyrs* do not scar, too," Darkheart said evenly. "This is another puzzle we should discuss."

He'd left then, accompanied by a grim-faced Dmitri, Jack and Mikhail following them. I would have preferred it if my sisters had left, too, I thought now as I stared out the window into the darkness. I wanted to be alone with my thoughts, not forced to listen to their platitudes and stilted sympathy.

As if she'd read my thoughts, Megan exhaled sharply and stood up, the movement restlessly indecisive. I spoke over my shoulder. "You two probably need to get back on patrol. I appreciate it that you came here to hold my hand, but it's not necessary. I'll be okay by myself."

I half expected Megan to come back with a tart response, but instead she exhaled again, this time in a sigh. "Patrol? Patrolling's been a joke lately. We haven't come within sniffing distance of a vamp for two nights now, and as for unearthing any undead in the daytime, forget it. I must be losing my touch."

"There was that biker-type you and Mikhail questioned three nights ago, sweetie," Kat said quickly. "I mean, too totally gruesome, with all those tattoos and that filthy beard, but before he tried to rip your head off he did divulge where Jasmine's daytime lair was."

I spun around from the window. "What?"

Megan gave a sour smile. "Kat's indulging in a touch of inappropriate sarcasm. Biker-vamp told us Melrose's lair was right under our noses—at the building where the Darkheart & Crosse office is, actually. The creep was just trying to yank my chain so I'd be distracted when he lunged for me. It didn't work."

"But maybe he was telling the truth," I said, with the first flicker of interest I'd felt since Brook's death. "I mean, Cyrus Kane's lair was that vast network of underground caverns beneath his brownstone. Maybe there's something similar under—"

"There's not," Megan said flatly. "Darkheart had it checked out by a Russian expatriate geological engineer. The building was constructed on the foundation of a previous structure, and beneath that it's solid bedrock."

"And you knew all that when you showed up at the meeting earlier tonight and told me you could handle the Jasmine situation without my help?" I felt my lips stretch into something that couldn't be called a smile. "Seems to me that you've totally fucked up on this one, Meg. In fact, maybe if you'd been more upfront about your spectacular lack of progress lately, Brook might not have been killed."

"You're upset, sweetie," Kat interjected sharply. "We all are, but that's no reason to—"

"*Upset?*" The image of Brook's mutilated body

flashed in front of my eyes. Fury burned through me, and the coins on my dress gave their faint, coffin-bell echo. "Upset is when the shoes you adore don't come in your size, Kat! Upset is what you feel if some jerk says he's going to call, and doesn't!"

"Okay, poor choice of words, but—"

"Upset isn't for seeing the best friend I'll ever have being blown apart by the murdering bitch my Daughter of Lilith sister was supposed to have *staked* by now!" I shouted. "Try the word *destroyed!* Or how about *devastated,* or *shattered,* or—"

"Stop it, Tash! Whatever it is you're doing, *stop it now!*" Megan was in my face, her hands clamped around my shoulders and shaking me violently. "You're about to bring the whole building down on us!"

As if through a black fog I saw her alarmed features. Behind her I saw Kat, her face white and drawn. For a moment I hated them both.

Then the fog dissipated and as my sisters came into focus, so did the room around me…or what was left of it.

Huge chunks of the ceiling lay on the floor. The window I'd been standing by only minutes before looked like it had been blown out, its frame empty except for a few knifelike shards, and the window wall itself was canted at an angle. A gaping slice of exposed lathe and plaster showed where it should have met up with the wall behind me.

Worst of all, from under Megan's short, honey-blond hair seeped a thin trickle of blood. A glittering shard of glass protruded from Kat's upper arm. I stumbled backward from Megan's hard stare.

"I don't…I didn't mean to…" I forced down the bile that rose in my throat. "Nothing like this has ever happened before. You don't believe I'd deliberately do anything that could get you and Kat *killed,* do you—"

"Just like you got my sister killed, vamp?"

The coldly accusatory words came from the direction of the doorway. I turned and saw Brook standing there—but a Brook with long, brown hair and hazel eyes, wearing a pale pink blouse tucked neatly into a conservative tan skirt.

"You're Xandra." I didn't make it a question.

Her nod was little more than an unsteady jerk of

her head, and I saw that under her controlled exterior, she was barely holding herself together. "And you must be Tashya Crosse. I was told I'd find you here."

"By whom?" Megan asked, stepping slightly in front of me.

"By a woman I came upon in an alleyway, sharing a rat with her cat," Xandra said, a faint spasm of revulsion crossing the features that were so like Brook's, and yet so different. "That was after I saw a group of men cutting down what was left of my sister's body from a lamppost. Nice town you've got here."

"Almost as nice as Smith's Falls, from what I hear," Megan said, her tone edged. "You want to tell us why you're accusing Tash of getting your sister killed?"

"I've been trying to trace Brook for months, and a couple of days ago a vampire I was about to kill told me he'd give me some information on her if I didn't stake him." Xandra's hazel eyes took in Megan's quick frown and Kat's narrowed glance. "Oh, I get it," she said in her colorless voice. "You think you have to go through some hereditary initiation process to know how to kill vampires, or even accept that they exist. Well, I took the crash course by staying in Smith's Falls the first night I got back from Italy. I soon found out what had happened to my hometown. You'd be surprised how fast a girl can pick up the basics of staking when her life's on the line."

"Okay, so you let a vamp go in return for some information on your sister," Kat drawled. "What information, and what does this have to do with *our* sister?"

I'd misjudged my sisters—misjudged them badly, I realized, taking in Megan's protective stance in front of me and Kat's confrontational posture as she faced Xandra. Under any other circumstances, they would have shown her kindness and compassion, but she'd made a fatal error that had canceled out the sympathy they felt for her loss.

She'd attacked me. And my sisters didn't let anyone get away with that. We might fight amongst ourselves, we might argue and disagree with each other, but when the chips were down we were the Crosse triplets, and no one messed with one of us without taking on all three. The feeling of numb iso-lation that had enveloped me for the past hour eased a little.

"I said I agreed to let the bastard go. I didn't say I kept to that agreement." Xandra corrected Kat with toneless precision. "Do any of you have a Kleenex? Never mind, I think I have a tissue in here," she said dully, looking down to undo the gold-tone clasp of her shoulderbag.

It wasn't just shock that had robbed her of any personality, I decided, my gaze narrowing on her bland clothes and her blah haircut and the boring shoulderbag she was rummaging in. She'd been like this for a long time, perhaps all her life. It was no wonder she and Brook hadn't had much in common.

"But before I drove my stake through his stinking heart he said he'd heard a rumor about a lesbian vamp in Maplesburg who'd fallen hard for the vampire sister of the local Daughter of Lilith. He told me that this Daughter's sister was involved in a power struggle with a Queen called Jasmine." Xandra's lackluster hazel eyes, so different from Brook's wicked green gaze, blinked tearlessly at me as she began to extract her hand from her shoulderbag. "He said that if my queer sister got caught in the middle she was probably dead already, and when I got here I found out that everything he'd told me was true. So that's why I've decided to stake you."

"Tash, watch—" Kat's warning came in the same instant that Megan threw herself at Xandra, but both of them were too late. The stake that Xandra Steinberg had thrown with deadly accuracy sped straight toward my heart.

I watched it fly in slow motion across the room. As it got closer to me it seemed to go even slower, and I took the time to glance at my sisters and the woman who'd tried to kill me. Xandra's arm was still outstretched, the tendons of it still tensed with the effort of hurling her stake at me. I looked from her to Kat, whose mouth was open as her shouted warning, low and distorted like a recording being played at slow speed, came to me as if she were shouting underwater.

Megan was defying gravity, or so it seemed. Her body was horizontal to the floor, her face twisted in an agonized expression as if she'd known even before she'd leaped at Xandra that she wouldn't be able to stop her.

Time hadn't slowed down, I decided. I'd sped up. This was yet another of my powers to reveal itself. Whenever I wanted, I could return to normal and watch Xandra's stake resume its deadly trajectory, hear the rest of Kat's screamed warning, see Megan's lunge at Xandra result in her taking Brook's sister down to the floor.

And I'd be able to see the tears that had appeared in Xandra's formerly tearless eyes spill over onto her lashes and pour down her cheeks as she grieved for her sister.

I walked forward and plucked the stake from midair. Slipping it into the sleeve of my dress, I walked out of my apartment without looking back.

Chapter 14

"Her name was Lola, she was a show—oh, shit, I shoulda peed before I left the kariloki…karaoke club." I giggled drunkenly as I stumbled down the dimly lit side street a few blocks away from my apartment. "Wunner if there's a bathroom around here? Those last two Long Island Iced Teas are totally *killing* me."

I was easy prey: a way-over-her-limit airhead who'd been on a toot with her friends and made the rash decision to walk home alone. Or at least that's what I wanted any nearby vamps to think. Problem was, I thought as I squinted through my drunk's half-mast eyelids, there didn't seem to *be* any nearby vamps. I'd left my apartment forty minutes ago, and my tipsy act still hadn't had any takers.

Unless you counted the five creeps pulling up beside me in the rusted-out pickup truck right now.

They were vamps, all right, I thought as the truck came to a rocking halt and its occupants piled out. But my guess was that even before they'd been turned, they hadn't been shining examples of the human race. They had worn identical expressions of violent stupidity, except for the runty speciman who'd been driving the truck. His face was ferretlike and hate-filled, and I had the feeling that if I'd been an ordinary female it would have been a toss-up as to whether this thug decided to try to maul me or kill me.

Or both.

"'Scuse me, fellas." I giggled, still in my drunken-prey mode. They were blocking the sidewalk in front of me, but as I took a wavering step, Ferret-Vamp moved aside with mocking courtesy to let me by. I took another step and felt myself being jerked to a stop.

I turned around, squinting owlishly. Ferret-Vamp's booted foot was placed squarely on the torn hem of my gown. He grinned at me, showing yellowed fangs, and I smiled uncertainly back. "Uh, you're standing on my dress?" I said, as if the danger I was in still hadn't penetrated my alcoholic fog.

"I guess I am, bitch," he said with soft menace. "But a ripped pretty ain't gonna be your biggest problem tonight."

He removed his dirt-caked boot and stepped back, his gaze avid with cruel anticipation. "You know the rules, boys," he said, turning away from me to his waiting buddies. "You can play, too, but she's mine in the end."

His voice seemed to reach me from a long way away. I stared transfixed at the muddy diamond-and-criss-cross bootprint on the diaphanous material of my dress.

My plan had been to dispatch all but one of them, and force the survivor to take me to his Queen. I raised my eyes to Brook's murderers, and knew I wasn't going to stick to the plan.

The books say there are two sure ways of killing

a vampire: with a stake through the heart or by separating the head from the body. Or as Kat once said with a delicate grimace, the neat way and the nasty way. As the four vamps rushed me and the single stake I'd whipped out of my sleeve, I did the math.

It wasn't rocket science. Two were lucky enough to go the neat way, staked and dusted with wham, bam, thank you ma'am efficiency. Two weren't. The whole process took less than thirty seconds, and when Ferret-Vamp turned around to see why the bitch his boys were supposed to be attacking wasn't screaming, his eyes widened in stunned disbelief as he took in the scene.

As I'd surmised, he wasn't stupid. His shocked gaze flew to me, taking in the spatter of blood across the back of my left hand and the stake I was holding in my right, and he turned to run.

But I was faster. My hand shot out, grabbing him by the neckline of his T-shirt and yanking him nearly off his feet. As he twisted futilely in my grasp, I pulled him closer and put my mouth near his ear. "Ready to take me, hell-bait?" I asked in a harsh whisper. "'Cause I can hardly *wait* to take you."

Abruptly I shoved him from me, and he stumbled and fell to the sidewalk. As I strode toward him he maneuvered himself into a sitting position and began scooting backward, his hands and heels propelling him as his shifting gaze looked for an opportunity to escape.

"The woman you and your late buddies tortured and wired with a bomb earlier tonight was my friend."

"She was your—" He swallowed convulsively. "Shit, you're the Crosse bitch. I'm not walkin' away from this, am I?"

"You got that right," I said tightly. "So when I tell you I want information you're probably thinking, 'I give the bitch what she wants to know, I don't give it to her, what's the diff?'" I jerked my head in the direction of the four piles of ash that had been his companions. "Big diff. Two of them went easy—easy for us vamps, that is. Two of them went hard."

"I know what you did to them. I saw the bodies before they dusted." He swallowed again. "I don't want wood going into my heart. If I tell you what you want to know, you promise you'll use the ax?"

I frowned. "What ax?"

"You mean you—" His face had been white with fear. Now it went pasty. "I'll take the stake," he said rapidly. "What do you want to know?"

"Where the Queen's daytime lair is, for starters. And where I can find her right now."

I hated myself for saying the words. I was making a deal with the scum who'd killed Brooklyn, when what I really wanted to do was to torture him as he and his cohorts had tortured her, make him suffer as he'd made her suffer. But Brook's real killer had been the soulless woman who'd set her pack of jackals on her. I would have to content myself with taking my revenge on Jasmine.

"Same answer to both." A sly grin temporarily replaced the fear on his face. "The building where you and your bitch sisters and the old man run your vamp investigation agency. The Darkheart & Crosse—"

"Do you think this is a *joke?*" I demanded furiously, yanking him by the collar of his T-shirt until his face was inches from mine. "You've got one last chance to give me a straight answer, vamp! Where's *Jasmine?* Where's her lair?"

"La, child, if I had known you were so eager to attend one of my *soirees,* I gladly would have issued you a personal invitation, if only to save you from the disagreeable chore of questioning this cur!"

The liltingly amused voice came from behind me. Letting go of Ferret-Vamp's collar, I slowly turned around to see Jasmine. She was dressed in a blue ballgown of colonial-era cut and style, and snapping an ivory fan open and closed in her hand. By the corner of her mouth was a dark beauty-mark that hadn't been there when I'd met her in Suzanne's shop. It disappeared briefly into the corner of her smile as she pointed the fan at me.

"Fine hunting. I almost wish that you and I could be on the same side, and hunt together. 'Tis not to be, however, so I fear I must—"

"I have the same wish," I said, meeting her jewel-like gaze with what I hoped she read as an expression of pride mixed with supplication. It was an odd mix and I wasn't sure I was achieving it, so I went on hastily, "I'll admit that when I heard you'd arrived in my town, Lady Jasmine, I saw you as my enemy. Since then I've realized that you and I can't be rivals, for the simple reason that no one can rival you. I thought my powers were something special, but compared to yours…" I let my words trail off and my gaze drop to my feet, as if I were too overwhelmed to go on.

If Jasmine was like every other vamp I'd met, she'd be lapping this up, I thought as I waited for her to respond. Of course, she'd fooled me before. Maybe she was shrewd enough or suspicious enough to set aside her vanity and simply kill me right now.

I didn't realize I was holding my breath until I let it out in relief. "You interest me, child," Jasmine said softly. "Continue interesting me, if you can."

I raised my gaze. "We've got a phrase that might not have been used in your time, Lady Jasmine. If you can't beat 'em, join 'em. Have you heard it?"

"No, but I have noted that the pungent Americanisms you rebels use often hold a kernel of yokel wisdom," she said, her eyes narrowing at me. "What means it in this situation?"

"It means I know now that I'm no match for you," I said, inclining my head slightly. "That being so, it would be an honor to serve you, my lady. I want to undergo the Binding ritual with you."

"'Tis a strange way you have of demonstrating your allegiance to me," Jasmine purred. "Including the cur you dispatched by burning earlier today, you have killed five of my vassals." Her gaze flicked to Ferret-Vamp, as if she'd just remembered he was still there. Throughout our conversation he'd been steadily backing away, but as he saw Jasmine's attention fall on him he froze.

"Me and the boys did like you ordered," he said, his tone tinged with feeble bluster. "Messed the dyke up bad, wired her and left her for her little girl-friend to find. Ain't our fault the bitch got the drop on us. How was we supposed to know she—"

"When I came upon this scene a moment ago, you were spilling my secrets," Jasmine said in a voice like a knife-slash. "In my day we had a special punishment for traitors. They were hung, drawn and quartered. Let me give you a demonstration, traitor."

I'm not going to go into detail about what happened next. For those of you who don't know what *hung, drawn and quartered* means, look it up; for those of you who do, trust me, knowing what it is and being forced to watch that particular gore-fest performed on someone are two very different things. And I did watch. My whole plan to take Jasmine down depended upon her believing I admired her, and to turn away in horrified disgust would have been a major tip-off that maybe I wasn't quite as enamoured of her as I was pretending to be.

I know what you're thinking. Only minutes ago I'd killed two vamps in a manner that, while it didn't rank as high up on the bloodthirsty scale as Jasmine's actions, was horrific enough. I can use the excuses that I was still reeling from Brook's death; that it was a situation where if I didn't kill them, they'd kill me; or argue the logistics angle. I had one stake. There were four of them. Even Zorro would have had a hard time with those odds.

But my excuses are just that: excuses. The reality is that by then I was slipping dangerously close to the dark side. About the only thing I can say in my favor is that my thirst for revenge against Ferret-Vamp for what he'd done to Brook didn't extend to executing him by Jasmine's medieval methods. By the time he dusted, I felt so sickened that it was an effort to take in what Jasmine was saying.

"Now, where were we?" She flicked her fan

open. "Oh, yes. How is it that you choose to demonstrate your allegiance to me by slaughtering my
vassals? True, they were lower than low, but they
were mine nonetheless, and you took them from
me. Why should I deign to enact the Binding ritual
with one who has robbed me?"

"Because I don't want to become just another of
your vassals, Lady Jasmine," I said, doing the re-
spectful-but-not-ass-kissy thing again. "You have
hordes of them and as individuals, they're as worth-
less as the traitor you just punished. The best way
of proving my worth to you is to act as you would.
You killed someone I valued. I killed four of your
minions. You know now that if I am Bound to you,
I will serve you with something of your own
courage and ruthlessness."

This was the moment, I told myself tensely as
Jasmine idly tapped the ivory fan against her chin,
her gaze thoughtful. She'd either buy my line of
bullshit or she'd see through it. And if she saw
through it, she would immediately attack. I was
ready for her, whatever she did...or I thought I was,
at least.

Without warning she snapped the fan away from

her face, tipped the long and lovely line of her throat back so that it gleamed white in the moonlight, and let loose with a merry peal of laughter. "Oh, 'twould have been a priceless jest on me, would it not, young Tashya?" She shook a lace-trimmed scrap of cotton from her sleeve and dabbed at her eyes with it, her laughter still pealing out. "For all these long centuries I have had but one regret—that I was turned before I had birthed a babe of my own, a child I could cosset and discipline and mold in my image. 'Tis a human vanity, of course, but it seems I retain the desire to have another version of myself to whom I can teach the ways of the world. I have searched all these years for a chit who might fulfill this desire of mine, and yet when she appears before my very eyes, I do not recognize my good fortune!" She slipped the scrap of lace back in her sleeve. "La, my love, I was about to deal with you in the same way I dealt with the cur. Would that not have been a delicious joke on me?"

Her words and her mannerisms were ridiculous, in an over-the-top, Dr. Evil kind of way. But Jasmine herself wasn't ridiculous, and if I let myself forget that it could be the last mistake I ever made.

She was mad. For all I knew, maybe she'd been a little mad before she'd become a vamp, but one thing was sure: those intervening centuries she'd just mentioned had turned Lady Melrose crazier than a shit-house bat, to put it bluntly.

"'Twould have been," I said, forcing a smile. "Does this mean you agree to Bind me to you, Lady Jasmine?"

"Come, we are like mother and daughter. No more Lady Jasmine," she said, leaning forward and tapping me playfully on the tip of my nose with her fan while I waited for it to turn into a switchblade and slice me open. "'Tis Tashya and Jasmine between you and me from now on. Yes, Tashya, the ritual will be performed tonight at my home. Let me escort you there."

She held out a slim, pale hand. I had no choice but to hold out my own, and let her grasp it. Her grip was painfully strong and I must have flinched, because immediately she released me.

"There, is that not a finer building than those of your age?" she asked with assured pride. "'Tis certainly finer than the one that currently takes its place."

I didn't have a clue what she was talking about, but there was a good reason for my disorientation. When she'd grasped my hand, we'd been standing on a side street a couple of blocks from my apartment. Now I was standing in front of the building that housed the Darkheart & Crosse office. It had to be a trick or an optical illusion of some sort, but why would—

I heard the low rumble of a familiar voice, and when I turned I saw the stocky figure of Darkheart standing beside the lamppost that had been the scene of Brook's final agony. He was all alone, and as I glanced above him and saw the cascade of flowers dripping from a hanging basket, I realized why. Every trace of the tragedy that had occurred here only hours ago had vanished, and with their work completed, the rest of the clean-up crew had gone. But why hadn't Darkheart left with them? As his almost inaudible rumble fell silent, I received the answer to my question. Reaching above him, my grandfather plucked a purple blossom from one of the trailing stems. He bent down and carefully placed it at the base of the lamppost, bowing his head briefly. Then he rose and took a step back.

It was the most insignificant of memorials: a single blossom placed at the site of her death…but with it Darkheart had paid his respects to Brook's spirit and courage. Just for a moment I hoped that wherever Brookie was, she knew what he'd done.

Then I remembered. Brook was in hell. The bitch beside me had put her there. And the fact that I could see and hear Darkheart meant this wasn't an illusion: Jasmine had instantly transported me halfway across town. For the first time since I'd come up with the plan of Binding with her, I felt a flicker of doubt.

Darkheart suddenly stiffened and looked across the street in my direction. Beside me, Jasmine frowned. "He senses something," she said with a tinge of disconcertment in her tone. "He should not be able to, but 'tis obvious he does."

She was crazier than I'd thought. "He probably doesn't just sense us, he can see us," I said politely. "I mean, we're standing right across the street from him and he's not blind."

"You think not, Tashya?" The beauty mark at the corner of her mouth lifted. "Yet you and your sisters have been blind to that which I do not wish you to see. Tell me, now that I have torn the veil from your eyes, what do you think of my home?"

Maybe she'd been a relative of King George III, I thought. His madness had cost him the Thirteen Colonies, hadn't it? Since I couldn't risk rebelling against Jasmine just yet, I turned obediently, prepared to make admiring-sounding noises about an ordinary office building I'd seen hundreds of times.

I blinked in shock as I saw that the Darkheart & Crosse building wasn't there anymore. Or wait— was it? Behind the massive cloud that seemed to have boiled down from the night sky, I thought I glimpsed a ghostly image of the building I was familiar with, but as the cloud parted I realized I'd been right the first time. The Darkheart office building *wasn't* where it had been only a minute ago. In its place was a wavering, ghostly image of the derelict ruin of a once-grand home, its exposed foundation and broken stone pillars all that remained of what it must have been.

The hair on the back of my neck rose as I saw more ghostly images overlap and bleed into one another, most of them small buildings I didn't know. Once I was sure I saw a teepee. A second later it was replaced by the office building again, and that building in turn seemed to slip out of focus and become a crude log cabin. More black clouds boiled out of the night sky, billowing like smoke from an oil fire. This time when the disturbance finally calmed down for good, the building that stood in front of me was one I'd never seen before.

It was a Colonial-style mansion. Except calling it a Colonial-style mansion makes it sound like one of those ugly four-car garage FrankenHouses that have sprung up on the outskirts of Maplesburg lately, and this was the real thing. It was all white; a breathtakingly beautiful dream of a building that seemed to glimmer like a jewel in the moonlight. Five shallow stone steps led up to a wide and gracious porch. White granite columns soared from the porch to support the classical-looking second-story portico jutting out over the entryway, and behind the portico on the flat-roofed top of the house itself I could just make out the delicate scroll-work of an iron railing.

Lights glowed invitingly behind the elegant double-hung windows, and more lights burned on either side of the open front door. A sweep of crushed stone curved in front of the mansion, and although I could have sworn that a moment earlier the drive had been empty, now I saw that it was crowded with gleaming horse-drawn carriages, each of them pausing for a minute to disgorge richly dressed passengers before moving away to where the drive split off to the back of the property.

It was the most beautiful house I'd ever seen in my life and there was something very, *very* wrong about it.

"I love it," I said woodenly, aware that Jasmine was waiting for my reaction. "But it's not supposed to be here, unless—" My frown smoothed out and I gave a relieved laugh. "For a minute I thought you'd somehow replaced the Darkheart & Crosse office building with this one, but you've transported us out of Maplesburg, haven't you? Where are we?"

"Upon my word, I swear we have not moved from the spot where you stood watching your grandfather, chit." Jasmine's dimples had disappeared. Her tone was sharp with impatience. "*Where* is the wrong question. I had thought it would not take you so long to ask the right one."

I thought of the jumble of images superimposing upon each other—the office building…the teepee and the cabin…the ruin with the smashed pillars… The hair on the back of my neck prickled as I raised my gaze to those same pillars, whole now and supporting the grand portico of the mansion in front of me.

I swallowed dryly. "Not *where* are we, but *when* are we. That's the right question, isn't it?"

Her blue eyes sparkled in approval. "I knew I could not baffle you for as long as I have done with your sisters! They search high and low for me—" she tapped me playfully on the chin with her fan "—and so have you, I wager, never guessing that I am right under their noses but some two hundred years in the past, in the house that was my home when your country was still struggling to be born. 'Tis a cunning trick, is it not?"

"'Tis," I said hollowly. "And I suppose the reason why they're finding fewer vamps lately is because they're all here? I mean, now? Back in Colonial times, I mean," I ended in frustration.

Jasmine nodded, gesturing toward the arriving crowds entering the mansion. "As you see, I extend the hospitality of my haven to all who swear allegiance to me. They are free to hunt in your time, and when they sense that the Daughter or her followers are near, they return here. In this time, Megan Crosse does not exist yet, and even your grandfather's grandfather has not yet come into the world. Come, enough of talking!" She held out both hands to me, her head tipped quizzically to one side. "Fie, child, we cannot have you attend your own Binding looking like a scullery maid! That dress will not do. First a scented bath, I think, and your hair shall be arranged by my Parisian maid in a more modish style. Then we shall find a gown for you that befits this occasion."

The next two hours passed in a blur. As we entered the mansion I got a brief impression of warmth and light and the gaily excited chattering of guests milling about the broad central hall. They were all vamps, of course; some in modern dress, but the majority of them wearing 1700s finery, the men in fitted coats and topboots, the women in ballgowns with deeply squared necklines that showed off powdered cleavage. Eyes slanted at me from behind fans and over intricately tied neckcloths, but Jasmine hurried me up an enormous curved staircase to the upper floor without stopping. With an equal air of haste she snapped out instructions to a bevy of maids, gave me a final playful tap with her fan, and disappeared down the hall.

Now, I'm the type who doesn't feel totally comfortable sharing a common change room at the gym. Not that I'm a prude, it's just that when all the other girls my age were beginning to develop those fascinating things called breasts I remained flat as a board, and although Grammie reassured me that I was a late bloomer, for a few months I was convinced that I was doomed to a life of Kleenex-stuffed trainer bras. My locker-room shyness never completely left me, even though everything that was supposed to be happening on my chest eventually did start happening.

But as Jasmine's maids stripped me, bustled me into a fragrant and steaming-hot bath and then attended to every detail of what was apparently the normal procedure for a lady's *toilette* in prerevolutionary America—powdering my bare skin, applying lavender water to the backs of my wrists and ears, piling my hair high in a tumble of curls that spilled onto my shoulders—I was too preoccupied to worry much about standing around in my birthday suit in front of a bunch of strangers.

Jasmine could bend the past.

I'd never heard of a vamp with such an extraordinary power, and the fact that she'd so casually revealed it to me made me wonder what other powers she had that I didn't know about. The doubts I'd had when I'd realized she'd transported me across Maplesburg in the twinkling of an eye had now become full-blown misgivings.

Dmitri had been right. Megan and Kat had been right. In fact, everyone had been right except me, I thought, my stomach clenching with fear.

I had no business going up against a Queen *Vampyr* of Jasmine's stature.

Chapter 15

My former confidence that I could beat Jasmine now seemed laughable but I wasn't laughing, I was concentrating on trying to find a way I could get myself out of this situation. I was in a time that wasn't my own, surrounded by Jasmine's lackeys, and I didn't have a single ally I could call on for help. I drew in a quick breath, and the woman who was lacing me into my ballgown murmured an apology.

It wasn't the cruelly tight lacing that had made

me catch my breath, however. Maybe I *did* have an ally here, I thought with a desperate surge of hope. Heath had passed on to Jasmine the information he'd gleaned from me that a Black Rose hit man was in town, but could it be possible that he hadn't seen that as a betrayal of me? After all, he'd known from my conversation with him about Dmitri that I was a Black Rose target, so why wouldn't he assume that I'd be relieved to know he'd passed the word to Jasmine?

"My Lady Jasmine awaits, Lady Tashya, but perhaps you would like to see yourself in a looking glass before you go to her?" One of the maids, a dark-haired female vampire in her early thirties who seemed to have authority over the others, bobbed her head deferentially at me. "The gown is a perfect match with madam's hair and eyes. 'Twould be truly tragic if madam did not see how beautiful she looks."

I glanced distractedly at her, still trying to figure out a way that I could delay the proceedings and find Heath. "Then I guess I'll just have to live with the tragedy," I said with a touch of impatience. "We're vamps, girlfriend, remember? You know, as in we can't see our reflections in mirrors?"

"Not in a silver-backed mirror, madam." Her smile was still deferential, but the tips of her fangs protruded scornfully over her lower lip. "But my Lady Jasmine would not countenance a home in which there was no way to view herself in the latest modishness from Europe. She has equipped each room with a glass that has been magicked to show the image of any vampire who stands before it. Is it not wondrous, madam?"

As she spoke, she moved aside. Looking past her, I saw an ornate, full-length mirror hanging on the wall facing me. Feeling oddly reluctant, I stepped forward to study my reflection.

The powdered and patched eighteenth-century fashion plate staring back at me was so unrecognizable that I bit back a shocked exclamation. My skin was alabaster-white, thanks to being fluffed all over by one of the maids with a swansdown puff, and in the paleness of my face my eyes blazed like sapphires. Rouge had been touched to my lips, and as I wet them nervously they gleamed ruby-red, drawing attention to the Cindy Crawford beauty mark that had been carefully placed on my top lip. My hair was pinned up with a single diamanté clasp, allowing a bed-tousled tumble of curls to fall sexily to my shoulders and down my back, but instead of being powdered to a matte dullness as had been the coiffures of some of the women I'd glimpsed in the entry hall, each red-gold strand glittered with something that looked like finely crushed amber.

But it was the gown I was wearing that made the biggest difference in my appearance. It was fashioned of a stiffly rich material, probably brocade. At first glance it seemed to be a somber green color, but at my slightest movement the fabric caught the light, flashing first bronze, then gold, then back to bronze again. A bell-like skirt swayed seductively just above the bronze toes of my heeled shoes, with a lace-flounced full petticoat peeping out from beneath its hem. Gazing at the plunging square neckline, I understood why the maid had needed to pull the gown's lacings so tight. My waist was whittled to a hand-span, and the powdered globes of my breasts had been forced upward until they looked ready to pop out of the dress's bodice like ripe peaches.

"I know my Lady Jasmine's tastes well,

madam," the maid said softly. In the mirror her eyes met mine and she gave me a small, not entirely pleasant smile. "Your appearance will be to her liking, I assure you. The Binding ritual can too often be tedious for my lady, but I believe that tonight it will be a singular pleasure for her. Come, I will take you to her now."

She laid her fingertips on my arm as we turned from the mirror and left the room, but as she escorted me down the long walnut-paneled hallway, I moved slightly apart from her and her hand fell away from me. Even for a vamp the woman was creepy, I thought with an inward shudder. "Singular pleasure"? Did she mean what I thought she meant by that? Because if she did, she'd just given me a second good reason to get the hell out of here as soon as possible. And to do that I had to find Heath, which might not be as easy as I hoped.

As things turned out, however, finding Heath wasn't a problem at all.

"My Lady Jasmine's bedchamber, madam." The maid stopped in front of a door and knocked discreetly. Without waiting for a response, she pushed the door open and gave me a nudge. I took an in-

voluntary step across the threshold and felt something inside me die.

A huge, four-poster, canopied bed dominated
the spacious room. It was in use, or had been up
until a couple of minutes ago, I guessed as I took
in the discarded velvet coverlet that had slipped
onto the floor and the rumpled linen sheet barely
covering Lady Jasmine's nudity. Her gaze met mine
as I stood in the doorway and a tiny smile curved
her lips, but my attention was focused on the prime
specimen of buck-naked male who had just risen
from her bed. Lieutenant Heath Lockridge was even
more gorgeously sexy without his uniform on, I
thought stonily.

Too bad he was such a total bastard.

"My dear Lieutenant, you have not met my new
protégée as of yet, have you?" Jasmine's purr
reminded me of a pampered Persian cat that had just
polished off a big bowl of cream and was now
eyeing a canary. "Or have you? La, what a topsy-
turvy featherhead I am when you have tumbled me,
my love! I scarce know whether I am up or down,
I have been so rough-ridden by you!"

"We've met," I said in a flat tone. I met Heath's

gaze. His eyes were fixed on me as if he was trying to convey a message to me without words, and my heart contracted painfully before I hardened it. I'd fallen for his act once, I thought, remembering how I'd hung on to his words about stars and doomed romance and what he felt for me. How stupid would I be to fall for it again, especially when he was standing by the bed of the woman he'd told me he wanted to break away from?

I broke off eye contact with him and let my gaze travel with insulting slowness down the hard, muscled length of his body. "'Tis topsy-turvy indeed," I commented with an amused smile. "My lady may well have been ridden hard, but I wager she has no trouble putting the spurs to this fine mount. He *is* a stallion, is he not?"

Jasmine's peal of laughter was immediate and merry. "I have chosen my newest Binding participant superbly, it seems." She slanted her gaze toward Heath, who was reaching for a pair of fawn-colored breeches that hung over a nearby chair. His features were rigidly unreadable, but as a hard flush of color touched his cheekbones Jasmine's smile became more catlike. "I had fancied that my lady

Tashya would learn from me like a child from a mother, but 'tis now clear to me that we will be more like loving sisters. She and I might be two peas from the same pod, think you not, Lieutenant?"

Heath had donned and buttoned his breeches and was pulling on his boots, chestnut leather with turned-over cuffs of gleaming black. He straightened up and shrugged bare-chested into his uniform coat before replying. "'Tis not my place to comment on your decisions, Lady Melrose," he said harshly. "If it were, I would repeat what I said before when you asked whether I thought Tashya Crosse would be a good subject for the Binding ritual."

"You advised against it, as I remember," Jasmine said silkily. "You predicted that she would never fully embrace the dark half of herself."

"Lieutenant Lockridge may underestimate me," I said with a light laugh. "Since I in my turn was wrong in my estimation of him, I do not hold it against him, my lady."

"But I do." Jasmine's tone was just as silky as before, but all trace of banter had left it. Lithely she rose from her bed and I saw that instead of being completely naked as I'd assumed, she wore a diaphanous white wrap only a shade or two paler than her skin. Unhurriedly she cinched the ribbon belt of the wrap around her waist and turned to Heath. "The ritual will take place in fifteen minutes in the gold drawing room. You will escort Tashya there and prepare her for the ordeal."

He stiffened as if she'd slapped him. "That is a servant's job, not a soldier's, my lady," he said in a low tone. "You have many who would see no dishonor in preparing a participant for a Binding, but this violates all agreements I have with you."

"'Tis too late for you to talk about violating agreements, Lieutenant," Jasmine said coldly. Her gaze flicked him up and down. "If 'tis dishonor to your uniform that worries you, there is an easy solution. Half-dressed as you are, you are no honorable soldier, but a lusty stud lately risen from his mistress's bed. You will appear in front of my guests without your military status." She narrowed her gaze at him. "If you are thinking of refusing my order, think again. You know from recent experience that I do not always punish the immediate object of my displeasure."

"Would that you had, my lady," Heath said distantly. He inclined his head in a bow. "Your orders are clear. I can do nothing else but follow them. My lady Tashya?" He strode to the door and opened it for me.

"Lieutenant." Jasmine's tone as we began to exit the room was once again purring and amused. I glanced over Heath's shoulder as he halted and saw that her amusement didn't reach the ice of her gaze. "Do not tarry," she said softly. "If you do not bring her to the drawing room when I am ready for the Binding ritual, my displeasure will be considerable." Her beauty mark flashed upward. "But here I am prattling on when I should be thinking of more important things, like what sad rag I can find in my closet that will not make me look like a complete hag beside you, dear Tashya! Go, now!" She flapped her hands at us, her expression droll as Heath closed the door behind us.

"She is mad and powerful," he said without preamble as he took my arm and steered me lightly toward the stairs. "You are in more danger than you know, every minute you stay here."

I jerked my arm away. "Is this something you

and the woman you just slept with cooked up during foreplay to trap me? You switch back to being noble Lieutenant Lockridge with an offer to help me escape and when I fall for it, she brands me a traitor and kills me like she killed the bastard who tortured and murdered Brook?"

Heath's expression looked haunted. He had quite a repertoire of expressions, I thought, pushing back the pain that rose in me as I remembered others that had played over his features: the naked longing in his eyes before he'd kissed me, the humor that had lifted a corner of his mouth when I'd said something that amused him, the grimness that had etched his face when he'd spoken of breaking free of Jasmine.

"The death meted out to your friend should have been mine," he said in a grating tone. "Jasmine has spies everywhere and she knew I had been with you. Instead of confronting me with her knowledge she chose to strike at an innocent, knowing I would realize I was responsible for the woman's death." Abruptly he pulled me into a small, windowed opening off the hall. "Yes, I tumbled the bitch," he said with sudden anger. "There was no pleasure in it for me, but if I had declined her someone would have paid for my refusal—a stable boy or a scullery maid or—" His jaw clenched. "I feared she would take her rage out on the woman I truly wanted to be with," he said hoarsely. "Make no mistake, Jasmine knows how I feel about you. That is why you must leave now."

"Fine," I said flatly. "Just shake up that big magic hourglass for me and drop me off in front of the Darkheart & Crosse office, Lieutenant."

Heath frowned. "That power is beyond me."

I gave him a thin smile. "How did I know you were going to say that? What am I supposed to do now, try to make a run for it so you and Jasmine can have a merry hunting party and chase me down before she kills me?" Anger thickened my tone. "That's not how I want to die, Lieutenant—fleeing for my life like a scared rabbit. Thinking I could take on Jasmine and win was probably the biggest mistake I ever made in my life, but I got myself into this mess and I'm going to go down fighting. Besides, maybe I'm stronger than I realize."

"That may be so, but Jasmine has found your weak spot," Heath said in a low tone. "She found out what you felt for me and she destroyed it."

I met his gaze. "She didn't have to. You did that all by yourself."

I swept away from him and after a moment he followed. In silence—his heavy and mine cold—we proceeded down the stairs to the main hall. The crowds that had thronged it when I'd arrived were nowhere to be seen now, but from behind one of the many closed doors that led off the hall I could hear sounds of voices and occasional bursts of excited laughter. I began heading toward it, but Heath stopped me.

"There is one possibility I had not thought of. Has your sister ever attempted a Heal on you, Tashya?"

"What's that got to do with anything?" My nerves were strung like tuning wires. I was about to pit myself against a Queen *Vampyr,* and the odds, to say the least, were definitely stacked in her favor. Whether or not Kat had ever tried to Heal me was the last thing on my mind at the moment. "When she was coming into her powers she was responsible for nearly getting me killed. She did something to bring me back from the edge, but even she's not sure it was a Heal, and I hadn't started turning vamp at that point, anyway."

"After you started becoming one of us?" His question held urgency. "Did she try again then?"

"No, for the simple reason that I wouldn't let her," I said, my patience thinning. "If Kat had Healed me, you'd know it, obviously. I mean, I wouldn't be a vamp, I wouldn't be here and you wouldn't be pulling this shit and trying to throw me off-balance."

"Even a partial Heal might have helped," Heath said tightly. "But if your sister has never attempted to do so, then all that is left is for me to give you the only advice I can. Lady Jasmine will try to overwhelm you during the Binding, but as you say, you are stronger than you realize. Hold on to that strength, even though she tries to pry it from you with all the power she has at her command." He hesitated. "Jasmine has decreed that I should be the one to prepare you for the ritual. Do you know what that entails?"

I shrugged. "You escort me to her, I assume. Why, is there something more?"

"Yes." A shadow passed behind Heath's eyes. He was losing his touch, I thought cynically. If the good lieutenant was trying for the haunted and sensitive

look again, he'd missed the mark by a mile. His
shadowed gaze looked more predatory than vulnerable. "But to perform my duties past this point I
must enter fully into my dark side," he continued in
a suddenly deeper tone. "Look into my eyes,
Tashya."

"The last time I was stupid enough to gaze into
your eyes I ended up falling for a bunch of lies," I
began, but then my words trailed off. He really was
the most incredibly *sexy* man, I thought, my impatience fading away as I gazed into those depthless
pools of navy blue. And it wasn't just the delectable
line of his lips or that broad expanse of bare chest
exposed by the open uniform jacket that made a girl
think of tangled bed sheets when she looked at him.
An almost tangible maleness came off him in
waves, lapping around me and washing away all my
reservations and inhibitions.

"You will feel pain, my lady, but only for a
moment," Heath breathed as his fangs lengthened
past his top lip and he bent his head to me. "After
the pain you will feel every sensation you have ever
yearned for in your most wanton dreams. Bare
yourself for me, Tashya."

My eyelids swept heavily down. There was something wrong here, I thought dazedly, but the heat that was rising rapidly in me was making it hard to think. Heath's hands were on my shoulders now, his breath warm on my skin. I arched my neck, exposing it fully to him, and felt the razor-sharp tips of his fangs pierce my skin.

And then they slashed downward. My eyes flew open in agony as twin knives seemed to plunge deeply into the frantically pulsing jugular vein at the side of my neck. I twisted in Heath's grasp but his grip only tightened, bringing me closer to him. Hampered by the petticoats of my gown, I kicked out, and then I felt the toes of my shoes kicking against thin air as he gathered me up into his arms. The pain crescendoed until I knew I couldn't endure it a single second longer. Darkness started to descend over me and I felt myself begin to lose consciousness.

"She will Bind with you, but I have drunk of you first, madam," Heath said hoarsely in my ear. "And it is from me that you experience your first taste of the dark pleasures. The pain is already becoming a memory, is it not? Tell me, what delights are beginning to kindle in you now?"

Even as his whispered words came to me, I realized he was right. The pain was subsiding, and in its place…

"Hot," I gasped. "Heat everywhere—on my thighs, lapping over my breasts, burning my lips. And images in my mind…images of things I've never done in my life, things I've never *imagined* doing. In…in my mind I'm doing all of them with you."

A shudder of pleasure ran through me, followed by another. I felt Heath's mouth on my breasts as he began to stride toward the closed door leading off the hall and more waves of liquid heat cascaded through me.

"Make them more than imagination," I said breathlessly, straining against him. "Take me somewhere, Heath, and do all those things I see you doing to me in my mind."

"La, you *have* prepared the chit well, Lieutenant Lockridge!" The mockingly amused tones of Jasmine penetrated the erotic fog swirling about me and I struggled to open my eyelids. "Lay her down on the chaise so that my guests can easily view my possession of my young rival, and then bring me to the enviable fever pitch you have aroused in this mongrel bitch of a pretender."

I forced my eyes open as an appreciative ripple of anticipation greeted Jasmine's speech. The room swam around me for a moment, and when it steadied I found myself looking at the exquisitely dressed crowd that had been in the hall earlier. For a second, however, my attention was focused on what Jasmine had just said.

She'd called me a mongrel bitch. Her former pretence of indulgence toward me had now given way to the reality of her intentions and she'd meant her words as an insult, but I didn't take them that way. I'd told Dmitri that the mixture of Daughter and Healer and Darkheart legacies that were part of me made me stronger than a mere vamp could ever be.

Jasmine's power came from only one source: the dark side. The mark that Zena had cursed me with ensured that I, too, could take power from the darkness…but if I chose, I could also borrow power from the light.

That meant I had a chance of defeating her.

The last of the fog numbing my brain swept

away and I turned to Jasmine, a smile of triumph already touching my lips. A moment later, my smile froze.

Jasmine's neck was arched in ecstasy and her body was molded so closely to Heath's that they seemed at first glance to be a single, writhing form. His fangs were sunk deeply into her neck, but even as I watched he raised his head and met my gaze.

His blue eyes looked blindly through me. He started to lower his mouth to Jasmine's exposed neck again, but she thrust him away and sank down on the chaise beside me.

"He is admirably suited for what he does, is he not?" she said with a tiny smile, her eyes watching me closely. "But what is this I see in you, sweet Tashya? Could it be that you still harbor a lingering *tendresse* for the gallantly degenerate lover you and I have now shared? If you do, I warn you— Lieutenant Lockridge may distribute his charms indiscriminately, but you can never hope to own his soul. I took that from him long ago."

Cold hatred filled me, blotting out everything but my overriding desire to smash the mocking smile from her face. "We're here for a reason,

Jasmine," I said, barely controlling the rage in my voice. "You'll either Bind me to you, or I'll Bind you to me. You can call this a ritual if you want, but you and I know it's a battle. I'm ready whenever you are."

"Then let us do battle, by all means." She laughed softly. "You know how the procedure is to be carried out?"

"You drink my blood. I drink yours," I said harshly, feeling my fangs lengthen. "Let's do it, bitch."

I moved swiftly toward her. She met me with open arms. At the very moment that my fangs sank into the vein Heath had opened on her neck, hers sank into the vein he'd opened on mine.

And as soon as I felt Jasmine begin to drink from me, the darkness came down and I knew I was lost.

Chapter 16

"There is something I wish you to do for me, my love," Jasmine purred as she idly wound a curl of my hair around her finger and let it uncurl again. "'Twill be no hardship for you. Will you say yes or are you unkind enough to make me beg?"

"You know your pleasure is my pleasure, madam," I said, thrilling to her light touch. "Say the word and 'tis done."

The Binding ritual was long over and our audience had melted away. My lady: beautiful, im-

perious and yet at this moment showing me a for-
bearance I knew I had not earned—I, who had been
so arrogant as to think I could best her!—lounged
on the chaise, my head in her lap and her cool
fingers in my hair.

"The soldier...he dared to defy me," she mused.
"He must be brought to his knees." I stirred, not
knowing why her words should spark unease in me.
Jasmine smiled down upon me. "La, my sweet lady,
I am no ogre," she chided. Had her tone cooled a
trifle? "I will not have you harm him, only prove to
him that what he thought you felt for him was a
delusion. You find him beddable, I believe?"

"As you said, my lady, he is good at what he
does," I said, a dark excitement kindling in me.
"You wish me to put him through his paces?"

"Of late Lieutenant Lockridge has shown a regrettable tendency to romantic posturing."
Jasmine's dimples flashed merrily. "Would it not be
a fine lesson to him if the object of his traitorous
yearnings makes it plain to him that while she may
enjoy him, she feels nothing for him?"

Again unease stirred in me, and my next words
were foolishly rash. "You are wrong, my lady. The

soldier never yearned for me, he merely dallied with my affections—"

Jasmine got to her feet so abruptly that I tumbled from the chaise. I looked up at her from my position on the floor, fear coursing through my veins like ice water.

"You amuse me, chit, but do not count on my amusement to shield you when you contradict me," she said with soft venom in her voice. "Will you carry out my wishes, or do I find another way to punish my rebellious lieutenant?"

I got to my knees, hot tears starting to my eyes. "I have disappointed you, my lady," I said, touching the hem of her gown with a trembling hand. "Please do not withdraw from me, but give me this chance to redeem myself in your eyes."

For a moment she did not reply. Then I felt the touch of her hand on my hair, and my world was righted again. "'Tis sometimes puzzling to me that I do not possess that quality others call mercy," she said with a low laugh, "but in its stead I enjoy a healthy curiosity. A better bargain, is it not? I am curious to see if my stallion's spirit can be broken by you." Her fingers moved to my chin and she tipped it up so that my tear-washed gaze met hers. "Yes, very curious," she said with a thin smile. "Listen carefully to what I require you to do, sweet Tashya."

The skirts of my green velvet riding habit swept moonlit spangles of dew from the grass as I walked toward the stables behind Jasmine's mansion. I caught the smells of hay and warm-blooded horse-flesh wafting through the night, but mixed with them was one that interested me more. I slapped my dainty braided leather riding crop against my thigh and walked faster, drawn by the trace of male scent I could discern in the air.

I had been honored greatly by Lady Melrose. I was Bound to her now for eternity; more than that, I was to be at her right hand two hours hence when she and her army took down the Daughter of Lilith, along with the Healer and the dangerous old man my lady called the Seeker Darkheart. In what I thought of as a previous life, I had been a sister to the Healer and the Daughter and a granddaughter to the Seeker, but the person I had been then was a stranger to me, and my time before Jasmine a hazy memory. There had been a woman, had there not been? I seemed to remember a pair of mint-green eyes—

Love you, Mata Hari....

A jolt passed through me, bringing me to an abrupt halt. A feeling like a knife through the heart—yes, *that* was what I remembered, I thought with a shudder. Great pain, and an emotion that I had called grief. I resumed walking again, a faint smile curving the corners of my lips. How blind I had been then! Had I really thought I preferred that hard existence to Jasmine's world of power and hedonism and amusement? Surely nothing I had experienced there had come close to the thrill I'd felt during this evening's ritual.

...and when you turned those crushed-violet eyes on me, I remembered what springtime had once felt like...

Again I halted, but this time my halt was momentary. The soldier had many impressive assets, but a truthful tongue was not among them. The foolish girl I had been in that previous life may have treasured the words he'd spoken, but as Lady

Jasmine's favored bondswoman I now saw them for the pretty lies they had been.

It would be sweet pleasure to carry out my mistress's wishes, I thought as I drew near to the stables and saw the dim yellow glow of the lantern that hung by the door. I stepped inside and my gaze lit on him immediately, although he showed no awareness of me. But of course he would not, I reminded myself, a shiver of arousal tingling up my spine. Jasmine had assured me that for this encounter she had given me the gift of seeing, but not being seen. I could feast my eyes on him without hiding my boldness, and he would be unaware of my hot gaze.

Until I *allowed* awareness to come to him.

He had just finished currying a mare. Lightly slapping the animal's glossy chestnut flank, he latched her stall and stepped more fully into the light. My breath caught in my throat as I let my gaze roam slowly over him.

The uniform jacket he had worn earlier lay discarded on a nearby mound of straw, leaving him bare to the waist. His stable tasks had raised a fine sheen of moisture on his chest, and the motes of hay-dust floating through the air had gilded his skin a dark gold, delineating every swell and bulge of muscle under his tanned hide with shimmering highlights and hazy shadows. He still wore the fawn-colored breeches he'd pulled on in Jasmine's bedchamber. They molded themselves to his thighs, and the double-buttoned front seemed to my approving imagination to be cut with the express aim of drawing female attention to that part of him it was meant to cover. His formerly gleaming riding boots were now flecked here and there with broken bits of hay, and altogether he seemed a much less gentlemanly version of the Lieutenant Heath Lockridge who had first introduced himself to me.

I had fantasized about that man making love to me in a bed. I found I had no regrets about altering my fantasy to a rough-and-tumble ravishment that included Heath lying naked and ready for me on a spread of sweetly ripened hay. Raising my riding crop, I lightly trailed the braided leather ends down his chest.

A shudder ran through him. Jerking his head up, he looked straight at me and for a second I thought I was visible to him. Then his gaze moved with wary alertness past me to scan the stable.

I raised the crop again but this time I let it trace the buttoned enclosure of his breeches and was gratified to hear his swiftly indrawn breath. "What lady of darkness toys with me?" Heath's voice was low and tinged with anger. "Show yourself, so I may know who attempts to seduce me."

I ran the riding crop upward from his heel, past the turned-down cuff of his boot and then even higher, letting it flick against a well-muscled inner thigh. His jaw tightened, but I noted with amused interest that his effort to conceal his reaction was defeated by the skintight tailoring of his breeches. I had a sudden need to feel the evidence of his arousal with my own flesh instead of a strand of braided leather.

I moved noiselessly toward him and ran my palm over the front of his breeches.

"Tashya."

My name came from him on a harsh gasp and I swiftly stepped back from him, a flicker of disconcertment running through me. He could not know my identity, I reassured myself. 'Twas a random guess, nothing more...but perhaps it would be intriguing to see how he reacted when I gave him proof that he had guessed correctly.

"Did I hear you ask what lady was *attempting* to seduce you?" I asked, my smile audible if not visible to him. I flicked the whip suddenly in the air, and as it curled around the back of his neck I caught the free end before it fell away. I pulled him lightly to me and placed my lips to his mouth. "It seems to me shockingly evident that my teasing is no attempt at seduction, but rather an accomplished deed. I know you for a charming deceiver, Lieutenant, but I think this is one part of you that cannot lie."

I ran a lazy fingertip over the bulge in his breeches. "Undo them," I whispered softly against his lips.

Heath's hands went slowly to the buttoned fly of his pants. Like a man unable to stop himself, he unbuttoned the first fastening. His fingers moved to the second, and then halted. "I once dreamed of how it might be between us, Tashya," he said hoarsely. "These dark tricks were no part of my dreams."

My voice became ice. "No? 'Tis hard to believe, coming from a man who used trickery and honeyed words to deceive me from the first. We should be Lyra and Altair, was that not the story you embroidered for me? Doomed lovers separated by a river of stars, dewing the end of each night with their tears." I gave a short laugh. "If I did not know it was a lie, I would say it was a heartbreaking future you saw for us."

"I have forfeited my soul. You still have one, even now," he replied evenly. "I like to hope that the damned are given a second chance to live their lives over again, but unless they are, a heartbreaking future is all we ever could have together."

"And if I am too impatient to wait for our lives to cross again in some future reincarnation, what then?" I said, moving closer to him. "If you cannot have an endless love, will you turn down an hour's passion, Lieutenant?"

As I spoke I allowed my invisibility to fall away. My fingers went to the velvet-covered buttons of my riding jacket, and by the time I had taken solid form, I had finished unfastening it.

"You set a new style today," I said with an innocent smile. "I thought 'twould please you if I copied it."

Under the velvet jacket my breasts were brazenly bare. I swayed toward him slightly, allowing the buds of my nipples to brush tantalizingly against his skin.

I knew from the groan of desire he gave that I had broken his resistance.

"If this is my lady's wish, I have no strength to fight against it anymore," Heath muttered, lifting my skirts and running his hands to the top of my thighs. My own hands were busy releasing him from the now cruelly tight confinement of his breeches, so his sudden excitement was impossible to overlook. "You came out wearing nothing under your skirts either, madam?" he said hoarsely. "I see now that you spoke the truth when you insisted you needed no romance from me, but just a rough and immediate tupping in the hay to temporarily quench the fires raging in you. Let me show you that I am as satisfactory a mount as you said I looked when you saw me earlier today."

His hands spread wide under my skirts. Lifting me up so that my legs were forced to wrap around his waist, he hoisted me into the middle of a stack of freshly cut hay. As we tumbled together into its scratchy fragrance Heath's tongue was already circling my nipples and his strong shaft was already pushing past my thighs to enter me.

He rode me harder and more thoroughly than I had hoped for in my darkest fantasies. I heard my gasps of passion mingle with his husky and erotic whispers in my ear, and as his thrusts became deeper and harder, the last vestiges of control slipped away from me. He gave one final thrust. I felt myself flying into a thousand sensations, as if fireworks were exploding in me and around me, and as the explosions reached their crescendo my eyes opened wide in ecstasy.

Heath's navy-blue gaze met and held mine. In his eyes I saw the same shattered arousal I was experiencing. His grip on my shoulders tightened as if he would never let me go, and my fingertips dug into his back as if I would keep him close to me forever.

Without warning, an icy fear pierced me, and from the desperation in Heath's gaze I knew he felt it, too. Although we were still clutching each other tightly, it suddenly seemed as if we were flying apart from each other, getting farther and farther away until whole universes separated us. A glittering river of icy, desolate light seemed to rush out of nowhere, obliterating my last glimpse of him.

"*Heath!*" The scream tore painfully from my

throat, but still I saw nothing but cold pinpoints of light. I squeezed my eyes closed to shut out their cruel brilliance. "I let her Bind me to her, Heath! Oh, God, what have I done? What have I *lost?*"

"Not me, Tashya. Never me, my love."

His voice was shaken, but his hand as he stroked back damp hair from my brow was reassuringly firm. I opened my eyes, my breath coming in shallow pants. "I went over to the dark side, Heath," I rasped. "I Bound myself to Jasmine. She's going to kill everyone I love, and I was ready to help her slaughter them tonight. I even let her use me against you," I whispered painfully. "I destroyed what you and I could have had, didn't I?"

His smile was bleak. "No, my lady, I did that long before I met you. I told you there is no future for me. But there is for you, and for your sisters if you hurry."

I buttoned my jacket with shaking fingers as he stood up and fastened his breeches. "You mean tell them they're in terrible danger?" Even to my own ears my voice sounded thin with desperation. "But Heath, we've gone through all this already! Jasmine's more powerful than I am. The fact that she Bound me to her is proof of that. Even if I could put up any kind of fight against her, I can't bend the past like she can. I'm stuck here with no way to reach my sisters and warn them!"

"Jasmine is more powerful than you?" His grip bit painfully into my arms. "If that is so, my love, how is it that you have escaped the bonds that were to tie you to her for an eternity?"

"How is it indeed?" At the sound of the mocking voice coming from the direction of the open stable door, I whirled in alarm. Jasmine regarded me with a quizzically arched eyebrow. "What is it I have interrupted here, I wonder," she said with cold amusement. "A lovers' tryst or a meeting of traitors? I underestimated you, chit…but not by a great deal. Still, you swore allegiance to me and now you have broken the Binding. You know the punishment I reserve for traitors, I believe?"

"Hung, drawn and quartered," I said, trying and failing to shut my mind to the horrific memory of Brook's murderer's death. "I can't stop you from considering me a traitor, Jasmine, but you need to know that Heath knew nothing about—"

"She can bend the past because that is what she

is, Tashya—the past," Heath said urgently. "But you are the future. That is what is behind—"

"*TRAITOR!*" Spittle flew from Jasmine's twisted lips as she screamed out her insane verdict. I felt something black and cold rush past me, and in sudden terror I spun around to see Heath turn to dust before my very eyes.

But before he was killed I saw the man I loved suffer a traitor's punishment.

I saw Heath being hung, drawn and quartered....

Chapter 17

Someone was screaming; a visceral expression of devastation that filled the air around me with endless sound, like a tuning fork that wouldn't stop vibrating. The howl of grief battered my senses in a physical assault that made me want to press my hands to my ears to shut out the raw, keening howl.

The scream was coming from my own throat. I spun away from Heath's ashes and directed it at Jasmine. "*Why?*" My voice was so thick with agony that the word I hurled at her was barely comprehensible. I forced past the barrier of pain constricting my throat. "It's *me* you want to destroy—it's been me right from the start! Why kill Heath and let me live?"

"You stupid chit." Her dismissive tone was a cool contrast to the destructively volcanic heat that seemed to be spewing from me. "Do you not yet see that I *have* destroyed you, so utterly and completely that I no longer have need to kill you?" Her smile showed none of her former coquettish charm, but only an icy triumph. "No need to fear you, either. You were never more than a false pretender to my throne, and now you are no longer even that. I will let you witness the deaths at my hands of all those you love, pretender, and you will be helpless to save them. Then I think you will kill yourself, will you not?" she added softly.

"*No!*" Her threat against my sisters and Darkheart galvanized me into action. I launched myself at her, prepared to rake her perfect face to shreds, to tear her nonbeating heart out with my bare hands, to—

My palms skidded along something rougher than strewn hay and my knees crashed onto a surface much harder than the horseshoe-flattened dirt outside the stables. I jerked up my head, expecting to see Jasmine's mocking smile as she shimmered just out of range, but she was no longer there.

And I wasn't on her Colonial estate anymore. I was back in Maplesburg, on my hands and knees on a sidewalk. She'd used her powers to bend the past once more.

As I lurched to my feet, a distracted part of my mind noted that the skin on my palms was scraped and bleeding. I sensed rather than saw someone behind me, and I turned around to see Joe, his eyes staring fearfully at me through his tangle of hair. I'd appeared out of nowhere, as far as he knew. No wonder he looked so terrified.

"It's okay, Joe, it's me, Tashya," I said shakily. "I was a friend of Brook's, remember?"

A spasm of pain crossed his weatherbeaten features. Grabbing the handle of his ever-present shopping cart, he began moving quickly away, his frantic gaze apparently focused on something he could see halfway down the block. I squinted against the glare of the setting sun and realized what he was heading for.

The Darkheart building was set on the site where Jasmine's mansion had stood in Colonial times, and the stables had been a slight distance apart from the mansion. I looked around me and saw that I was about half a block away from the Darkheart offices and the familiar knot of people standing outside it on the curb.

The sun was slipping below the horizon. My sisters and the others were obviously checking their weapons and giving last-minute instructions, preparing to head off in different directions for a night of patrol. What better time for Jasmine to take them all out in one fell swoop?

"*Megan! Kat!*" I began running down the sidewalk, keeping to the shadows that had already cloaked this side of the street, although a few stray shafts of orange-tinted light still fell on the other side. "Jasmine's on her way! *Take cover!*"

The bitch had defeated me at every turn. She'd killed my best friend, made me betray everything I believed in, and destroyed a man whom I'd realized too late I would always love—destroyed him in the most violent and sadistic way possible before ending his agony on Earth by sending him to an eternity in hell. Heath hadn't hidden his past from me; during his centuries as a vampire he'd committed unforgivable acts. He'd been right, there'd never been any possibility of a future between us. Even if he'd undergone the agony of a Heal from Kat and survived the process, he would have spent the rest of his mortal life torn apart by guilt and remorse.

And none of that mattered. I'd loved him and Jasmine had killed him, just as she'd killed Brook. I'd send her to hell before I let her kill anyone else I loved.

I wasn't running anymore, I was skimming over the sidewalk, the coins on my dress shivering in the rush of air flowing past me. As I registered the icy ringing sound I looked quickly down at myself and saw with no surprise that instead of the riding habit I'd been wearing only minutes ago, I was now in the Galliano-that-wasn't-really-a-Galliano. It made a confusing kind of sense. I'd rejected Jasmine's world and she'd cast me from it completely, right down to the clothes on my back. I was glad she had, I thought as I slowed down and let my feet hit the ground running. I was going to die tonight. There was no question in my mind about that, and no regret, either, since I intended to take Jasmine down with me. But it gave me strength to know I was going to take my final breath as myself, not as her protégée.

"Don't come any closer, Tash!"

Ignoring Megan's shouted command, I sprinted toward the group of people watching my approach. They were all there, I realized—Megan and Kat, Mikhail, Ramon and Jack, Darkheart and Liz Dixon. There were others I didn't know, but I vaguely recognized one or two of the tall, hard-eyed men and the slimly muscled, frowning women from a month ago, when Mikhail had called on his shadowy Russian contacts for help in the battle against Cyrus Kane's followers. Megan had gathered extra troops, I realized. That was good. But it would also give Jasmine the opportunity to take out more vamp-fighters at one go, and that wasn't so good.

She wasn't going to get that chance, I told myself. "Meg, Jasmine's got an army!" I said as I ran up to her. "As soon as the sun completely sets you'll be surrounded! There isn't time to explain, but—"

"Make time, Tash," Megan said as she swiftly

pulled me to her and jammed the point of her stake into the flesh just above my left ribcage. "Hold your fire unless I give the word, people!" she snapped to the group behind her.

"What the—" Megan's stake pressed harder into me, and I swallowed my words. Jack's nail-gun was trained on me, I realized as I scanned the crowd without moving my head. Some of the Russians held compact-looking crossbows. They were locked and loaded, each steel arrow gleaming dully silver at the tip, and they were all pointed in my direction. Even Ramon, standing beside a white-faced and unarmed Kat, was gripping a stake and watching me tensely.

"What are you waiting for? Just do it!" Someone was stumbling through the crowd. As I saw the long, brown hair, now tied back, and the pink blouse she was wearing, I recognized Xandra Steinberg. "If you don't, I will," she said, her voice choked and uneven. "Someone's got to send this bitch to hell for what she did to my—"

"Dmitri, stop her!" Megan snapped without taking her eyes from me. "The deal was that she could only join us if you kept her under control. She pulls another stunt like this and you're both out."

I saw a grim-faced Dmitri grab Xandra by the shoulder and halt her progress toward me. With his other hand he plucked a stake from her grasp. Xandra's expression had been set in ugly lines, but now it went blank. With surprising gentleness, Dmitri pulled her unprotestingly to him and guided her to the far edge of the crowd.

I let out a breath. "What's this all about, Meg? I'm not the enemy, Jasmine is, and in a few seconds she'll—"

"What it's all about is that you left us pretty abruptly yesterday," Megan interrupted. "As in one moment you were there, and the next moment you'd disappeared."

"It's another vamp power I've developed," I said, slanting my gaze at the shadows darkening around us. "Megan, you've got to listen to—"

"Another thing it's all about is that a few hours later, Darkheart thought he saw you and Jasmine together outside this building," Megan continued coldly. "Did he, Tash? Were you with Jasmine?"

"Yes," I said impatiently. "But that's not important right now."

"I think it's damned important to know why

you're suddenly hanging out with Jasmine," Megan said thinly. "I also think it's important to find out whether you've gone over to the dark side, because if you have—"

She was wasting seconds we didn't have. I closed my eyes and concentrated on the stake she was holding at my heart.

It felt like I was flexing a muscle in my mind; a stiffly protesting muscle that I'd never used before. A moment later, I was holding Meg against my body like a shield, with her own stake at her throat.

"What the—" Her eyes, wide and shocked, cut sideways at me. Then she switched her glance to encompass Jack and the huge black wolf snarling up at us. "Jack, fire straight through me and get her. Mikhail, if for any reason she doesn't—"

"I'm on *your* side, Meg!" I shouted, shoving her from me and hurling her stake at her. "I went over to the dark side, but I came back, dammit! And I'm trying to warn you that at any moment we're all going to be surrounded by an army of vamps!"

"Not possible, sweetie." Kat spoke rapidly. "Meg'll tell you, there isn't a single, solitary vamp left in Maplesburg. Present company excepted, of course. It looks like we might actually have cleaned up the town. We brought in reinforcements tonight just so we could scour every corner of Maplesburg to make sure we hadn't missed one."

"Maplesburg's crawling with vamps," I contradicted her. "Except the Maplesburg I'm talking about is Jasmine's Maplesburg—the one that existed back around the time of the American Revolution. She's created a lair that no one will find, a haven for every bloodsucking, undead bastard who swears allegiance to her. She can bend the past, dammit! She's probably standing in front of her mansion right now, surrounded by her army and just waiting for the sun to set here before she—"

"Sun *has* set, Granddaughter." Darkheart's rumbling tones were edged with tension. "And I think she is already here."

"Oh, no." Megan's voice was strained. "Am I seeing what I think I'm seeing, Tash?"

I followed her gaze. Massing the street and sidewalks in both directions were the ghostly outlines of what looked to be hundreds of vamps, but even as I watched they became less ghostly and more solid-looking. I caught a wavering glimpse of an imposing white mansion with elegant pillars, but then the image steadied and became the Darkheart office building once more.

Of Jasmine there was no sign, but Darkheart was right, she was here. When she was ready, she'd show herself.

"If you think you're seeing an undead army, then yeah," I said hollowly. "Got a plan, sis?"

"Do I have a—" Megan swung angrily on me. Then the corners of her mouth lifted in a wry grin. "Oh, I've got a plan, all right," she said steadily. "We stake as many of them as we can. Then we keep going and stake a bunch more."

"Simple yet effective, sweetie," Kat drawled. "I like it."

Jasmine's vamp army was almost completely solid now. I let out a breath. "One for all and all for one, and all that Three Musketeers crap," I said, giving Meg and Kat a tight smile. "But the bitch is mine, okay?"

"Not okay," Megan said. "She's mine."

"Nuh-uh, Meg." I shook my head. "She's got powers you've never even dreamed of. Leave her to—"

"Heads up, ladies, incoming vamps at six o'clock," Kat said nervously. "And seven, and eight—oh, hell. As a Healer I might not be able to kill vamps, but there's nothing in the rules that says I can't keep loading fresh clips for my nailgun-totin' boyfriend, is there?"

"Nothing at all," Megan replied. She raised her voice. "Okay, people, circle the wagons! Try to stay in formation as long as you can, and protect your neighbor's back! Good hunting!"

I tugged at her sleeve. "Say something about me."

She scowled, then looked appalled before turning quickly back to the Darkheart contingent. "People! Tash is on our side! Don't—repeat, *DON'T*—stake her! Happy now, brat?" she said, giving me an apologetic grin. Her grin faded. "Tash, if we don't both make it out of this alive, I want you to know that—"

I put my fingers lightly to her lips. "I do know, Meg. The three of us might not have said the words as often as we should have, but we've always known how we felt about each other. A lot's changed in these past months for us, but not that."

Her eyes held mine for a moment. Then she gave a quick nod and strode over to her group as the first wave of vamps came pouring toward us.

History books describe epic battles as if they had some kind of order or organization to them, and maybe to the generals directing them from behind the front lines, they do. But when you're right in the thick of things fighting for your life, a battle is a series of noise and jumbled impressions, at best.

If Megan hadn't ordered our side to circle round, we wouldn't have stood a chance. As it was, the fighting was grimly fierce on the perimeter where the two armies clashed. Almost immediately I saw one of the Russian women go down, her life's-blood streaming away from a jagged wound at the side of her neck. The man who'd been fighting alongside her tightened his jaw as he saw her fall and then, with a stake in both massive fists and a spare clenched between his teeth, he methodically took down ten or twelve vamps before a horde of them swarmed over him.

It was gruesome. We were fighting for our lives, and some of us lost the fight. When the second wave of Jasmine's shock troops raced over the scattered piles of dust that moments before had been their comrades, I saw an older male vamp batten on to Liz's neck, his fangs slicing through her flesh like knives. Darkheart was a few feet away, occupied in thrusting his stake into a vamp I recognized as being the lady's-maid who'd dressed me, and even as I started toward Liz I knew I wasn't going to be in time to save her. Then I saw a short man in a garishly patterned bowling shirt whirl around and quickly take in the situation. Ramon, Kat's best friend and the manager of her club, launched himself at the vampire who was attacking Liz. Snarling in fury, the vamp shoved Liz aside and instantly switched his attention to Ramon.

"You wanna piece of me, hell-bait?" Ramon taunted him, ducking under the vamp's arm as it tried to grab him.

The vamp's face contorted in a sneer.

"Suck on this, boyfriend!" Ramon grunted, moving quickly under the vamp's arm again and straightening up directly in front of him. He slammed his stake into the vamp's chest.

"Ramon—behind you!" Kat's shouted warning came too late. As Ramon turned from the vamp he'd just dusted, two others jumped him from behind. One of the two slashed extended fangs swiftly across Ramon's throat, and I didn't need to see the bright crimson mark to know he was dead. As I saw Kat and Jack take on Ramon's attackers, I turned away.

I killed my share of vamps that night, using my own powers whenever I needed to, all the while keeping my guard up for Jasmine's arrival. Her first target would be Megan, or possibly Kat. As long as I didn't let my sisters out of my sight I would be ready for her.

But when she finally showed herself, I wasn't ready for her at all. And her first target wasn't one of my sisters, it was an innocent bystander.

"La, what a crush this affair is, to be sure! I scarce know where to begin carving out some room for myself, but 'tis no great matter. This unfortunate cur will do for a start."

The bored drawl was unmistakably Jasmine's. I pushed to the edge of the fighting and saw her standing a few feet away, her fangs extended and her iron grip around Joe's shoulder. From the look of dull fear on his face, I realized he didn't fully understand what was happening.

"Let him go." I moved quickly toward her. "He's nothing to you, Jasmine, but I am. I'll take his place."

"You are right, chit, this wretch is nothing to me." Her dimples deepened. "But he is something to you, and that makes him a fine target to begin with."

I shook my head, not willing to make a move on her until she released Joe. "You're wrong, bitch. He's a confused old guy without a home, that's all. I hardly know him."

"Would you care to place a wager on that, madam?" Her eyes glinted with secret amusement. She was as crazy as Joe was, I thought—probably crazier. But she was holding his life in her elegantly manicured hands right now, and I didn't want to push her into making a move against him.

I stepped forward. "No wagers, just me for him. That's fair enough, isn't—"

She moved with the speed of a striking snake, her free hand blurring toward me and fastening on to my upper arm. I reacted with equal speed, giving Joe a violent shove that knocked him from Jasmine's grasp before clamping both my hands on her upper arms.

"We're going down together, you abomination," I said, thrusting my face into hers. "You've killed enough people I care about, and I'm not about to—"

The scene around me wavered. I dug my fingers into Jasmine's arms. "Oh, no, you don't!" I snarled. "You're not taking me back to your—"

Cold hit me in an icy blast. It was another one of her tricks, I thought furiously, but if she thought I was going to release her she was wrong. I could take cold. I could take standing thigh-deep in snow. I could…

Standing in snow? I blinked, and the scene around me came into dim focus. Massive pine trees, their branches laden, ringed a clearing in which a man was being set upon by three attackers.

Three vamp attackers, I saw with sick dread. Whoever the man was, this had all happened in the past. His fate had been sealed long ago, and I couldn't do anything to change it.

The vamps fell upon him, dragging him down into the snow. I heard a shouted snatch of Russian, and suddenly I knew what Jasmine's game was.

"I'm witnessing my father's death, aren't I?" I

said hoarsely. "You want me totally shattered before you kill me, is that it?"

"Shattered? La, what nonsense you talk! It may well have shattered your father to violate his Healer heritage by killing these scum, but I thought you would be overjoyed to know he survived."

I glimpsed David Crosse thrusting a stake into one of his attackers before turning to the second and dusting him, as well. His stake flashed in the moonlight a third time but the snowy scene was wavering into insubstantialness and being replaced by another.

"Survived physically, at least," Jasmine said with silky cruelty in my ear.

I was looking at a squalid street. The hard faces of the hurrying passersby stared straight ahead as a young woman was suddenly dragged by a tall, pallid-skinned man into the opening to a garbage-strewn alleyway. A pallid-skinned vamp, I corrected myself, as I saw his fangs lengthen. From farther back in the alleyway a drunk stumbled toward the vamp and his screaming victim. Lurching closer, the drunk put his hands on the vamp's shoulders.

The stumbling man wasn't a drunk, he was David Crosse, I realized—but a David Crosse who looked years older than any pictures I had of my father. And it wasn't only time that had ravaged him. His face was carved in lines of pain, his hair and clothing unkempt. As the vampire bent to his female victim's neck and began drinking deeply of her blood, David Crosse stumbled away, blundering into the night.

"He lost the power to Heal," I said unsteadily. "What I don't understand is why that vamp just let him walk away."

"What a dull-wit you are, to be sure," Jasmine said chidingly. "Is it not staring you right in your face? David Crosse became an outcast from vampires and humans alike. His mind was broken when he failed to stop Zena from killing his wife and marking his child, and it shattered completely when he turned away from his Healer heritage. He became human flotsam…but in some corner of his broken mind he must have remembered something of who and what he had once been."

The squalid street scene flickered oddly, like an old silent film running off the reel. Another image began taking its place, and as I recognized it I felt my heart squeeze painfully in my chest.

"He must have," I said from between lips that felt frozen. "In the end his wanderings brought him back home, didn't they?"

The woman walking gingerly along the dark laneway had red-gold hair reaching halfway down her back. She stopped suddenly, looking at a man sleeping by a shopping cart. Then she moved cautiously toward him, her gaze on the disreputable running shoes he wore on his feet. The woman was me, I knew. The sleeping man was Crazy Joe.

And Joe was David Crosse.

Joe bore no resemblance to the photographs I had showing the vital, handsome man my father had been before his whole world was smashed beyond repair. But in the past moments I'd seen that vital man change, first into a grief-torn husband and father who'd violated the code he'd lived by; then aging further into a man shunned even by his enemies and finally hitting rock bottom as the homeless derelict Brook had nicknamed Joe, for his coffee-drinking habit.

I knew now why Jasmine chose him as her first target. She had no interest in killing a homeless derelict—but she had every interest in killing my father while I watched.

"So that is why you were not fully Bound to me!" she exclaimed in a very different tone than the silky one she'd been affecting up until now. "The wretch used the final dregs of his power to taint you!"

I looked again at the scene. Not only did I know what I would see, I thought, I finally understood what had happened to me two nights ago in the alleyway. "He didn't taint me, he partially Healed me," I said hoarsely, my vision blurring as I watched an unconscious Joe convulsively gripping my ankle as I expelled the poison that eventually would have led me to embrace the dark side forever. "David Crosse saved his daughter's soul, even if he didn't know what he was doing. But that wasn't his last Heal, that was his power stirring back to life in him again."

Love you, Mata Hari.... I'd stared at what remained of Brook's body long enough to burn the sight into my brain. Yet I'd missed the most jolting revelation of all: torn and mutilated as it was, it had been a body, not dust and ash. Brook hadn't died a vamp, she'd died human.

And moments before she'd died, the homeless man she'd befriended had laid a healing hand on her.

I turned and looked Jasmine straight in the eye. "You got screwed over by a homeless guy and a punk-girl. Do you know what that means?" I said, almost conversationally. "It means we're going to beat you, bitch. Some of us won't be there to see it happen, but that's okay. Wherever Brookie is, she'll know, and so will Ramon and the rest who fall before you do. Heath knew," I added huskily. "He said you were the past, and he was right."

For a long second Jasmine stared at me, her bright blue eyes hard with disbelief and the dimples at the side of her mouth replaced by two lines. With an almost visible effort, she forced a cold smile. "You have just signed a mass death warrant, madam," she said in a whisper that shook with fury. "Now I shall begin executing it."

This time there was no wavering transition between realities. Jasmine and I were face-to-face, each still gripping the other, when a body crashed into me, shouts and screams assailed my ears, and I realized we were back in the thick of battle again.

"Tash!" Megan's appalled shout came from directly beside me and I jerked my attention away from Jasmine for a split second to see my sister leap to her feet. She'd been the one who'd crashed into me, I realized. From the horror on her face it was obvious she saw Jasmine's grip on me and feared the worst.

"Stay out of this, Meg!" I yelled, but it was too late.

"Mikhail, get Tash out of the way so I have a clear target!" Stake in hand, Megan came at us in a crouching run, the massive black wolf at her side speeding up and springing toward me. A moment later he smashed into me like a battering ram, breaking my hold on Jasmine and knocking me to the ground.

"La, chit, I have been killing Daughters before your great-grandmama was born. If you think yours is the stake that will find its way into my heart, you are as deluded as your poor father is."

I staggered to my feet. Jasmine held a barely conscious David Crosse as a barrier between her and Megan's weapon. My sister's expression hardened. "What are you talking about? What do you know about David Crosse?"

"Why do you not ask your sister what she knows about him?" suggested Jasmine with a small smile.

"What does she mean, Tash?" Megan's voice was strained. "Was the report Dmitri received wrong? Is our father still alive?"

Her glance, bright with fearful hope, flicked to me, and in that moment Jasmine acted, thrusting David Crosse into a leaping Mikhail and smashing Megan's stake from her grip. She grabbed Megan by the throat, lifting her off her feet and spreading her other hand wide on Megan's chest.

"Your stake has pierced the hearts of many of my kind, Daughter," Jasmine mocked. "'Tis only fitting that I should finish your life by pulling your still-beating one from your body."

Her hand clenched into a fist and drew back. Megan closed her eyes, her lips moving in a silent last prayer, and in desperation I flexed the muscle in my mind again.

This time it responded with a surge of eager power that ran smoothly through me. The coins on my dress gave out an icy tinkle, and at the sound Jasmine blanched.

I couldn't blame her. Now it was my throat she

was gripping, and her own throat was being gripped by me. Megan, her mouth open in an oval of shock, was lying on the ground a few feet away where my power had thrust her.

Jasmine recovered quickly. "I knew you had some small talents, pretender," she said, beginning to rise in the air. I rose with her, both of us locked together and gripping each other's throat. "I had not guessed your powers had progressed so far. 'Tis best that I kill you before they increase further."

Behind the facade of coolness there was a thread of real fear in her voice. The coins on my dress shivered mockingly, and all at once I could hear Heath's final words in my mind—the words that had angered Jasmine so much that she'd killed him before he could finish uttering them.

She can bend the past because that is what she is. But you are the future. That is what is behind— What would the end of his sentence have been? In Jasmine's eyes I saw a flicker of the same apprehension I'd heard in her voice, and suddenly I knew.

She was powerful, but her powers were fed by the past. I was the future—something new, a mongrel mix of vamp and human that had never been seen before. I walked a thin line between the dark side and the light, and for the rest of my life those two opposites would battle for my soul. But that was what made me strong.

I hadn't come into my full powers yet; they were still ahead of me. And Jasmine suspected that—suspected and feared that a day would come when I could defeat her easily. That was why she wanted to kill me now, while she still could.

She'd left it too late.

If my full powers hadn't come to me yet, I'd just have to go to them. And Jasmine was coming along for the ride, on a one-way ticket only.

We were twenty feet off the ground now, locked together in our death-grip. I flexed the muscle in my mind and immediately everything around us began to waver. The fear in Jasmine's eyes was overlaid for a moment by triumph, and I decided it was time to burst her bubble.

"Guess again. It's not you doing it, it's me," I said, tightening my grip around her throat. "And I'm not taking you back to the good old days, either. We're going to fight this one on my turf, bitch."

"*No!*"

As she spat the word at me, she tried to break free from my grasp, but I was already too strong for her. The air around us steadied. "Welcome to my world," I said with a thin smile. "Get used to it, because you're going to die here."

"What have you done, chit? Where is this place?" The fear in her eyes was back again, and I had a feeling it wasn't going away anytime soon.

"You can bend the past." I shrugged. "That's your strength, Jasmine. But I'll come into my full strength here, in the future. Too bad for you that I'd gained just enough power to bring us here so I could tap in to the woman I'm going to be."

I released my grip on her. I didn't need to hold her with my hand anymore, not when I could hold her with my mind. I saw and thwarted her instant impulse to use her own powers to escape my world and return to her own, and when she realized she had no option but to stand and fight, she tried other tricks.

I could have killed her simply by raising a finger, but I let it go on way too long…and at some point during my one-sided battle with her I realized I'd gone over to the dark side. What was worse, Maplesburg had gone over to it with me.

I think that was when I realized just what my future would be. I looked at the grimy streets and the abandoned buildings around me, and then turned back to Jasmine and finished her off.

There was no changing the curse Zena had put on me. I was fated to be a *Vampyr* Queen, I thought as I stood trembling over the pile of ash and dust that was all that was left of Jasmine. But what kind of queen I became was up to me. I could draw strength from my sisters and my father and Dark-heart, or I could turn my back on the light and fully embrace the dark.

If I did the latter, Maplesburg would become a second Smith's Falls, and Brook and Heath would have died for nothing.

I turned away from Jasmine's ashes. A moment later I was back fighting alongside my sisters.

Epilogue

Maplesburg looked prettiest at dusk, I thought as I stood at the edge of the town square and stared up at the memorial that took pride of place in the little park. Of course, evening was a good time for me, too, since I couldn't go out in the daylight anymore, but my dusk-till-dawn lifestyle didn't interfere with hanging out with my sisters. Megan's Daughter duties were mostly performed at night and Kat, who still hadn't filled Ramon's manager position, spent her evenings at the Hot Box. Now that Grammie and Popsie were back home, however, they'd start asking questions pretty soon.

Although right now they were pretty much occupied with getting to know their son again. And their son was occupied with getting to know his three daughters.

In the weeks that had passed since we'd defeated Jasmine's army, Meg and Kat and I had spent as much time as we could with David Crosse. He still wasn't fully healed and maybe he never would be, but no one would mistake him for a street-person now. The evening when my sisters and I had heard him humming *Barbara Allen* under his breath we'd known we had our father back.

But even that didn't help ease the pain that sometimes caught me unawares, lancing through me with the same intensity I'd felt when I'd seen Heath die.

Which is why I came here at dusk. The Revolutionary War soldier standing with his horse on top of Maplesburg's memorial to those of her sons who had fallen in battle looked a little like Lieutenant Lockridge, I'd decided. Enough, at least, so that I felt I was closer to him here than anywhere else.

"We hoped we'd find you before we left."

At the sound of Dmitri's voice, I turned to see him and Xandra standing behind me. Her gaze on me was cool, but it didn't have the hatred it had once held. She made a gesture at the pack she was carrying.

"Our bus leaves in a couple of minutes, but Dmitri wanted to say goodbye and I wanted to say—" She paused, then shrugged. "I just wanted to say I'm glad my sister was with someone she cared for at the end."

I nodded. "I'm glad, too."

Dmitri broke the small silence that followed my words. "I made things right with Darkheart yesterday, told him about Black Rose and that I'd come here under false pretenses. He wasn't happy, but before we parted he wished me luck."

"You're going to need a lot of that," I said sharply. "Why can't you two wait for things to settle down here? Megan and I are still cleaning up pockets of Jasmine's army that are hiding out, but in a couple of months we could go to Smith's Falls with you."

"And in the meantime, how many people will be killed or turned?" Xandra shot back. "You've heard the weird rumors, just like I have. The vamps in my hometown are starting to spread out, traveling by night, finding places to hide by day. That farm family we read about in the newspaper—even if the authorities are chalking up their deaths to a serial killer, you and I both know that from the description of the bodies, it was a vamp slaughter." Her face flushed with emotion, she turned to Dmitri. "The bus will be here in a minute. I'm going across the street to wait for it."

I couldn't help but notice the expression on Dmitri's face as he watched her walk stiffly away from us. When he turned back to me, I raised an eyebrow. "So, did I lead you to your fate like you thought I would?"

"What do you mean?" His skin was slightly flushed now, I noted with interest, and he had that jaw-clenching thing going on.

I took pity on him. "Nothing, Malkovich. Nothing at all. You'd better make tracks. I think that's your bus."

He glanced across the street to see the Greyhound coming to a stop near Xandra. "I guess this is goodbye," he said awkwardly.

"I hope not." Leaning forward, I pressed a quick kiss on the corner of his mouth. "Come back safely. Make sure your new girlfriend does, too."

He just made the bus. As it pulled away from the curb I saw that it had obviously deposited a passenger while picking up Dmitri and Xandra. The man standing across the street with a duffel bag slung over his shoulder was in uniform, and for a moment I froze.

Then I turned back to the statue. I had to get over this, I told myself impatiently. Every time I glimpsed a man with broad shoulders and dark hair my dumb heart jumped up like a jack-in-the-box. The man I'd loved had been taken from me. He was never coming back and it was time I learned to live with that.

"Nice old statue," a voice beside me said. There was a soft thump, and I saw a duffel bag lying on the grass in front of highly polished shoes.

I didn't look at the soldier. "Yes," I said flatly, hoping he'd take the hint and leave.

He didn't. "All the time I was doing my tour, I promised myself that when I got out I'd come here and take a look at this. My grandmother always told me that the Revolutionary War soldier on this statue was supposed to have been an ancestor of mine."

Slowly I turned. Navy-blue eyes gazed down at me. His hair was still service-short, but I knew that when it grew out there would be a renegade strand that would fall across his brow.

"Heath?" I whispered.

Even before I saw his quizzical smile I knew I was wrong. The man standing beside me had a small scar at the side of his mouth that Heath hadn't had. His shoulders seemed just a little broader, his stance more relaxed, his manner more casual.

"That's right, Heath Lockridge." He stuck out a hand. "I was named after him, but how did you know?"

I smiled weakly. "Just a lucky guess?"

He grinned back. "You going to tell me your name now or wait until we're sitting over coffee together at that diner across the street?"

"Tashya Crosse." I disengaged my hand. "And thanks for the offer of coffee, but I'm meeting my sister in a couple of minutes."

He was a babe. He seemed nice. But he wasn't

the man I'd lost. Perhaps one day I'd start taking nice, sexy men up on their offers, but not just yet.

"Maybe another time then." With a smile, he stooped to pick up the duffel bag. Turning away, he paused, his gaze on the sky. "Altair and Lyra," he said, jerking a thumb upward. "There were times during my tour when I wondered if I'd ever get the chance to stand beside a pretty girl and look up at the night sky from the good, old U.S. of A again," he added softly. "Take care, ma'am."

I watched him walk away, feeling frozen with shock. Did it mean anything? Was it just a coincidence, or was it something more?

I like to hope that the damned are given a second chance to live their lives over again...

"Were you given that chance, Lieutenant?" I whispered, blinking back the dumb tears that had sprung to my eyes. "Is this my chance to find you again?"

I ran fast enough that I caught up with him before he entered the diner.

SUPER NOCTURNE™

Coming next month

DARK SEDUCTION
by Brenda Joyce

Already responsible for a young woman's death, powerful Master of Time Malcolm is determined to keep the darkness within him at bay, even if that means denying himself all pleasure...until fate sends him Claire.

Since her mother's murder, Claire has done everything possible to make a safe life for herself. But nothing can prepare her for being swept back into the medieval age with powerful warrior Malcolm. Now she needs Malcolm to survive, yet she must keep the dangerously seductive Master at arm's length. For Malcolm's soul is at stake – and fulfilling his desire could prove fatal for Claire...

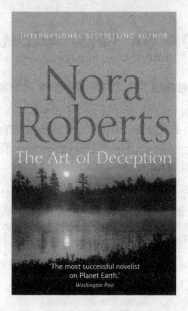